THE WAY OF SEX

SAVANNAH M. NEEDS

COPYRIGHT NOTICE

The Way of Sex

Savannah M. Needs
Copyright 2021
All rights reserved.

Ex Parte Press

Find announcements about more of Savvy's books at
SavvyMNeeds.com.

ISBN (ebook) 978-1-927607-59-6

ISBN (paperback) 978-1-927607-58-9

Thanks to Kit Foster for his cover design.
Special thanks to Robert at Ex Parte Press for his assistance with
this project.
Please direct media and rights inquiries to Holly at
expartepress@gmail.com.

FORWARD WITH THE FOREWORD

This is the story of how I changed my life after divorce, from bitter to better. My days weren't always about reading on sun-bleached beaches, writing books under palm trees, or enjoying sex-drenched afternoons. When people ask how I transformed, the short answer is, I committed to becoming a new person.

Longer answer: At a strange and luxurious retreat on Vancouver Island, I crawled out from under the weight of disappointment to discover my purpose. Before the spa, I spent way too much time thinking about what might have been instead of stepping up and making my new future happen. Confronting my delusions was one way my life got better. Fear is heavy. Once I dropped my fears, I freed both arms to embrace lust and love. I grip pleasure in two hands and wring as much fun as I can out of every day.

As you read this, the answer to the question on your mind is, yes, *The Way of Sex* is my trip out of the trap of other people's expectations. I hope you enjoy the journey, or at least masturbate furiously to the sex scenes.

I sometimes joke about going to wizard school. Before I could moved forward into the luscious life, I waffled a lot. We can waffle until we die or finally decide we can't take living tiny lives anymore. Is it time to read some self-help smut, find your purpose, and live larger?

We both know your answer. Welcome to *The Way of Sex*. Your adventure is just beginning, too.

~ Savvy M. Needs

Sipping jasmine tea and listening to nightingales sing outside the Alhambra in Granada, Spain.

1

———

If I'd looked, I could have spotted trouble in my marriage early on. Too soon after the honeymoon, Doug and I rarely had sex while the sun crossed the sky. My Dark Ages featured routine sex in the dark. We were so busy trying to make enough money to get by, we forgot to have fun. We screwed up instead of screwing each other.

Oh, is it Saturday night again? Sex night. Oh, is it Valentine's Day already? Fine, we'll dress up and go out before we have sex. Sadly, intimacy became more about duty and a date on the calendar instead of a real show of love, lust, and caring. When I look back on that time, I remember feeling tired a lot. I didn't save enough energy for me or for my husband.

Life is like a book. Each day is a chapter. We're making things up as we go and sometimes we forget to make it exciting. I thought I knew what my life story would be based on my early chapters, the married ones. Divorce, and what happened after, taught me a lot of things. Now I have orgasms during the day again!

When I was playing dutiful house frau while trying to achieve lift-off with my business, I was lost. I didn't think I could rewrite my book in the middle and come up with a new (and sexier) happily ever after.

I finally stopped writing each chapter of my life as if it had to be like what came before. Since I dared to change, gorgeous people gladly suck my nipples every day. (Once the juices are flowing, I love having my nipples sucked hard — really hard.)

Kelly Forester was my best friend since I moved to Vancouver and, later, my business partner. When our work at the travel agency dawdled — business was often so slow I'd call the pace glacial — she spoke in excited whispers about a rich guy who changed lives. "This crazy hot rich dude operates a sex spa! He's a bodyworker who caters to one woman at a time. Wouldn't that be great? You get treated like a queen. Wouldn't you love to be treated like sexy royalty?"

"That reminds me, let's go to Dairy Queen for lunch. We can blow the morning's profits on a dilly bar as long as we share just one."

Undeterred by my withering stare, Kelly seemed particularly focused on how the perv wanted to save the whales between orgies. "He must be a good guy!" she reasoned.

"Nah. Sounds to me like that creep wants to stage orgies with whales."

"He's for real, Savvy! I swear. And not a creep. I heard it from a friend of a friend."

"A sex spa? Too weird."

"You sure?"

I rolled my eyes as aggressively as I could to underline my certainty. "Imagine the carnal bliss. All those STDs, just a ferry ride away!" I envisioned a greasy guy with a lot of gold necklaces chaining up women to massage them to goo and orgasm. Sure, that might possibly be fun for a hot minute if I closed my eyes and dreamed of Ryan Reynolds and Ryan Gosling. Double Ryan delight! That would inevitably be followed by dark regret, stinging humiliation, and persistent burning when I peed.

"It's only kinda weird," Kelly said.

"You don't think it's strange?"

"Not terribly. The scope of human sexuality being what it is ... I mean — "

"Kelly? Really? C'mon!"

"Okay, maybe it is weird but you could use some of that weirdness in your life, Savvy."

"I'm not the sort of person who goes to a sex spa, whatever that is."

"What would you be like if you were that 'sort of person?'"

The words *adventurous* and *bold* sprung to mind first. "Different from what I am, I guess. Much."

"Would that be so bad?"

I didn't answer. I turned back to my computer and pretended to work. Kelly's question made me uncomfortable. It seemed she was telling me I should be someone different, that I wasn't good enough or doing well enough. Later, I figured out what she was really saying: I could be me, but more. I couldn't hear the love and hope behind her words at the time. I was still wallowing in the Dark Ages, looking backward not forward. When it came to my divorce, I was a paleontologist, endlessly picking over the bones of the past. It's hard to move on when all you think about is failure and regret.

But the seed was planted. I kept thinking about the sex spa and what the mystery man might be like. I'd been to a couple of spas and had massage therapy for a sore neck and tension headaches. I figured Kelly didn't know what she was talking about. A whole week at a sex spa? Typically, people can only stand to visit Las Vegas for three days. Seven days at a spa would be exhausting. As soon as you had your first orgasm, wouldn't you want to go home, have a shower, curl up with a book, and try not to feel dirty?

Kelly brought up the magic masseur a lot. The more she talked about this strange rumor, the more she complained about her husband. For months, I was almost sure Kelly was going to divorce Paul. At the end of my beginning, Kelly's relationship was not diseased. She stayed with Paul. It was my marriage that drowned in boredom.

On a cold day in April, I, Savannah Melissa Needs, divorced Douglas Nelson Needs. The process took three years, start to finish. The scene that launched the divorce proceedings was pretty ugly. I came home early from a business trip to find my husband in our bed with Patsy, the service manager from his Subaru dealership.

I did not throw things and scream immediately. That precious life moment came a few minutes later. In case you find yourself in a similar situation, ceramics make the most satisfying crashes. If you don't have dishes or figurines handy, you could opt to knee the cheating bastard in the balls.

When Doug had dropped me off at the airport, I pulled my heavy bag out of the trunk alone. He didn't get out of the car or kiss me goodbye. We'd argued about money. He wanted me to make more. I wanted him to be more understanding and helpful. Looking back now, we weren't fighting about a lot of money, but at the time a little felt like a lot. As I boarded the plane, I wondered what my life would look like if switched to a one-way ticket and kept going.

With all that recent friction in mind, I'd planned to wake my hubby with a nice blowjob. I knew from experience that would take the fight out of him. The door to the bedroom was open as I crept up the stairs. In the dim light, I found Doug standing on the bed. He was bent at the knees and thrusting at Patsy's ample cleavage.

They didn't hear my sharp intake of breath. Struck mute, I stood there in shock. She was on her knees, looking up, smiling at him. He held her breasts, crushing them together around his cock.

Patsy looked so much like me I could have been watching myself. Doug had a type and Patsy and I were it. I felt woozy. I leaned against the wall. If he was going to cheat, why do it with a woman who looked so much like me? Why not a younger blonde who wore glasses or an older redhead with one leg and an Irish accent? It was like he wanted me, but not me.

Patsy had one hand on his balls, kneading gently. With her other hand, she rubbed between her legs, driving herself to orgasm. "C'mon, Doug! C'mon, baby! You can do it!"

Confused by the flood of feelings washing over me, I froze. Until you find yourself in the middle of extraordinary circumstances, you never know what you might do. A coward, I did nothing at first. Doing anything meant ending the fiction I'd believed in. My life wasn't what I thought it was.

I was furious, of course, but turned on, too. Doug looked good. So did she. In retrospect, the woman peering in from the darkened hallway — the voyeur — was the real me. The shock yanked my true self to the surface, if only for a moment. Absently, I slipped my hand under my skirt and touched myself, rubbing through my white panties. I wouldn't have predicted that, but you can deceive yourself with thoughts. Emotional reactions are real.

"I'm going to come again!" Doug cried.

Again? What was this "again" shit? He was always one and done with me!

Patsy stopped what she was doing and immediately flipped over on all fours. "Do me again!" she pleaded.

Again with the "again?"

My husband quickly slipped to his knees. Patsy moaned as he maneuvered his prick into her from behind. As he buried it, she shook and let out a long, "Yes! Oh, fuck, yes. Fuck me!" Hers was half a plea, half an order. He grabbed her hips as he pounded her. With her face smushed against the sweaty sheets, she crooned a tuneless song of connected moans. She reached between her legs once more to play with her clit.

I rarely said the word fuck in the bedroom. I used to think good girls only talked about making love. Watching Doug and his mistress fused in fleshy delight, I was reminded of an old joke: People talk about making love, but when it's true love, it sure looks like fucking. From where I stood, their connection looked like real passion. I couldn't remember when Doug was so excited about me.

In the race to release, Doug and Patsy crossed the finish line before I did. The sight of their orgasms broke my spell of silence. Everything was broken. Amid the many feelings rushing and pulsing in my blood and bones, I chose naked rage over their naked lust. Why couldn't Doug fuck *me* like that?

Most interesting was that moment before they came: me, masturbating as I watched them fuck. Until I put ink on paper, I never told the truth of what I did in the doorway to my bedroom. Not even Doug and Patsy knew. I was too ashamed. I've let go of shame now. Writing the truth is freeing.

As those scenes go — wife walks in on husband with the other woman — I shouted a bunch of exhausted cliches. I won't replay my tearful screaming fit, but for one exception. Doug did reluctantly agree he probably shouldn't have fucked Patsy with my pillow under her swampy ass.

The marriage crashed. There were no survivors.

At first, we believed our split could be amicable. Doug suggested we wouldn't need lawyers and a judge to work out the sad business of dividing our belongings. I agreed, but Doug was slow to sign the paperwork. Kelly told me to get a lawyer because Doug certainly would. She was right. Doug lawyered so I did, too. In the end, the lawyers won. My husband and I almost bankrupted each other in the fight to be free.

I won't bore you with the details of our divorce, either. You know the drill: anger, accusations, recriminations fair and unfair, last-minute doubt, apologies, marriage counseling, hopes of last-minute reconciliation dashed. People don't talk about how exhausting divorce is. It's a marathon. You can't see the finish line, but you keep running and stumbling toward freedom.

If I'd gone to the spa first, I would have saved a lot of time and pain. I was taught marriage was kisses, bliss, kids, and mutual support. My mother told me from a young age, "A woman needs a man to keep her warm when it gets cold. Sooner or later it's going to get darn cold. When you're not hot anymore, the world gets down-right icy."

All our movies end with heroes and heroines getting together in the final shot. Even when the movie is about somebody trying to kill the president, there's a cliched romance. You've just stopped insectile aliens from destroying national monuments? Doesn't matter. Heroes and heroines must smooch as moviegoers fidget in their seats, brush off the buttery popcorn, and start to wonder where they parked the car. It's implied that eternal love and lifetime commitments are the only happy culmination. All those stories end with a hug and a kiss as two perfect people wander off into the sunset to a bright future in which they never die or even get hemorrhoids.

We are trained to idolize people who have peak experiences. We are not encouraged to go out and get peak experiences for ourselves. That could be dangerous. Keep your head down, do the work, forget your childish dreams. Be useful, quiet, and normal. We are cogs made of meat caught in the steel gears of society's machine. While others are off saving the world, we burrow into our cubicles and do menial tasks. We are the worker drones, fulfilling other people's dreams and never saving the world. It's as if we're bred for disappointment.

Women who stay single are almost always portrayed in the media as sad, lonely, and loved only by way too many unbathed cats. No wonder so many people fantasize about the end of the world. We want to go outside, step over the dead bodies of our enemies and loot a Walgreens for the happy drugs. We want to feast on an endless supply of free potato chips and never balance a checkbook again. We want to get laid without having to talk before or after. Talk is for during, and only then if the message can be formulated in a moan.

Stuck in a deep hole, I needed a light to find my way out. Luckily, forces were gathering to help me escape the darkness.

2

——————

"My new life started with a party." When the movie of this book is made, that will be the opening voice-over. The studio will insist on skimming over my marital misery so there won't be much of a character arc on display. That's the difference between movies and books. My L.A. agent says the first draft of *The Way of Sex* is making the rounds of various directors. Because of the smut, I won't be invited to the Oscars. They'll probably shoot my story like *Fifty Shades of Gray*: lots of T and A, but still no delicious dick to ogle.

The day before the party, I stopped at the grocery store on the way home. Though I knew the store was busy, I went in anyway. The crowd made my heart beat faster. The buzz of the fluorescent lights melded with the muddles of idle conversation around me. Every noise seemed loud, jarring, and jagged. I stood at the end of a long line to wait my turn at the cash register. Overheating in a heavy coat, I watched the procession in a daze. As people ahead of me paid for their groceries, they seemed to move in slow motion.

A sneaking suspicion crept out of the darkness behind my medulla oblongata: are these people fucking with me? Are they aggravating me on purpose? What's taking so long?

I assumed I was sane so I dismissed my rising paranoia. Paranoia is a boomerang: it comes back and smacks you in the forehead.

This isn't easy enough, I thought. Something in my life should be easy!

Tearing up, I wandered away from my cart full of groceries and hurried for the exit.

"Ma'am? Ma'am!" someone called after me.

"It's abandoned," I shouted back. "By international law, that grocery cart is salvage! Claim it if you want!"

Everyone stared at the crazy lady and she was me. It was as if I stood outside myself watching the scene unfold. I didn't look back. My scalp was on fire. I never returned to that store in case the staff recognized me. Somebody had to put all my groceries back on the shelf, but I couldn't face waiting anymore. The metaphor was clumsy but heartfelt. I was waiting for my life to start again. There were too many obstacles between me and Happy: me, money, failure, me, the past, the future, me, me, me.

On the way home from the abandoned errand for groceries, I pulled into a drive-through. Emptying my wallet, I wolfed down twenty-three dollars worth of junk food in the parking lot. I made it home, working on automatic, driving in a trance. My apartment building's elevator lurched, and that got my stomach rumbling.

As I walked down the long hall to my apartment, my pulse pounded in my ears. I struggled to fit my key in the lock. I was dreaming underwater, drowning slowly. I didn't make it to the bathroom before throwing up. I didn't just vomit, either. My panic attack made my hands shake uncontrollably as I hosed my tiny apartment. After a while, I fell asleep on the bathroom floor. I woke up alone in my apartment. The acidic smell made me want to vomit again, but I had nothing left to give. I fought the dry heaves as I cleaned up the mess.

Once, when Doug and I were newlyweds, I got really sick. (End of Day Sushi Sale! Old raw fish! What could go wrong?) Doug held my hair back and made soothing sounds as I threw up. When I was done, he tucked me into bed. He cleaned up the mess while I lay with a hot pack on my stomach and a cold compress on my forehead. Fast forward ten years and there goes Doug, off to work for Patsy in the Hair-holding and Soothing Sounds Department.

I had Kelly on speed dial. I told her about leaving the grocery cart behind while a dozen strangers gawked at me. She drove me to the hospital to get a prescription to deal with panic attacks. I'd quit the cheap wine by then, but my friend wasn't convinced. "Anti-anxiety medication doesn't mix well with wine, Savvy."

Little did I know, Kelly's next suggestion would take me far away from the straight and narrow. "What you need is a party."

"I don't."

"Sure, you do. Everybody gets a divorce party."

"Even if they don't want one?"

"Especially then."

"Seriously, I'm not in the mood."

"Then it's agreed," Kelly said. Before I could object, she put up one index finger. "*Sh!* This is what friends are for."

The next day after work, a limo arrived to pick me up.

As I climbed in, I couldn't conceal my surprise from Kelly. "A limo? Really? Are we going to prom? Did you get me a corsage?"

Undeterred, Kelly announced, "I've got several orders for you and they all begin with D. Don't mention Doug. Don't even think of Doug. Don't say the word divorce, either."

"Sure. Anything else?"

"Well, we do need to get you off the dildo before you develop a callous."

"Kelly!" The barrier between us and the driver was up, but I'm sure I heard him guffaw.

"If you use electronics too much, you'll get dependent on them. You don't want to end up with an industrial German sex toy that requires gas and a pull cord like a lawnmower."

I was laughing and feeling a little sick, too. "Kelly! Stop!"

The driver let out a high giggle.

"Am I wrong?"

"Shut up."

"I'm not wrong."

She had more planned than a girl's night out at TGI Fridays. We ended up in Kitsilano, my favorite part of Vancouver. We drove up to an enormous iron gate. Far beyond it, a mansion dominated the landscape. Fancy sports cars and limos were parked along the great circle of a driveway.

"Look at the house!" Kelly said. "Turrets and towers and gables! Oh, my!"

"Screw the house. Look at the driveway," I said. "Bright white concrete...you know, I think they vacuumed the driveway! It's the nicest, cleanest driveway I've ever seen in my life."

"That's my girl," Kelly replied, "always looking down instead of up."

"What is this place?"

"Would you believe TGI Fridays renovated?"

"I would not. Applebees, maybe but — hey!" I leaned close and whispered so our driver couldn't hear. "This place reminds me of the mansion in *Eyes Wide Shut*! You aren't taking me to an orgy are you?"

Kelly burst out laughing. "You're so close, but no."

"Good. I know you want me to date but I'm not ready."

"Even if Tom Cruise is here?"

"Especially if Tom Cruise is here. He scares me. Way too intense. He'd be too intense eating oatmeal."

She laughed. "Relax. Trust me. It's a little party."

"Look at this place. There's nothing little about it. Are you sure it's not a soiree, or possibly a cotillion? It's definitely not a hootenanny. Way too ritzy for a hootenanny."

"A get-together," she said.

"How did we get invited? Who owns it? Is it Tom Cruise?"

"I know somebody. And, no, not Tom Cruise."

I didn't know it yet, but the Dark Ages were already getting smaller in my rearview mirror. My Big New Life was coming quick and I didn't suspect a thing.

ike any city, Vancouver has an elite. The breast cancer research charity had brought the rich and powerful out from behind their stacks of money. I noticed a local politician I recognized from the news. Servers in cream jackets and white gloves sifted through the crowd. They carried silver trays of champagne flutes and offered intricate hors d'oeuvres I vaguely recognized as Thai food, but fancier than I'd ever seen.

As we entered the great room, we spotted a tall grinning adonis in a tux. The stunning woman at his elbow wore a white sheath dress that must have cost more than my rent. The crowd seemed to swirl around them. "Who are they?" I asked.

"The power couple? Our hosts," Kelly replied. "They are hugely successful on the production side of Hollywood North."

With their air of celebrity, these weren't the sort of people who would hang out at our rundown mall. They looked vaguely familiar. I might have seen their pictures somewhere. "First a limo and now this? How did you get an invite to this shindig, Kelly? This isn't our circle."

"I have ways. I know people. I'm in other circles."

"I had no idea."

"It's nice to maintain a little mystery. If there weren't more to discover about me, you might get bored."

"I did donate to breast cancer research last year," I mused. "It was maybe forty bucks. I don't think that's enough to get us in the door here. I'm going to pass on the hors d'oeuvres. I don't deserve them. When a donation doesn't cover one of the caterer's — "

"Savvy? Please chill. You need to chill." Kelly's gaze was still fixed on the power couple.

"Don't stare," I said.

"Why not? They're beautiful."

I gave the power couple another furtive glance. "Yeah. They are. It's intimidating. So...TGI Fridays next? Now?"

"We're staying. Get comfortable."

I didn't want to appear creepy, but the hosts drew every eye as they worked the room. Transfixed, I felt like a fat tourist on safari in an exotic land peering at rare creatures from behind the bushes.

"Their latest movie is with Lionsgate," Kelly said.

"They aren't in front of the camera? They look like actors."

"He used to be a model. She was in several Canadian TV shows."

"I never watch Canadian TV. Too many jokes about living on the prairies, hockey, and Tim Horton's coffee. As long as I've lived in this country, Canadian celebrity has been an oxymoron."

"Jealous much?"

"Hell, yes. Not proud. I'd take her life. He's hunky in a suit and tie sort of way."

Kelly giggled. "I'd crawl through rotten mayonnaise and spoiled eggs to eat her ass after he fucked her."

"Kelly!"

"What?"

"The shit you say sometimes! We're fancy tonight. Tell me about the movie they're making."

"I saw the trailer. Looks good. A scorcher set in World War II."

"Great," I said. "Against a backdrop of war, they found love, blah, blah, blah. Let me guess: Ryan Gosling with his shirt off. Amy Adams looking adorable."

"It won't be Ryan Gosling. It's one of those brothers who plays Thor. I can't keep those guys straight."

"You didn't see the trailer?"

"I avoid sappy movies, romance books, and love songs since the divorce."

"You said the D-word."

"I'll put a quarter in the swear jar at work."

Guests milled nearby, obviously waiting their chance to shake hands and maybe pitch a screenplay to our hosts. I wished I had a screenplay to sell. Or, better, I wished I was her. They looked so happy and I felt shitty for resenting them.

Kelly whispered in my ear. "It's not all Maybelline, either. She's working on an advanced mathematics degree at UBC while she's producing movies."

"At the same time?"

Kelly nodded. "Girl's got brains *and* tits."

"You've been cruising celebrity gossip sites at work again, haven't you?"

"We don't have enough work to do, so yeah."

"What do you think their lives are really like, besides being philanthropists who live in a mansion and apparently being everyone's friend?"

"Hard decisions every morning," Kelly said, "like whether to take the Lexus or let the limo driver deal."

I surveyed the crowd. I wasn't one of these people. I felt like the skunk who snuck into the barn, pretending she was a cat. "Let's look around the house," I said. "I'm turning green."

"Envy is one of the seven deadly sins you know."

"What's your deadly sin, Kelly?"

"Lust."

"Good for you. Paul must be very happy. I might have to lose you in the crowd soon, just so you know. I don't know what's gotten into you."

"Dick," she said. "Dick got into me."

"You're bad."

"When I'm very good, yes."

Kelly and I wandered. It was the biggest house I'd ever been in. The bar was free and most people seemed to gravitate to it when they weren't trying to kiss the hosts' rings. We drifted from the throngs to listen to a string quartet. They wove back and forth between classical and smooth jazz. It was the one place it was okay to stand still and not talk to anyone. I lingered, glad of my opportunity to slip into a socially sanctioned anti-social bubble.

My Gremlins of Sadness crept in. Gremlins of Sadness are what I call those thoughts that take something good and make it bad. If it's a sunny day, the Gremlins say, "But it will rain soon."

Kelly broke my pattern. "I want you to meet someone." She pulled me away, and we soon found ourselves in a glass room at the rear of the mansion. The owners called it the Orchid Room. There was a sign on the door.

"Your house is too big if you have to label the rooms to figure out where you are," I whispered. "Imagine a big sign like at the mall: *YOU ARE HERE.* Don't forget your compass, GPS, map, and local guide. Follow the breadcrumbs to your kitchen. You'll find it between the mansion's Baby Gap and the Apple Store. If you find yourself in the Batcave, you've gone too far."

Behind me, a woman with what sounded vaguely like a German accent said, "Savannah Needs! Good afternoon! So lovely to finally meet you!"

I stiffened, wondering if I'd been overheard. One of the upper crust was speaking to me. Worse, as I looked to her for support, Kelly turned and walked away.

4

I turned to find that my best friend had been replaced by a short, blonde woman with startling blue eyes. It was hard to pinpoint her age. I sensed she was older than me, maybe forty, and stunning. I'm not tall but she was so tiny she barely came up to my shoulder.

"Forgive me for saying so, darling, but you look like someone stole your puppy." She pronounced darling *dahlink*. Someone stole came out as *zomeone ztole*. Puppy sounded like *poopy*.

"Are you a mind reader?"

"No, nothing mystical. There is an interesting book about the science of empathic connection called *Mirror Touch*. I do recommend it. It's about a doctor who has a superhuman ability to feel what his patients experience. Fascinating things, mirror neurons. Anyway, our friend Kelly has told me so much about you." She seemed to study me, her gaze lingering on my lips and eyes.

"You still grieve. That high level of attachment this far out from the divorce is unhealthy. I'm sorry if I sound too presumptuous, but time is not of the essence, it is of our essence. Time to move on, don't you think?"

"You do sound presumptuous," I said. "Where I'm from, we don't talk about personal problems with strangers. Or friends. Or family. We only gossip about other people's problems behind their backs, where it's safe."

"You make a joke to ease the tension between us. Good. You accommodate people well. That is positive, if reasonable and socially adept, negative if it cancels out your capacity for self-assertion." She bobbed her head as if confirming I'd passed a test.

No one had ever told me anything like that. I didn't know what to do with my face. A microscope was on me and I was heating up under the glare of its light. "Uh...oh. I see," was all I could manage.

"Not yet, you don't, but I suspect you soon will. Please let go of your self-consciousness, darling. Reading people is an occupation and a preoccupation of mine. I make people uncomfortable."

"What? You mean, like, professionally?"

"Discomfort and dissatisfaction are critical to every successful transformation process. Those elements lead us to change in healthier directions." The woman extended a hand. "My name is Sabine Ali."

I shook her hand cautiously, the way you might shake the paw of a strange dog with big teeth. "Savannah."

"Yes, darling. Kelly asked me to speak with you."

"Is this an intervention? Do you have a bunch of my old friends waiting somewhere to tell me how disappointed they are with my life choices? I told Kelly I was off the boxed wine. She doesn't seem to believe me, but I really am."

Sabine smiled. "Your friend is genuinely worried about you."

"Are you a shrink? I can't afford a shrink. I had one but my insurance ran out so...." I shut up when I realized, too late, I was babbling.

"Let's find a quiet place to talk."

I wanted to strangle Kelly. I also considered smothering her in lemon meringue pies. Too many murder methods are cliché, so yeah, death by lemon meringue pies. She'd never see that coming and it would confuse the police.

"I'd like to tell you a story about the man who changed my life."

"Oh, no."

"You are alarmed."

"Mildly. Are you about to ask me if I'm saved? Or are you trying to get me into a pyramid scheme? Either way, my money's tight and — "

"This isn't about Jesus or Odin. I'd like to talk to you about the guy who teased me deliciously until I begged him to fuck me. When he finally did, everything changed for the better."

"Um ... what?"

"You heard correctly. I'm quite sure you'll find my proposal interesting."

"Proposal?"

"If you accept my invitation, everything might change for you, too."

"Yeah, I should go."

"Kelly tells me you are intelligent and, when you loosen up, funny. She intimated that you haven't let your hair down in a long time."

My gaze lingered on the exit a moment too long.

"You don't want to run from me because you're shocked. You want to run away because I'm making you uncomfortable by speaking plainly."

"It sounds like Kelly has been spilling her guts. Things said between friends in confidence — "

"Life's too short not to be honest. Please don't blame Kelly. She's trying to help you, as am I."

"I better go, Sabine. This is too weird."

"You have nothing to fear from me, Savannah. Please hear me out before you reject what I have for you."

"I'm no prude, Sabine, but this is strange cocktail party conversation."

She cupped my elbow gently. "The alternative is you walk out of here and never learn what I wanted to tell you. You'll go back to your place in West Van. You'll wonder what my story was and why I wanted you to know it. It will nag at you for years and you'll never learn the amazing opportunity that slipped by. If you give me a chance, you could change your life. The worst-case scenario is you have a funny story to tell about the crazy lady you met at a cocktail party once."

"If this ends up as a bizarre pitch for me to start selling Tupperware or Amway, I am going to be so pissed."

Sabine laughed. "You are funny."

"I still haven't ruled out killing Kelly. Okay, what's your pitch?"

"I want to tell you about a retreat I suspect you would enjoy."

"I'm not sure — "

"It's a retreat on Vancouver Island."

"The secret sex spa?"

"The same!"

"Kelly mentioned it. Sounds silly. There are plenty of places like that for men, I guess, but — "

"I've been there. It is real. It's wonderful." *Vonderful!*

"I guess I have to say tell me more ... just for the funny story, though."

She stepped close to whisper in my ear. "It's not just a story. I could tell you in elaborate detail about how he knelt before me and licked my pussy until I cried. Or how he bent me over a chair in his magnificent library and gave me the fuck of the century until my legs shook and my knees gave out. How he did things with my clit most men lack the imagination to even think of. Or would you rather hear about how we made sweet love at dawn? I could skimp on the details and keep my pornographic descriptions softcore?"

My temperature rose. "No, Sabine. You...you...um...."

"Yes?"

I reddened. I could feel heat shoot into my cheeks. "You had my attention the way you put it the first time."

"Sensational, passionate sex sounds good, doesn't it, Savannah? Do you want to be fucked by a gorgeous young man like you're the last woman on Earth? Do you ache for a hard cock so much sometimes, you can't satisfy yourself? Are you ready to handle a sexual adventure to fuel your masturbatory sessions for the rest of your life? I'm offering you a fantasy made real. People will look at you for years to come and they'll ask why you are smiling. That smile will hide the memory of your secret history."

I could feel my cheeks flush even more. "I admit, I'm intrigued."

"Then you've passed the first test."

I knew it! This was a test, mainly of my patience. "If I don't pass the oral is there a supplementary anal?"

"If you'd like. Courage and curiosity is the mark of the seeker." *Zeeker*.

"Does this story end with you training me in the ways of the Force? 'Cause lightsabers look really dangerous to me. Jedi knights lose limbs and — "

"You are amusing."

She told me that in such a deadpan way, I thought she was screwing with me.

"Please," she said. "Let's talk outside. You're about to become a much more interesting person."

If I were a cat, my back would be up and the claws would come out. Sabine was so tiny I was sure I could knock her out in a fair scrap.

"Relax," she cooed. "I mean no offense. Quite the opposite. I mean you're about to become you, only more so: Savannah to the fullest. The world will be better for it, I'm sure. We need more of you in this world instead of trapped inside your head."

"You've got a lot of chutzpah, Sabine."

"My mother was Jewish. She would agree. My father was Irish. He would say I have a lot of what the cat licks his ass with."

"Tongue?"

"I'm not clear on that idiom. It's possible he meant I was full of shit."

I relaxed a notch. By that I mean I didn't run away screaming.

"Jewish and Irish? Where did you get your accent?"

"I grew up in Riga."

"Where?"

"Latvia's capital."

"Ah." I couldn't picture Latvia on a map. "How'd you end up there?"

"My mother taught business at the university in Valmiera."

"Oh." I wondered if she was making all that up. I was pretty sure Riga was an alien planet or a character on *Star Trek*.

"Come with me if you want to come a lot," Sabine beckoned. I followed her outside as if in a trance. I did not stride out, itching to start anew and meet my destiny. It wasn't nearly so easy. Old habits grow strong and die hard. You can't allow them to expire on their own. You have to murder those ingrained ways with a chainsaw and use a blowtorch on the roots so they don't grow back.

I'm embarrassed to write these words now. I was given a great gift, but Sabine had to drag me into the light. I went to my bright future kicking and screaming. She was very persuasive, though. "You want to be different," she said. "To achieve that, you must do different. It's a sex-positive retreat, but you don't have to have sex with anyone."

"Then the questions are what, why, and how much?"

"To change things up and explore your options. Take time for yourself. Vacations are important for everyone, but free vacations in luxury are exceedingly rare."

"*Free* time off? And I don't have to have sex with anyone?"

That's how I ended up on a seaplane headed to a retreat on Vancouver Island.

5

I do love travel but small planes make me nervous. Check that: little seaplanes whisking me off to mysterious destinations make me squirrelly. I went through a mental list of celebrities who died in small plane crashes: John Kennedy, Jr., John Denver, the Big Bopper, Richie Valens, Left Eye Lopez .... There was that golfer whose little jet kept on flying for a while after all the oxygen was inexplicably shut off. I was sure there were plenty more to freak out about — there's always more to freak out about.

It wasn't a long flight from Vancouver to the Island, but as we took off I could feel the city's gravitational pull at my back. Vancouver doesn't have the tough reputation of being a dream crusher like Los Angeles or New York. Even though I wasn't happy with my status quo, leaving the familiar scared me.

Since Doug and I moved from the States, I had a complicated relationship with my adopted home. The people are nice — not so nice you worry they're up to something, like asking for money or following you home. There are the vegetarian restaurant cliches and B.C. bud dispensaries, of course. Business is cloaked in sharp suits, glass, and steel. The city rarely acknowledges its seedy underbelly, wherein heroin-addicted unfortunates are trapped and slowly digested. Because it's cheaper to produce a film there, Hollywood Northwest is a TV and movie-making mecca. Visitors on the lookout for celebrities rarely find them. Instead, they battle traffic to see Old Town's steam clock, Stanley Park Zoo, and the Kitsilano suspension bridge.

Everybody loves the view of the Rockies. Most breathe a sigh of relief the moment they leave, too. As with any cosmopolitan city, much is demanded of its inhabitants. Vancouverites are in a hurry. The city sets a quick pace and exerts subtle pressure on the skin. It's a living machine pushing you to make enough to pay the rent. If you can manage that, you can be a cog. Make more and bingo! You're a sprocket! Make a lot more and maybe you, too, can retire to Victoria someday.

Canadians say that Victoria is made up of the "newly wed and nearly dead." From what I knew of it, Victoria is for people who are content and wish they were British. The city doesn't want to get bigger. The expense of traveling via ferry, plane, and seaplane discourages idle wanderers. Vancouver Strait is a moat against the mainland's rigors and North America's coarseness. Victoria is the refined old neighbor lady who tends her garden and takes four o'clock tea seriously. As my daddy would say, "She wouldn't say shit if her mouth was full of it." (Note to tourists: Victoria's older population adores lawn bowling with a fervor usually reserved for jacking off to porn. They don't put it that way in the pamphlets, though.)

I thought we'd land in Victoria, or at least in the water beside it. Instead, my pilot brought the Cessna into an inlet down the coast. A smooth concrete runway is a comfort. Putting down on water is rougher. I squeezed my hands, fingers hurting and knuckles white. The pilot pulled us close and, by wizardry or instinct born from years of experience, cut the engine to glide into position perfectly.

A tall redhead with short spiky hair stood on the floating dock ready to greet me. Long slits up the sides of her sleeveless red dress showed her limbs were covered in colorful tattoos: all roses. With her button nose and large green eyes, she reminded me of a badass Tinkerbell. "Hi! I'm Rose Sinclair," she said. "Welcome, Savannah."

The pilot looked her over appreciatively and tipped his baseball cap.

"Hey, Bud."

"Hey, Rose. Any new tattoos?"

"Not where you can see them."

"Can I?"

"Depends," she smiled. "Did you get an OB/GYN degree since I saw you last?"

The pilot chuckled. "No, but you are encouraging me to expand my education." Bud handed me my bag and climbed back into the Cessna. He took off, but he looked back to stare at the woman in roses. I worried he was too distracted to fly safely.

"I trust you had a pleasant flight?" Rose asked.

"Yeah. Um, this might seem like an odd question, but does Bud know about the retreat?"

"One of the guests might have told him. He's never said anything to me about it. Why do you ask? Did he say something that bothered you?"

"No, but I feel like my granddad just gave me a ride to a sex shop."

Rose burst out laughing. "Don't worry about Bud. He's a sweetie."

"He did seem nice, I guess. He sure likes you."

"Yes. Please don't judge him for it."

Judge him for it? I communicated more in my tone than I'd intended. "His stares don't bother you?"

"Nope. Should they?"

"Well, he's ... you know." I mimed primping a big handlebar mustache.

"You mean because he's older?"

"Older? He's ancient. Plus, there's the problem of the male gaze."

Rose shrugged. "Men are men, women are women, and I don't feel threatened by Bud. The spirit stays willing, even if the flesh is weak. He likes my look. I enjoy his adoration. He comes from a generation where a man looks at a woman and isn't ashamed of what he's thinking. I appreciate his honesty. Too many men feel like they have to say they love you for your mind. Many of them are lying, even to themselves. It's the dance we do."

"So he doesn't make you uncomfortable at all?"

She shrugged. "Not for nothing, but I don't dress the way I do and get all these tattoos to avoid attention."

We watched the seaplane lift off into the dimming light. Feeling awkward, I was reminded of the first time I went to the drugstore to buy condoms because Doug was too embarrassed to do so. "Sorry, I feel like we're getting off on the wrong foot."

"Not at all." Rose's smile reached her eyes, genuine in her warmth.

"I'm not sure I'm in the right place."

"You're very welcome here, Savannah. Sabine chose you, so I'm sure you're meant to be here."

"Sabine sure is ... confident, isn't she?"

"That can be grating, can't it?"

" Talking to Sabine, I felt naked."

"Naked should be a good feeling."

I turned red. Rose gave my shoulder a friendly squeeze. "When she first meets someone, she feels the need to impress them. I don't blame her. Putting her sensitivity on display helped her get you to come."

"She was convincing and ...."

"Formidable?"

I nodded. "I was going to say pushy."

"We had an opening in our schedule and Sabine felt the urgency of filling the spot. She told me to pass on her apologies, but she's also very pleased you've come. She has made some great changes. When she came to us, she was living in her head too much, torturing herself. Now she's immersed in her body and mind. She's an incredibly giving person who cares deeply about spreading the benefits of our work."

"How did you manage to get her to change?"

"Oh, we can't change anyone. Everybody has to change themselves. I just nudged her in a new direction by suggesting there was more she could do with her tongue besides argue."

"I see."

"You're uncomfortable again."

"No, I'm more uncomfortable than I was before. So ... more and still, not again,"

Rose stepped close and gave me a hug. "I can see why Sabine used her talented tongue on you and wants to do it more and again." She giggled and, as she pulled away, let her hands slip beneath my breasts briefly, feeling their weight. I gasped and she let out a great belly laugh as her lips formed an "O" and her big eyes widened. "Nice tits!"

"Hey! Is this some kind of test?"

"I had to know if they were real. Sabine wasn't sure."

"They aren't that big!" Instinctively, I stepped back and teetered on the edge of the dock, almost falling in.

Rose's arm flashed out and caught me by the wrist before I could tumble back into the cold water.

"They're more than a mouthful." She giggled like a schoolgirl again. "They look delicious."

My first impulse was to get mad at having my personal space invaded. My irritation competed with my gratitude for not getting dunked into the saltwater along with my cell phone. Rose's laughter was infectious. Despite her innuendo and frankness, there was something girlish, impulsive, and playful about her. She somehow seemed innocent, like she might ask me to play doctor one moment or challenge me to a race up the dock the next.

As she pulled me safely away from the dock's edge, she asked if I was hungry.

"Am I too late for dinner? Should I take a cab to Victoria?"

"You can always have whatever you like here." She looked at me the same way the pilot had looked at her. Her flirty grin made me think she was offering more than a meal.

I wanted to ask if Rose and Sabine had been lovers. Instead, I looked around and played dumb. "Is Victoria far?" In case I wanted to take off in the middle of the night, I needed an escape plan.

"Not far at all. I'll take you myself tomorrow if you'd like. There are a couple of bookstores I have to show you. I absolutely adore them. They are two of my shrines."

Shrines? I wondered what her other shrines might be. If I dared to ask, I worried she'd say, "The masseur's magic cock."

Contemplating the possibility, I dissolved into giggles as I walked up the dock toward the house on the hill among the trees.

6
―――

As we climbed the zig-zagging stairs from the dock, rows of terraced gardens in scalloped patterns punctuated the steep hillside. A thick latticework of low manicured hedges protected rows of root vegetables, arugula, broad beans, kale, and spinach from the ocean wind. I glimpsed a discreet network of hoses that fed the plants fresh water. Plastic domes sheltered some flowering plants while others were backed by a reflective material that, at a glance, looked like tinfoil.

I paused and pointed. Before I could ask, Rose said, "Some need more protection, heat, and sun to grow. Others thrive with more moisture and a delicate touch. I strive to accommodate all comers."

The way she looked at me when she spoke, I felt like I was the only other person in the world. I had her full attention. A tingle of desire pulsed through me.

At the top of the stairs, we came upon another garden that obscured my view of the first floor of the house. Since Sabine had made a point of referring to the master of the house as the masseur, I expected a mansion. It was a mansion of sorts but the house on the hill wasn't what I expected. The long two-story glass house was topped by solar panels interrupted at intervals by skylights.

"Besides solar power, we use the big roof to collect rainwater. The pool is saltwater, fed by the ocean," Rose said. She touched my arm and pointed back the way we'd come.

I took in the view to the east. The seaplane had already disappeared. A wind turbine spun slowly but steadily in the distance on a finger of land to the south. Whitecaps played across the waves.

Rose gestured toward the point. "Like the view? You can't see it from this side of the point but, through the pine trees on the opposite side, there's an old lighthouse at the edge of the next bay. The lights are all automated now, but you can still climb up to the gallery. It's a great view. Our boathouse is out there, too, if you're up for a ride. I suggest the moonlight cruise. It is spectacular."

"Don't you get a bunch of tourists coming around to check this place out?"

"The trees and private drive seclude us. The beach is public access along the point, but up here it's secluded from prying eyes. Walk around naked all you like. I do."

I smiled and thought how, even when I thought our marriage was good, I rushed to change clothes so Doug wouldn't catch me naked and unprepared. If he was already in the bedroom, I'd slip into the bathroom to change for bed. I wouldn't be walking around nude anytime soon. I thought people who changed clothes in front of their pets were daring and weird.

I looked around, desperate to change the subject from whatever the hell it was. "The gardens must be a full-time job."

"It's not too bad, actually. I've got everything plotted out and cross-referenced on a spreadsheet, a calendar, and a weather app. The schedule breaks down to categories: prepping, seeding, weeding, watering, blooming, transplanting, harvesting and frost. There aren't that many deadlines with flowers and veggies. Half the time I ignore the computer, look at the sky, and eyeball what needs to be done."

Transfixed by the little Eden before me, I heard Rose's words but I wasn't processing much. As we made our way toward the house, we took a circuitous route so I could see more of Rose's design. The garden was planted in concentric circles that alternated in great arcs of colorful flowers and vegetables. Hummingbirds flitted back and forth from feeders hung above an herb garden. We watched the tiny birds, furtive and quick, hovering and then flicking away.

"We have more birdhouses around the front of the house that serve more species. The hummingbird feeders are my favorite, though." She added, "Beautiful little creatures with such long tongues. They reach deep into the flower, past the petals, to get the sweetness, you know?"

I glanced up. Rose gazed at me in a way that made me think she was wondering about the length of my tongue. My lips twitched, and I cleared my throat. "It's surprisingly warm up here even though we're beside the ocean."

"It's the trees, hedges, and landscaping." Her large Tinkerbell eyes didn't leave mine. "This is an oasis, safe from the mundane shit that curdles the milk everywhere else."

As we walked through the labyrinth of plants, the aroma of lavender and mint stole over us. "I feel like I just walked through a perfume department at a mall, but this is so much better. It's a sweet cloud, subtle but...I don't know — "

Rose brought her head forward as her hand went to her cheek before slowly it sweeping down over her mouth. Her little finger pulled her lower lip slightly. "Seductive?" she suggested.

My God, I thought, *that was a pure Marilyn Monroe move, if Marilyn had been a thin red-headed Tinkerbell covered in rose tattoos.*

I gulped audibly.

"I love the earthy smell of cedar most," Rose said. "Sometimes I just lie between the hedges. The cedar is so sweet. Ooh, but to lie on a bed of moss naked in the sunlight? That's even better, better than any mattress."

She was putting a spell on me. I wanted to snort cedar chips and get laid on a bed of moss. I wanted to feel the length of Rose's tongue up and down my body. Well, on my clitoris mostly.

I inhaled deeply to breathe in the garden's aromas and to slow my heart's pounding. Calm and relaxation eased into my muscles and penetrated my bones. If the smell of cedar hadn't settled my nerves, the distinctive pungent odor of marijuana that wafted my way might have done the job.

"Your bougainvilleas are beautiful," I said, pointedly overlooking the marijuana smell.

"My bougainvilleas?" Rose looked down at her small breasts. "If that's your best innuendo, we'll have to work on your pillow talk."

My jaw moved up and down but no sound came out.

"Ease back, right? No worries. I won't be relentless. I just want you to know I'm available for all your needs, Ms. Needs."

"Thanks," was all I could think to say. I hadn't been hit on this hard by a woman since ... I was about to say, "ever." However, Kelly was bi and enjoyed flirty lesbian jokes that weren't all jokes. My cheeks felt hot again and the slight sheen of sweat on my forehead wasn't just because of the climb up the stairs.

Rose blessed me with another easy smile. "If you like adventures in floral design, we can do the touristy thing and I'll take you to Butchart Gardens. Brentwood Bay is about forty minutes away. I get a lot of inspiration from the flowers at Butchart."

"Sounds great." Flowers? Who had time to look at flowers? Didn't people have work to do?

That's where my mind was: I literally didn't have time to stop and smell the roses. Despite all the distractions Rose offered, floral and sexual, I was not fully embracing vacation mode yet.

"How many gardeners do you have here?"

"I take care of most of what you see. Sometimes we bring in extra help for big projects. Mostly, we have Ryan. He's a young, local guy who started in construction pouring concrete. When the boss built the house, Ryan stayed on to mow the front lawn, do the trimming and maintenance. The kid was interested in hydroponics so we sent him off to college for four years. He came back a man who knows much more about managing vertical gardens than I do. The greenhouses are his domain. He helps me more with my work in the spring and fall. I help him out in the winter with the greenhouse."

"Ryan can talk about the nitty-gritty chemistry of botany all day and not get tired, but he's cool. Really hot bod, too."

"This still looks like so much for you to do." I was really thinking how hard it was for me to drag my ass out of bed each morning. I went to a job where I sat that ass at a desk for many hours each day. For sheer calories burnt, I had it easy compared to Rose. However, I sensed she loved her work as much as I hated mine.

"About two-thirds of our food comes from within a few hundred feet of the house and we've got some to spare. We're not totally self-sufficient."

"Still, when the zombie apocalypse comes, you'll be ready."

"I hope it doesn't come to that. I'm not a fan of apocalyptic scenarios," Rose said. "We did have a guest who was deep into zombie porn, though. She was fun. We got to play around with some very inventive make-up. We hired a makeup artist for a week. I do cosplay sometimes and it's a riot. We — "

"Hold up. Zombie porn? That's a thing?"

"When it comes to sex, everything's a thing. Tentacle porn, cow lactation porn, werewolf porn. You name it, somebody wants to stick a dick in it or sit on its face."

"Oh," I said. What I meant was: Oh, my God! I have to get the fuck out of here and back to Normal.

7

A hedge and a wall of climbing vines hid the back of the house along the first floor. Ivy stretched along the edge of the garden to form a living border by a sunken pool. As we emerged from the greenery, the riot of color was a sight I'd only thought possible in a paint store. Banks of tulips surrounded the pristine pool. I looked from the garden to my guide's many tattoos. "I should have guessed."

Rose flexed a bicep. "You like?"

"It's amazing. Er, your arms and the garden, yes."

"You should see it covered in massage oil. My body, I mean, not the flowers. Imagine me, naked, shiny, and slick."

"Heh." The way she slowly enunciated the word slick sent a shiver through my vulva that made me cross my legs nervously. "Looks like your boss has enough money to be a Bond villain. Unusual for a masseur, huh?"

"He's flower power and solar batteries all the way. Not many Bond villains are into harnessing the wind to power pumps for wells in rural Sudan. You might think of him as a bodyworker who employs sex for the greater good. He's trying to get away from the stereotypes of the word masseur. Try to avoid it. I know Sabine insists on saying masseur for marketing purposes, but it's really not accurate."

"Okay. Can I ask? You mentioned, 'We live like this.' Are you guys a couple?"

She smiled. "Couplehood isn't for me. Rick calls me his majordomo."

Rick! I finally had a first name for the mystery man!

"I like majordomo," she said. "I take care of the place and make sure things go smoothly with our guests."

I kept my attention on the house and tried to remain as pure in thought as my mother. Lousy at keeping to pure thoughts, I took a deep breath. "The air is richer here."

"More green, more oxygen. My head is clearer here, too, like in the rainforest. That's the beauty of Vancouver Island, lots of sea and forest air, mixing and cleansing. Sabine tells me you've traveled a lot."

"Kind of a thing of the past now," I said.

"You seem stressed. I hope you'll find the spa is a palate cleanser."

Standing next to Rose, I'd never felt so old, stuffy, and grim.

"Is Rick in there?"

"Kayaking, but he'll be back by dark. Sorry about that. When he left, we weren't sure you were joining us today. Otherwise, he would have greeted you personally."

"I don't even know his last name. Sabine said the rule was I didn't get to know until I got here."

"That's just a Sabine rule. She thinks mystery closes the deal."

"In my case, mystery helped."

"We don't get along well all the time, but Sabine's good at what she does. She had me in bed within five minutes of meeting her. She took one look at me and said, 'You like getting your hair pulled.' A few minutes later, I was on my knees, spread like butter as she — "

"Rose!"

"Oh, right. His name is Barrister. Rick Barrister."

8

R ose pointed to a gate to the left. "That path is the way to the cabins."

I hefted my little bag, ready to retreat. "Oh, will I be in a cabin?"

"We have a guest room for you in the house. The cabins are usually for staff unless we host a group or someone visits for an extended stay."

Groups? Extended stays? I had visions of orgies in secluded cabins, human sacrifice by blazing campfires, and chattering mental patients wandering lost and naked among the pines. What guarantee did I have that I hadn't wandered into a surreal trap, a hellish scenario somewhere between *The Wicker Man* and *Shutter Island*?

Rose pointed out a gate to the right. "That way takes you on a lovely trail through the woods and back along the shore, the boathouse, the windmill, the greenhouses, and the lighthouse."

"And all this time I thought utopia was a hopeless mission."

"Rick's premise is that the best ideas with the best outcomes are already tried and tested," Rose told me. "We just have to live them."

"Rose? Between the solar panels, hemp, and the free-range everything...are you guys running some kind of hippie commune here? I don't want to end up wearing a bed sheet and sell flowers at the airport."

"I don't think selling flowers at airports is a thing anymore, anyway."

"Sorry for all the suspicion and questions. I sound as paranoid as a mouse in a glue trap factory, don't I? I'm stupid nervous."

"Many are a little weirded out coming here the first time. The visitors who are too eager and don't think we're strange are the ones I worry about. For some, this place is about taking time to get healthier. Others come just to be heard. It feels to them like their family, friends, and lovers are deaf to their needs." Rose shrugged. "Varies, though. Maybe you need me or Rick. Or is this time for you to downshift in solitude? If I had to guess, I'd say you need to calm your tits. They're lovely but you seem pretty amped up."

I allowed a grudging smile. "I am amped up. Day before yesterday I didn't know I'd be here in Shangri-la and, yes, the price tag is free but — "

"I never forget how weird we seem to people still plugged into the common paradigm: work, pay, consume, work, pay, consume, pay, consume, die."

"Nice."

"Give me a couple minutes and I could probably come up with a way to say that so it sounds ten percent less shitty," she replied.

Rose slipped off a sandal and dipped one pale foot in the pool. "Eighty-one degrees. Not too hot, not too cold. We run pipes around the solar panels to heat the pool. I love swimming here at night. The flowers that open at night are the most fragrant. With the steam rising off the water in the moonlight and the view of the mountains? Beautiful. I skinny dip. Feel free to join me. Our house is your house. You can even keep your bathing suit on if you want to. Or let me take it off with my teeth."

"Wow."

"Too much?"

"Little bit."

"I've been testing around the edges to see how receptive you are to my advances, in case you hadn't noticed."

"In case I hadn't noticed? You're Captain Innuendo! If you were a guy I'd have slapped you so much it would sound like applause."

"Good thing I'm not a guy, then. I get it. You aren't open to skinny dipping with me. It's cool. Just wanted you to know I'm not much good with subtlety on the vertical but I am delightful when horizontal."

"Delightful? There's a foreign concept. Life is a struggle to be endured."

"Suffering should be optional, Savannah. It's not a commandment."

Rose operated on laws of physics that were alien to me. She was an organic engine, a life driver. I was still a cog in the machine.

9

―――――――――

"We're a retreat, first and foremost," Rose said. "If we're successful, the sex comes as a natural result of our work. When everything is working, sex is one of the beautiful expressions of acceptance. There are other acts of acceptance. You can always decline and the door swings in and out. We are not possessive people and we do want the best for you."

"Sorry, but you're being kind of vague."

"I guess this is why Sabine is in sales and I'm not."

I stopped at the back door and inhaled the mix of cedar and rose perfumes. "I'll try not to jump to conclusions and confusions, but I'm still not sure what Sabine sold me. She might have hypnotized me or hit me over the head and this is a pleasant coma."

"She sold you possibility," Rose said. "People fear that circumstances will change. They're also afraid things *won't* change. You're slightly more afraid your life will remain static so you ended up here."

I went cold as I processed her words. "Since my divorce began, I've been afraid a lot."

"Probably since before that."

I couldn't decide whether to be sad or annoyed.

"You aren't alone, Savannah. People are afraid all the time. Illness, violence, death, sex, money...we are conditioned to respond to all kinds of issues in an unhealthy way. Feeling shame about fear is like piling shit on top of shit. Won't taste like layer cake."

"Where I come from, you're never supposed to admit you're afraid."

"That's a disorganization of the mind you could choose to reprogram this week. You don't have to throw everything out in the trash. However, make decisions using your judgment. Past experience can inform mature decisions instead of dictating your behavior."

"What do you suggest I do, Rose?"

"About what?"

"I mean, how should I change my life?"

"As the boss would say, I just provide stimulation: neocortical, neural, vaginal, and clitoral. Anal, if you're lubed and ready."

"I'm trying to be serious here."

"Me, too. I'm telling you, the path you choose is up to you. If I'm irritating you. Please ask yourself why."

My cheeks flushed. I knew what she was getting at. "I'm a little pissed at you because I'm asking you to tell me what to do."

"I don't want to be your mama, but I'll let you suck my nipples if you want."

"I'm asking questions when I should be coming up with my own answers."

"That, and the other thing. About sucking my nipples."

"Message received." Despite my embarrassment, I allowed a smile that probably looked like I was gritting my teeth.

"Is that a little crack of sunlight I see? A little breakthrough?"

"Do you cry, Rose?"

"Of course, but I rarely have reason to."

"I cried this morning. I was embarrassed that Kelly thought I needed this place...worrying about money...my past, the future I don't have...."

"You can make new decisions at any moment, Savannah. I believe that. I've done that. People do."

I stared at her.

"Am I as annoying as Sabine yet?"

"I'm only holding back on scratching your eyes out because I believe you're trying to help me."

"How can I help in a way that would bypass your nervous brain? Would you feel better if I showed you to your room and licked your pussy before you have a siesta? I'm an artist in the garden, but you really should feel what I can do with your clit."

Stunned, my jaw dropped. "Whoa! Whiplash from the sharp turn, Rose!"

"No? Okay. No pressure. Getting licked always makes me feel better when I'm afraid. That makes me feel better no matter what's going on."

I chuckled uncomfortably. I also felt a tingle between my legs. I was reminded of something Kelly said about the difference between turning down men versus refusing a lesbian's pass. "With men, we say no and if they get uptight, we get uptight and angry and afraid. I don't fear women so I just say no thanks. With chicks, I don't have to reach for my bear spray."

Kelly had told me recently that if she hadn't married Paul, she'd take me to bed "just to shut up your boohooing about your goddamn divorce. That's what friends with benefits are for, Savvy."

Rose beckoned me to follow her into the house. "Dinner's at 8:30." Rose threw me a flirty wink. "Whatever you desire is always on the menu. If Rick were here, he'd say, 'Welcome to Fantasy Island!'"

———

10

The layout on the first floor was open concept. The sparse furniture was luxurious, all warm earth tones that contrasted drastically with walls of buttercream. Doorways between rooms were wide welcoming arches framed with intricate spirals of interlaced designs that reminded me of the knots on Celtic crosses.

At the top of a spiral staircase, Rose showed me a semi-circular room. I peeked into the dimly lit room. A bright yellow hammock hung under a skylight, dominating the center of the space. Ropes stretching up to anchors along the ceiling secured it. "This is the Recovery Room," she said.

"I've never seen a hammock inside a house before."

"We've got several outside, but on rainy days this is one of my favorite rooms," Rose said. "It's so wide you can pull the sides over you so you don't even need a blanket. It's like it's a cocoon."

"It looks like a banana."

"It's comfy, whether you want to come here to think or to not think."

A thick exercise mat lay to my right. An antique rolltop desk and chair stood off to one side of the door under a brass reading lamp.

This was the coziest room so far. I felt a pang for my little apartment. It wasn't homesickness. I wanted to move into this room and never leave.

"You'll find pens and stationery in the big drawer, chargers for your devices if you need. If you want a quiet place to sit and think where no one will bother you, I recommend this room."

Rose showed me a sliding pocket door. "For privacy. When this door is closed, no one comes in. Like I said, we don't have a lot of rules but that's one."

"Good to know, in case I need a place to hide and cry."

"Or relax, read or meditate. Sometimes the bodywork sessions are intense and guests need some time to decompress, relax, and process.

I walked around the mat to peer out of the window to the right. Sunflowers and petunias encircled a sunken hot tub protected by glass walls. Beyond the greenhouse, a chestnut tree sheltered a two-person swing and a shuffleboard court. A dozen magnolia trees skirted a pine forest with a floor carpeted with green moss. A fence entwined with thick ivy screened the greenhouse and hot tub from the front yard.

I left that room reluctantly. As nice as it was, a sliver of worry began to nag me. How could a bodywork session be so intense that I'd need a special room to recover? Was this going to be sex, massage, torture, or surgery?

Rose opened the double doors to a huge round room that took up half of the front of the house. Before me stood a vast library with shelves stuffed with books from floor to ceiling. A ladder on wheels on a track allowed a browser to reach any book. Three big leather massage chairs sat in the center of the room around a glass fireplace.

"What must it be like to live here? I'd love to be more like you, Rose."

Rose paused, stepped forward, and gave me a bear hug. "Thank you, Savannah. What a nice thing to say! See? You're not such a cynical bitch after all! Come on, let me show you your room. Wear whatever you like for dinner. Clothing optional, if you like."

"Dinner naked? I don't want to put everyone off their food."

"And there it is. Savannah Needs, Queen of Self-deprecation. I knew I was moving too fast, your highness."

"What if we have soup? I don't want to burn myself."

"If hot soup is the only thing keeping your clothes on, I'll make vichyssoise."

11

The soft scent of lavender wafted through the open door as I peered in my bedroom. It looked like a photo spread straight out of a *Better Homes & Gardens*: rich hardwood floors the color of coffee, pot lights casting subtle warm glows, textured walls in a deep wave pattern of dark blue, sliding glass doors to a small private balcony. A white linen canopy hung above the king-sized four-poster bed.

How many women had been tied to that beautiful bed? Would I be next? Would Rose or Rick bind my wrists and ankles in soft ropes? Would I end up spread-eagle, vulnerable, moaning, screaming, arching my back in ecstasy?

It had been a long time since I felt joy in my body. I'd denied myself as a physical being. Instead, I pondered the same worries over and over but arrived at no conclusions. At that moment I realized the economy, beauty, and profundity of the phrase, "getting my brains fucked out." I had associated that expression with empty frat boy bravado and aggression. But what if I could get railed so hard I'd stop obsessing over death, disease, and taxes? All those celibate monks and nuns have it wrong. Fucking my brains out doggy-style would be a relief from my existential rage. Very Zen.

"Savannah?" Rose pointed to an intercom by the bed. "If you need anything, just let me know. Press that button and you'll reach me anywhere. The bathtub in the en suite fits two comfortably, by the way."

She leaned close and, for the first time, I noticed a scent so light it might have been perfume. Maybe it was the flowers she nurtured all the time. Rose smelled like rose petals. I felt her breath on my left ear. I thought she was going to whisper something, the wifi password, maybe. Instead, she took my earlobe between her lips and sucked gently.

I gasped and felt a zing of electricity shoot straight to my pussy. I froze in shock. She sucked harder, and the tingles continued until she slowly let go, reluctant and lingering. "I can't wait to get to know you better, Savannah. I'm so glad you're here."

"I-I don't have sex with women, Rose."

"You haven't so far and you don't have to, but you're curious, aren't you?"

"I have wondered, sure. I came close to trying a couple of times." I thought of Kelly's flirty jokes that weren't really jokes. They were tests. I took my friend a little more seriously after we drank too many beers together. There was also the college roommate who looked like the idealized Disney Arabian princess. The princess turned me down, but the ache I felt for her was still memorable.

I could still feel Rose's lips on my earlobe, a phantom signal lingering along the length of nerves that reached between my legs. A rush of heat washed over me like a fever, a confusion of embarrassment and arousal.

"How are you so goddamn sure of yourself?" I asked. "I envy that."

"If you don't put out invitations for multiple delicious orgasms, you don't get many." She grinned. "We get as many heartbeats as we are allotted but we can maximize our orgasm total."

"You're braver than me."

"Anybody can be brave, Savannah. You just have to decide which you want more, being alone or being more social? Do you really want to be left alone? Or do you want me lapping at your clit and fucking you with my tongue until you beg me to stop?"

She kissed me on the mouth gently.

I kissed her back.

The kiss deepened. Warmth spread through me. Her palm found one of my nipples through my shirt. I didn't stiffen in shock this time. I leaned into it and closed my eyes. It was as easy as letting it happen. No. Easier. It had been a long time since I experienced a first kiss. I wanted to be wanted.

Slowly, Rose pulled away an inch. "When I go down on you, I might not stop right away. You'll just keep on dancing on the tip of my tongue. I love the sound of ecstasy. That sound when you come? That's one of the best sounds in the world, don't you think? I love discovering that sound. Screaming, squealing, moaning? Each orgasm is unique."

Her hand lingered a few seconds more on my breast before she slipped away. "Dinner's at 8:30 in the kitchen. Rick's looking forward to meeting you."

Rose left me panting in the bedroom doorway. I thought of the last time I stood in the doorway to my old bedroom, watching Doug and Patsy fuck. I'd been turned on and angry then. I was conflicted now. For the first time, I wondered if I could have saved my marriage if I'd been more open to possibility. I'd been so furious with Doug for cheating. I hadn't considered joining him and Patsy on the bed. I dismissed that idea immediately.

Almost.

The stress of the divorce had brought out the worst in both of us. Might I have held on to Doug if I'd been more flexible? Statistically, most husbands and wives forgive infidelity. I'd briefly tried to salvage our marriage with talk but maybe the occasional threesome with Doug and Patsy would have defused the bomb.

"Aw, fuck it." I wouldn't waste a week in hippie sex spa paradise thinking about Doug. That was over. We were over. The trouble was figuring out what would come next.

I flopped on the bed and stared up at the white canopy. "I don't want Doug," I told the empty room. "I don't even know why I'm so pissed at losing him anymore. If I think about it much longer, I'm sure I'll remember. Be it resolved, my week is about me, not Doug and Patsy. Fuckers."

I rolled on my back and ran my palms over my nipples through my shirt as Rose had. Still rock hard. Her description of her prowess with cunnilingus pulled my mind away. I would hem and haw. It's what we hemmers and hawers do. Would I give in to the temptations of this strange trip? Deep down (between my legs), I knew the answer was: probably.

If I accepted Rose's offer, would scissoring prove to be the fairly pointless exercise it appeared to be? I imagined soppy sounds as we ground our pussies against each other. Was a double-headed dildo required? Would scissoring be truly hot? Or was it an oddly cheery prelude to the serious business of what we could do with our fingers, tongues, and toys?

I still had to meet the masseur — excuse me, bodyworker — legendary and mysterious at the same time. The term 'bodyworker' made it sound like he worked on cars.

What would Rick Barrister be like? How long would I have to wait before it was a man feeling the weight of my breasts and reaching down to — as they say in romance novels — stir my slick silkiness? I was ripe and ready to get into the sex spa swing of things.

For the first time in a long time, I surprised myself.

12

Rick found me in the library after dark, huddled under a blanket and slouched over *Eat, Pray, Love* by Elizabeth Gilbert. When I glanced up from the page, the dark silhouette of a tall man loomed in the doorway. His shoulders were broad, his waist small. From the downward cast of my reading lamp, his face remained in shadow. I don't know how long he'd been watching.

I stood quickly, as if I'd been caught doing something wrong. The book slipped to the floor as the blanket puddled at my feet. The man stepped into the light and bent quickly to scoop up the book. He held it out to me and smiled. Numbly, I accepted.

Only his feet were bare but his wetsuit was so molded to his muscular body he may as well have been naked. It was like meeting a superhero while he was changing into his mortal disguise.

"Welcome! Rick Barrister, pleased to meet you, Savannah." His deep voice rumbled, sounding almost metallic.

No, not metallic. *Magnetic.*

My hand trembled as I swept my hair out of my eyes. I drank him in: light brown skin, high cheekbones, strong jaw, and a bit of stubble. His long black hair was slicked back as if he'd just stepped out of a shower. He was obviously gifted with good genes. Some well-muscled guys are too thick through the neck, as if an air hose up the ass inflates them into cartoonish balloons. Rick's long, defined contours looked like they'd been earned by work, not bench pressing forever. His dark eyes — bright intelligence softened by kindness — held my gaze.

He was younger than me, twenty-six or twenty-seven, maybe. He might have been a Calvin Klein model except for his nose. A little dent and turn just below the bridge told me it had been broken more than once. Rick didn't care to get it fixed. He was the perfect balance between pretty and rugged.

"A strong wind came up on the way back so my kayaking trip took a little longer than expected. Sorry, I didn't mean to surprise you. Finding you here, I wanted to see you in an unguarded moment. We are most ourselves when we are alone."

Flustered, I managed half a smile and blurted the first thing that came to mind. "Unguarded moment? Spying, you mean."

I blamed nerves, but the roots of my anxiety went deeper than that. Upon meeting the rich, successful, and gifted, resentment was my reflex. I knew that twinge well: "You think you're better than me?" If my mother or father said so-and-so from high school was "doing well," my financial failure was the not-so-subtle subtext. If we measure ourselves by money alone, only the gold-plated prick with the most money gets to be Jesus.

"I gave in to temptation," Rick admitted amiably. "I have no excuses for observing you unannounced, but I have reasons."

"Such as?"

"Sabine and Rose told me you were lovely. I wasn't prepared for how lovely."

"Bet you say that to all the girls."

"With you, I especially mean it."

"Aw! My father would call you a silver-tongued diplomat, the sort of salesman he'd shoo off the porch with a shotgun. He actually did that to an insurance broker once, no kidding."

"Shotgun diplomacy?"

"I'm from the South. We lived a long way from the sheriff, so that sort of thing happens quite a bit. It's different farther north. I imagine people in Connecticut trade strongly worded letters when they get angry."

"And since you've moved to Canada?"

"Up here, if you piss somebody off you invite them in for coffee to say sorry for an hour."

"How's this: Let me tell you a bit about the roots of what we do here. I won't try to sell you anything. Would that put you at ease?"

I gave him a grudging nod to let him know I was not to be messed with. He smiled and I relaxed a notch. He had nice teeth, white and even. I pictured him playfully biting my ass cheek. A little nip could make me giggle. That idea made me smile.

Rick got me on track gently, coaxing me so I wouldn't pull back and kick. "The greatest challenge is to be honest with ourselves. Everything flows from that."

He gestured for me to sit. As I returned to my seat, he retrieved the blanket from the floor and, without a word, covered me. A kind gesture. His face harbored no hint of calculation. He could have had me in bed that night. I knew it from the moment I saw him. As soon as Rick stepped out of the shadows and into the light I'd felt the hot ache of arousal.

"What do you want me to be honest about?"

"Anything unexamined that might trap you in a rut."

"Such as?"

"Conventional attitudes, living inauthentically, materialism without end. It's up to individuals to find meaning in their lives, if there is any meaning. If we just take philosophy that's handed down to us, we're not really engaged with our lives.

"You guys are hippies for a new century, am I right?"

Rick tilted his head back and forth in a way that let me know he disagreed but neither of us should be bothered too much.

"Bad news," I said. "I'm a cynic."

"Some things, we should be cynical about," Rick conceded.

"I don't want to put a pin in your big ol' balloon of altruism but

Sabine described what you do as some sort of sex club. Those weren't her exact words...."

"First, we have to focus on what you need. Then we can talk about what you want. After that, possibilities open up."

"Possibilities?"

"You're in control of where this time goes, Savannah."

I wanted to tell him I was most interested to explore his notions of sex positivity. I imagined pulling off that wetsuit, showering with him, and spreading my legs to feel his tongue explore me. The fantasy turned up the heat between my legs.

13

R ick was studying me again. I laughed nervously.

"You feel naked?" he asked.

I nodded.

"Are you embarrassed to be naked? I can't imagine that as a bad thing."

From another man, that line might have sounded lecherous. It wasn't his tone that saved him from sounding sleazy. I forgave him because I was so attracted to him. Beautiful people get away with just about anything except skinning puppies alive. Don't let them tell you different. Beautiful people get a pass on their first few murders. Put that on a bumper sticker.

"What were you about to say?" he asked.

"Nothing."

"C'mon. Rip off the bandaid quick, less pain that way."

I took a deep breath and plunged in. "I'm humiliated that my best friend thinks I need to be here."

"I'm certainly glad you're here."

"I'm told you strive to be a people pleaser. Please be as kind to Savannah Needs as you would to a stranger," he suggested. "The world is full of critics. You don't need to add to their number when you talk to yourself. We can help you feel better about life by changing your perception," Rick said. "Reframe the perception and you change the experience."

"Are you a shrink?"

He laughed. "Nah, we're just talking. I've studied a lot of body-work that's on the psychological end of the spectrum, a bunch of postural analysis and body reading — "

"Body reading? Is that like Braille? You use your fingertips to read my body and your eyes to read my dark, filthy mind?"

He laughed. "Something like that. Stepping back from stress and getting a change of scenery can help you reboot your operating system. Let's hope we can help you out of complacency before you run out of time."

"Run out of time? Am I going to die tomorrow? Is that on the schedule?"

"Kelly and Sabine are worried you're already dead. The world makes us zombies if we let it."

"But you won't tell me what to do?"

"Is that what you want?"

I felt heat rise in my cheeks. The honest answer was yes. Instead, I said, "My ex used to tell me what to do and I didn't like that. On the other hand, if I knew what to do, shouldn't I have done it by now?"

"Have you spoken to your doctor about your feelings?"

I nodded. "And a psychotherapist. 'Low-grade anhedonia,' I was told. In other words, I've forgotten how to have fun. And...well...here we are. They said to exercise more and to wait before I try pills. That was almost three years ago. I haven't really followed up medically. I didn't want to be the kind of person who takes pills so I run a few times a week even though I kind of hate it. If I didn't have Spotify to listen to, I couldn't exercise at all. Running does help. Without it, I don't think I could get out of bed. I'm broken. What else would you suggest?"

"I don't know if I have answers for you but I hope to ask the right questions and you'll make the changes you need to make."

"So, you're useless, too, then?"

He laughed, thank god. "If someone comes up with solutions for you, those easy answers tend to stay theoretical. We each have to figure out what we can do to optimize our experience. You aren't broken. You feel suboptimal, but everything can change."

"How do you know?"

"Because everything does." Rick leaned forward and took my hand. His hands were big and warm. "This is not an intervention unless you want it to be, Savannah. This is your time away from routine life. You'll know you've spent your time here wisely when you return home and find normal doesn't feel normal anymore."

When he looked me in the eyes, I saw gentle compassion. Somehow, that made me want to cry. "Until I got here, I didn't really believe people and places like this existed outside of expensive rehab centers."

"For some, church is their refuge. For others, universities and libraries are their shrines. I like to think of this place as a bit of both."

"If this is a university, what course am I taking?"

"You're studying Savannah Needs. And, if you like, I will worship you."

His gaze slipped over my body like a light warm caress. Rose wanted me, I wanted her back. I felt the same fire with Rick. My lust burned bright.

14

"Maybe thinking too much is the problem. I think I think the same thinks all the time," I said. "Feels like I'm on a Nascar track, always turning left at high speed, same view, same terror I'll crash at any moment. I probably deserve it. I thought I'd be a competitor in the human race. Turns out, I'm not even a pace car. I'm a spectator."

"Self-deprecation is one of your habits," Rick said.

"A steady diet of hate is pretty healthy, but wrath is slimming, right?"

"Maybe I am a terrible person. Have you considered that possibility? I'm thinking maybe — "

"Even if you're right, you're wrong."

"Come again?"

"Reinvent yourself. You've invented yourself at least once, I'm sure. Do it again until it sticks. It's a daily commitment. Sometimes hourly or by the minute."

"Sounds exhausting."

"You matter, Savannah."

I wanted to wrap my legs around his head. Then I wanted to wrap them around his waist and hump the night away. *Give me that prescription for dick quick, Doctor!*

An old-timey radio announcer popped into my head: Ladies! This hottie is brought to you by Dick Quick! Dick Quick! Ask your doctor if a good, hard fucking is right for you. If the sexual bliss lasts more than four hours, good for you! Consult a physician for rug burn and use more lube. Dick Quick! Because when you have a chance at Rick Barrister doing you, do him!

I slipped into another daydream: Rick bending me over my chair and sinking to his knees to worship my pussy with his tongue. Rick peeling off his wetsuit, pulling me to him, then down on him. I pictured him slowly impaling me on his cock, inch by inch, until I was full. I'd gasp. He'd moan.

I'd cling to Rick as he quickened the pace, unable to contain his lust. I'd be on top, riding him to orgasm. As the pressure built, we'd hurry to the end, working together until I collapsed on his chest. I'd cry out and bite his shoulder as I came. Then I'd come again. And again.

I snapped out of the daydream. Rick was talking. I was wet.

"As you debated about visiting us, you were trying to avoid pain instead of pursuing pleasure."

"Coming here sounded weird and dangerous."

"I'd call it unfamiliar, new, or challenging."

"Do you blame me? We're all scared of fucking up."

"Worry is a waste. You believe in the power of pleasure. Otherwise, you wouldn't be here."

Trying to sound clinical and detached, I said, "Orgasm do sound...therapeutically useful." I stole another glance at his body. New energy fired through me. Alert with anticipation, I sat up and let the blanket fall away. I scooched to the edge of my seat, getting closer to Rick as I planted my feet wider, subtly widening my stance, opening my legs to him minutely. Straightening my spine, I pushed my tits out.

The searing heat of my blistering lust got in the way of understanding how Rick planned to help me. He could have had me upon our first meeting. Ogling him, I was not particularly open to delayed gratification. I wanted a passionate, deep dicking: hard, thorough, and sweaty. I stopped short of tearing his clothes off, but I came dangerously close to that.

15

"People who are motivated by pain are always eager to tell you what they hate," Rick said. "They wallow in their misery and spread it around. Happy, successful, productive people focus on what they love. They spread the love eagerly. Put it in practical terms: don't tell me about movies I shouldn't bother seeing. Tell me what you love. I want to know your peak experiences so I can share them. See what I'm saying, Savannah?"

"I'm going to need a personality transplant," I said. "You got a golden retriever puppy somewhere I can switch brains with? Nothing much makes me wag my tail."

"Your cheeks are flushed pink. That's the energy of the sex drive firing up. That drive gets goosed with greater mental and physical health. Everything can improve. When we relax, inhibitions drop away. We must question the restrictions we put on ourselves. The world's changing and what used to make sense doesn't necessarily work anymore."

"Example?"

"Outdated rules of sexual morality, for one. Operating on old instructions is fine as long as people evaluate and really believe. If you aren't sleeping with someone because of mindless inertia or baseless fears, that's not a conscious, informed choice."

I thought of how hot Rose was, how hungry she was for me. Her pure animal magnetism had set my sexual compass spinning. "It is time I stopped holding back and reevaluated."

Rick's smile warmed me. "I can hardly wait to get to the promise of pleasure that brought you here."

I didn't want to wait at all. Rick was my ideal. I needed him and a bed.

"We change mindsets," Rick said. "People do better and feel better when they let go of what does not serve them. Clients work it out for themselves, mostly. They already know what they need to do. They have to stop doing what's not working. Sometimes medication or financial support is a component. Social support is always needed."

His earnest and humane style had my full attention. The high-minded talk of personal growth appealed to me. He could be talking nonsense, though. I'd still be rapt. I stole lusty glances at his body. *Look at you,* I thought. *Can we please just fuck?*

Rick's handshake was firm, his palm warm. I held on a little longer than was strictly necessary, struck again by how big his hands were.

The chime on his diving watch pinged. "I rinsed the salt off, but I was in such a rush to get here, I haven't had a proper shower and shave. I'll go get changed and meet you for dinner in the kitchen." He rose and strode to the door.

"Rick?"

"Yes?"

"You said you hate to waste time. What happens tonight?"

He beamed his big grin at me. "Dinner."

"No sex?"

"I wouldn't want to rush."

"It's been a long time since I had sex."

"You're not ready."

"Ready? Who says I'm not ready?"

Cobwebs! I've got cobwebs down there! I didn't give voice to that thought. There's funny and there's gross and sometimes I know the difference.

"Sex would be lovely, but we should take our time, don't you think?"

"How much time?" I asked.

"When we're both ready and it feels right."

"So you're not disappointed at a sexless evening together?"

His smile didn't falter. "I'm crushingly disappointed, but you are our guest. I'm at your service. We give what you need first. Then we focus on what you want."

The fact that he would not pressure me made my hunger for him turn into an ache.

"You do want me, though? Wait. Forget I said that." I'd spoken too soon, revealing even more self-doubt in a dumb rush of words.

Embarrassed, I put on my best professorial tone using an arch British accent: "No need to answer, dear heart. No one should have to explain why they don't want something, especially when it comes to physical interaction."

"I felt the attraction between us immediately. When it happens, it has to be at the correct time so we'll feel right about it afterward. Are you disappointed, deep down, Savannah?"

"You're teasing me."

"When I tease you, you'll know it. You'll feel it, deep down."

I felt a tingle up my legs and down my spine. The electrical surges met at my groin.

"Hunger is the best spice," he said.

"Get that from a fortune cookie? It sounds wise."

"You like that one? How about: We enjoy our arrival most when the journey is long."

I glanced at his crotch again. His wetsuit was so tight, I didn't know whether to be impressed or scared at his sleeping monster. My gaze lingered a second too long so I made a point of staring him in the eyes. That tactic didn't spare my heart much racing, either.

I focused on his tight ass as he walked away. He looked good walking away, too. I took a few deep breaths to calm down. "Holy shit!"

The library was so big that my exclamation echoed. I hoped Rick hadn't heard me but of course, he must have. I was hot, embarrassed, and excited in equal parts. I wanted to reach between my legs and give myself some relief then and there.

16

I wandered into the kitchen. Rose cut vegetables beside a steaming pot on the stove. I offered to help so she pointed me to a bowl on the counter. "Cool. Please cut up the cordyceps."

"The who?"

"Cordyceps mushrooms."

"Where I come from, we just call them mushrooms. 'Shrooms if you're a teenager."

"But there are many kinds of mushrooms. A bunch look really freaky, like some kind of alien life. Mushrooms are the octopi of the fungi world."

I gave Rose a pained squint and a strong what-the-fuck eyebrow spasm.

"Octopuses — octopi, whatever — giant squid at the bottom of the ocean...all those weirdos have gotta be alien, right? It's their heads that freak me out. Cephalopods are just too weird, as if they've got balloons for brains. They store no body fat and die soon after mating. They don't seem to enjoy the act of reproduction much. Like I said, aliens!"

"Okay. Weird that you know that."

She smiled. "Once upon a time I thought I'd be a marine biologist."

"What happened? Did the scary octopus balloon heads change your mind? I wouldn't blame you."

"Deep dives into the dark weren't for me. If the swim isn't in warm clear tropical water, I don't scuba. Too cold! Fortunately, cordyceps mushroom coffee got me interested in fungi."

"So then you switched to studying plants?"

"I've had a circuitous career route. Couldn't settle down. I flirted with a few ideas along the way, seriously thought about becoming a firefighter. Settled on botany eventually."

"Mushroom coffee, though? Really?"

"Tastes awesome."

"I'm sure."

"Don't say it if you don't mean it. And don't be too polite. You don't want to end up getting mushroom coffee every day when you really want mochas topped with whipped cream."

Was Rose really asking about my hopes for the sex spa experience? Would mine be a lesbian odyssey of discovery or a long hard ride on the Rick Dick Express? I didn't want to choose one over the other.

Pushing naughty thoughts aside, I tried a pattern break of my own. "I had some vegan friends. They were always offering me fake meat. It was mostly tofu in meat molds. They said it would taste as good as the real thing but it never did."

"Meat is like orgasms. Don't fake it."

I fumbled a couple of mushrooms and they dropped to the floor. Chopping carrots expertly, Rose worked her knife like a professional chef.

"I eat meat off and on," she said, "but I never try to mimic it with unreasonable facsimiles. The trick is, don't try to fool the taste buds. They're sensitive, especially when the mouthfeel is wrong. But the mushroom coffee is for real. You might like it. Supposed to help with cognition and libido."

"Libido. Of course. I forgot where I was for a minute."

"Exercise, happy hormones, and keeping circulation moving are keys to healthy brain meats and satisfying sex. Also, doing it more," Rose enthused. "Sex is the only sport that looks the same whether you're an occasional hobbyist or a professional."

"I'm not so sure," I said. "Amateur or professional, curling all looks the same to me. It makes me want to kill myself."

"Curling?" Rose crowed with laughter. "Yeah, amateur or pro, curling does kind of suck."

"It's the nadir of the Canadian experience. A sport with brooms doesn't inspire drama or Olympic hopes. It reminds me I need to clean out my closets. Dust bunnies meet to discuss bunny business under my fridge and I gotta sweep."

I liked the way she threw her head back and shimmied a little when she laughed. She didn't hold anything back. I was still pondering Rick's bulge in his wetsuit, his big warm hands, and dark eyes. But I treasured the sense memory of Rose sucking on my earlobe, too. I wanted them both.

She picked up a piece of mushroom from the cutting board and held it out to me. I took it between my lips and slipped the tip of Rose's index finger in my mouth. I looked in her eyes as I did it.

Maybe I was getting the knack of slowing down and paying attention. She didn't shudder like women do in romance novels. However, for a second, I thought there was a flutter around her eyelids. A change in her breathing suggested she had enjoyed a subtle pleasure. Rose smiled prettily as she slowly withdrew her hand. I hadn't flirted with a woman in a long time. It was easier than with a man, especially since she'd already been so forward.

She stared at my tits. I hoped my smile was pretty, too.

"I think a lot about the things I take into my body," Rose said. "Fresh air, tongues, and fingers. Toys are fun. I think about that sort of thing all the time. I'm pondering it right now."

I blushed.

"You're pink. I love pink."

But I wasn't ready. I chickened out. I stepped back, too nervous to close the small distance between us. Too scared to pull her to me and kiss her full lips.

As I leaned over the bubbling pot, my stomach growled. "This smells fantastic. I eat way too much processed food. Say what you want about all the crap that comes in boxes, it tastes really good. It's easy to heat up and eat quick, too."

"Pseudo-food!" Rose declared. "Even if they're eating healthy, people are still in too much of a hurry. They don't get to enjoy it. Taste, chew, then swallow. Do not speed eat."

I looked around the immaculate kitchen: bright yellow and orange peppers, a full spice rack, fancy dishes, and linen napkins of azure. Everything looked so clean and neat and pretty. "I don't cook much. I couldn't eat like this at home."

"When I lived in the world," Rose said, "I used Sunday afternoons to plan. I cooked meals and froze them for the coming week. I ate then pretty much the way I do now. It is different in that just about everything's organic and fresh here. I hope you like borscht, by the way. I made borscht."

"Then I'll like it."

"Between the beets and the carrots, it's really sweet."

"How long have you been here?"

"Rick brought me in to landscape the place three years ago. After about three weeks, I thought I'd figured out what was going on. I was sure he was some kind of vapid playboy with a different woman lounging by the pool each week. I didn't like him. I thought he was hiding something. I love surprises but I hate secrets. When I handed in my two-week notice he told me what the retreat was all about. I've been on board ever since. The world needs optimizing."

She put down her knife and reached out to squeeze my hand gently. "We are all on a mission, whether we know it or not."

"When Kelly asks how my trip went, what am I allowed to say? That this is a hippie commune?"

"The hippies were on the right track but we bathe more."

"Sorry if I'm being rude. Back home, I'm not this awkward."

"Take your time. You're a refugee. Regular life is a war zone. The so-called normal is dangerous. I know you have doubts about being here but it's the status quo that scares me. I have no fears working with Rick. Maybe we're a little crazy by everyday standards but we're friendly and safe."

"What scares you about normal?"

"It's all spiraling down fast. This is arguably the best time to be alive in all of history. Still, people lack patience, civility, understanding, and compassion. They rush to get to the end of everything. They want it all yesterday for free but they aren't satisfied when they get it. Everyone's afraid, even people in power — maybe especially them. They're lucky people only want equality instead of revenge. There's also the anti-intellectualism."

"Sabine told me she likes intellectuals."

"Yeah, she's a sapiosexual, which is a fancy way of saying she loves to suck smart dick," Rose replied. "That's not where a lot of the energy in the culture lies. It doesn't help the brainiacs to lock themselves in ivory towers."

I looked around the most fabulous house I'd ever been in. "Isn't this an ivory tower?"

"That's what I tell Rick. We have to be open about all we do and invite people outside of our little circles."

"And here I am."

She nodded. "And here you are. So, thinking outside the box, could you do your job online, without an office? Arrange travel for people from a laptop? Or have you thought about what you would do if you weren't a travel agent?"

"I don't know." I didn't tell her my secret ambition was to write books. I wasn't writing then so I felt stupid even mentioning it.

Rose was as comfortable with silence as she was working with her chef's knife. She gave me time to think about her questions.

Rick walked in: freshly shaven, blue jeans, a white linen shirt, and shiny black shoes. He wore no watch or rings. He looked almost as good as he had in his tight wetsuit. I caught the faint whiff of lime. It wasn't strong enough for cologne so it must have been his shaving cream.

Acting cool, I said, "Hello again," as if I didn't want to tear his clothes off right there. As if I didn't need Rose to strip naked and worship me with her tongue. As if I didn't want to fuck them both fast and come three times before soup was served.

Sure, I thought. *I'm chill. I exude casual elegance. I can pretend. I belong here. I won't poop on the floor or eat ice cream with my hands.* It's almost as if I hang out with handsome rich guys and hot horny lesbians every week and twice on Sundays.

My mother would say, "Nice pecs, model looks, and a good butt. Watch out for that one. He's the devil. He'll drag you to hell. And her? The she-devil? She'll send you to damnation, yodeling all the way down."

That sounded like a delicious way to go.

17

R ick's gaze slipped over my body a moment before his eyes met mine. "Feeling more comfortable?"

"Take it easy on her," Rose said. "Sabine was too pushy again."

"Sabine knows what she's doing," Rick said, "but she can overdo the missionary zeal sometimes."

"I have no doubt her heart is in the right place," I said.

"Savannah was pushed our way on short notice," Rose added. "Glad we had a hole in our schedule. I do love tight holes — "

Rick cleared his throat. "Rose. Behave."

She laughed and I wanted to join in. Unfortunately, I was still stuck on the fact that I was a charity case.

Before I could slap on a smile, Rose caught my frown. "Don't feel bad, Savannah. I like that you decided to jump in without testing the waters more. Too many wait too long before they commit to anything."

"Then the first toast of the evening goes to Sabine," Rick said. He stepped to the huge fridge, pulled out a red wine bottle, and poured us three large glasses. "Red wine should be served at room temperature. However, we got this special beverage just for you."

I looked at the glass of red on the kitchen counter and hesitated. Was I about to be drugged? Would I wake up tied spreadeagled in a sex dungeon? Would I mind? Rick and Rose picked up their glasses and drank first.

As I brought the glass to my lips, Rose touched my arm gently. "Remember, slow down to savor the flavor."

I did so and burst out laughing. "Cherry Kool-aid!"

"Kelly told Sabine you don't like wine," Rick said. "We strive to accommodate."

I raised my glass, still laughing. "To Sabine and Kelly!"

Rick made the next toast and, to my surprise, did an amazing imitation of Ricardo Montalban. "Welcome to Fantasy Island! Smiles, everyone! Smiles!"

"I already did the Fantasy Island welcome," Rose told him.

"Damn. Stole my jam."

"I'm your Tattoo," Rose said. "I'm in charge when you aren't around, Mr. Roark."

Rick asked me, "You know that old show?"

"I've caught reruns late at night. Two nights out of five, I'm an insomniac."

"That show is Rick's true inspiration," Rose said.

"Well, all that and Epicurus," Rick said. "Epicurus believed in a life of simplicity, avoiding pain and maximizing pleasure — "

"Yeah, yeah, Ancient Greek philosophy, blah-di-blah," Rose cut him off breezily. "I'm sure you'll get into it but don't feel you have to, Boss. I'm here for the rockin' sex not Philosophy 101."

Rick's face fell and he pushed out his lower lip. "Oh."

I blurt laughed as Rose mimed an exaggerated yawn and rolled her eyes.

"I prefer your Sean Connery impression," Rose said. "Make a note. Next time you're screwing me up against a wall, talk dirty to me in the original James Bond's voice."

"Noted, Mish Moneypenny." He did sound like Sean Connery.

I looked away, a little shocked by Rose's request. I also wondered what it would be like for Rick to fuck me while holding me against a wall. I'd seen that move in movies but never experienced it. Would that be face to face or would he pin me from behind? Would I feel the cool kiss of the wall on my nipples with each thrust? Rick wouldn't need a Sean Connery impersonation for me to be happy.

"You know, on second thought," Rose continued, "if you're going to do impersonations, I prefer names and voices I know from this century."

He shrugged. "I'm still working on my Obama impression. All I've got so far are the hesitations."

We all laughed and the tension — okay, my tension — was broken. "Guys, I have a request."

Rose broke into a wide grin. "You want to take me up on my offer from earlier?" Maybe she was teasing, but she looked eager. It crossed my mind that if I asked, she would drop to her knees and lick me while Rick watched...or massaged my breasts and pulled gently at my nipples or.... My breath got shallow.

"Savannah?" Rick touched my shoulder. "Your request?"

"Please call me Savvy. My friends call me Savvy."

"I like it," Rick said. "After dinner, how about we give you your first session on the table?"

"You, me, and Rose?"

"It's a slow introduction to bodywork," he said. "No worries."

"The first session is always the same," Rose said. "Clothes stay on, damn it. Rick's massages are like chocolate-dipped strawberries. They're orgasmic ... even if they aren't really orgasmic. This first one is a braingasm. You know what I mean?"

I didn't know what she meant. I was excited to find out.

"We'll take it slow," Rick assured me. "Raising awareness is the first step."

"First step to what exactly?"

"Embodiment."

I was in a slow cooker. Things soon heated up in unexpected ways.

18

Rick and Rose led me down a dim hallway. As I descended to the basement, I entered a darker, cozier, and warmer place. A fountain bubbled softly at the bottom of the stairs. The air held the faint scent of peppermint and a sweet violin played. Overhead, potlights came on ahead of us. The violin music fell away behind us and a softer chorus greeted us from hidden speakers. The corridor widened and tilted downward slightly as the air cooled.

"This is the oldest part of the house," Rick said. "My mother built into the hillside. Underground homes were popular. Some interesting below-ground designs are coming back."

"Oh, good," I said. "For a moment there, underground and going down farther, I thought this was a Hell metaphor."

Rose giggled. "Think of this as the place you ascend from, angel."

We stepped into a circular room. I heard a soft electric ping and hum as the room slowly illuminated.

"This was a sunken living room," Rick explained. "We took out the old orange shag rug and remodeled."

I'd expected a dungeon. Instead, the room was light and airy. The floor was of light bamboo. Tiny, tubular yellow and white flowers filled the perimeter. The room was large enough that the lamps over the flowers provided diffuse illumination to the center of the room where a massage table awaited me.

Nervous, I looked away from the table and examined the flowers. "That perfume. What is it? I know that smell."

"Jasmine," Rose said. "The flowers are night-blooming. I call this the Jasmine Room."

"Rose knows her stuff," Rick said. "These flowers bloom in spring and fall. I like using this room to introduce clients to the work."

"The work is play and the play is work," Rose said.

"What do I do?" I asked.

Rick stepped toward the table and offered me his hand. "Would you like to climb aboard? We'll ask little of you besides lying down and letting go. This is your time."

I took his hand instinctively and, as I came closer to the table I noticed a step. I climbed it and sat on the table as Rose pulled back the blanket, woven in the pattern of Van Gogh's *Starry Night*. "Would you care to lie on your back?"

I did as I was asked. The table's cushion was a thick memory foam heated to gently warm my back, buttocks, and legs. Rose covered me with the blanket as the spotlights began to fade. Above me, a single point of light shone like the North Star.

Without a word, Rose and Rick took their places on each side of the table. Gently, Rick took my left hand and began to massage it. Rose did the same with my right. I never realized how much tension I held in my hands until they began to squeeze it away.

I relaxed into the warm foam, settling down as they worked the heels of my palms and gradually worked toward the end of each finger. As Rick gave a firm pull, I heard a satisfying pop and snap in the joints of my left middle finger. The movement was a surprise, but relieving, too.

"Don't worry about that," Rick said. "The joint was just a little jammed. You do a lot of keyboarding."

"Yes." It was such an innocuous comment but I felt regret at my admission. I did a lot of keyboarding at work, it was true. It was a reminder that I worked at a keyboard too much. I was always fulfilling other people's dreams but not my own. I planned their trips. When I was in university, I was sure I'd be a celebrated novelist by thirty. Thirty had come and gone and I'd hardly written a word I liked. I had allowed mundane days to build up. I'd sacrificed time with nothing to show for it.

Rose slipped away from my hand. I missed her touch. She returned after a moment with a pillow to slip under my knees. I relaxed further, surrendering to gravity. I considered talking but Rick and Rose were silent. I squinted up at the ceiling to that one pinprick of light. Before they finished kneading my hands I allowed my eyes to close. My defenses were down. Whatever they decided to do, I was for it.

After some time, Rick moved down to my bare feet. I felt his warm hands envelop my ankles. "Just a little traction," he assured me. He pulled my legs slowly, steadily increasing the pressure. I felt muscles in my low back ease. Knots I didn't know I had came loose.

Rose joined him at my feet and, just as they had kneaded my hands, they massaged my feet. I thought I'd be ticklish or self-conscious. Instead, I reveled in the firm pressure as they squeezed in a slow, determined rhythm. Working together, their pace matched. Heaven.

I lost track of time and fell into silent appreciation of all they were doing for me. Eventually, I fell into a light doze. I was waking up as Rose slipped one cool hand to my forehead. Her other hand rested lightly above my belly button.

This is it, I thought.

In a moment, I was sure Rick would pull off my jeans and underwear and spread my legs. Rose would slip down, spreading my lips for him to feast. He'd tongue my clitoris while she sucked my nipples. I'd moan. My breath would come ever faster. Eventually, I'd cry out and beg for mercy. I would not resist in the least. I'd surrender. They'd tease me, keep me teetering on the brink of orgasm. I'd spread my legs wider, rocking my hips, urging Rick to lap at me, faster, harder, deeper.

Instead, Rose began to rock the hand on my belly back and forth. Rick pulled on my legs gently again and then took up her rhythm. I hadn't been rocked since I was a baby. The movement was subtle and welcome. I imagined myself still in the womb, slowly rocked to sleep, awash in warmth and safety as my mother sang a tuneless song.

I closed my eyes and took a long breath in through my nose. Afloat on a sea of jasmine, I was finally truly idle. This table was my ship. My new friends formed the waves that rocked me. Each movement was kind.

New heat rose in my cheeks as tears slipped down my cheeks. These two strangers seemed to care for me more than I did. They worked on me patiently, giving without expecting anything in return. They worked in silence.

Back in Vancouver, noise followed me everywhere and there was no escape. I rushed back and forth and called it living. I hurried about with little purpose and no quantifiable results. Now that I had real quiet, the realizations came quickly. I'd paid attention to the wrong things. I rarely focused on any one thing for very long. I sabotaged myself by spending money I didn't have to try to feel better. I bought self-help and business books I didn't read. I made jokes not for the enjoyment of others but to deflect, to soothe my nerves, to mask anger. I pitied myself too much. I'd made no plans. All I really expected was to die alone and friendless. I had committed to nothing and to nothingness.

The rhythm of the waves stopped. Rick and Rose just held me. I was dimly aware that Rose had moved down to my feet. Rick appeared above me and slipped a practiced hand beneath my neck. He held my head and placed one fingertip between my eyebrows. Soon, ever so light and ever so gentle, he made a small circle. His fingertip barely touched me but, with each slow rotation, I felt myself falling asleep. I fought to stay awake. I wanted to feel all my muscles melt into the heated table. I wanted to feel my bones sift away like desert sand on a breeze.

No movement was forced or hurried. Rick and Rose could have been one person with four gentle hands. Their care was kind and terrible because they treated me better than I had treated myself. I'd been a fool and a whiner. Worse than that, I was sure I'd be a foolish whiner again. I doubted that I could rise to the heights others said they saw in me. I didn't believe in myself. How could I? I'd fucked up a lot. Changing would mean giving up all I'd been and done.

Fresh tears came with great racking sobs. Embarrassed, I tried to get my breathing under control. The more I tried to hold back the flood of tears, the more I lost my grip on my emotions. My dam was breaking and I panicked at the prospect.

Rick asked me if I wanted him to stop.

"I feel like I'm flying apart," I said. "Mom always said bawlin' and blattin' don't get shit done."

"Crying lets the pain out, Savvy," Rose whispered. "It's okay if you want to."

"Denying our tears and fears closes us off from humanity," Rick said. "The more we hold back, the more we hold on to pain."

I felt like I was five years old again. In a memory as clear as this moment, I saw my mother's face. Mom Voice came to me as clear as if Rick or Rose had spoken: *Grow up! Life is hard, girl. You have to be harder. Life is war and you have to be a warrior. Warriors are fearless.*

"I was supposed to be tough," I said.

"You are human," Rick said.

When I closed my eyes, I saw my mother's disappointed face.

I did try to grow up, Mom. You and Dad wanted to live through me, to grow up to be a constant success. I couldn't. I can't!

"Your tears are honesty leaking out," Rose said. "What are your tears telling you, sweetie?"

"I don't know!" I whimpered.

They must have known this was a lie. I choked on my sobs as the truth bubbled up past the lump in my throat. "My parents want me to be a robot. I know that sounds stupid but — "

"You don't sound stupid," Rick assured me. "When we hold ourselves to impossible standards, we become rigid. Our muscles tighten. We go through life braced for impact. We hold on to pain.

You don't have to do that if you don't want to, not anymore. What do you want, Savannah? Are you ready to choose what you want?"

"I don't want to try so hard at doing things I hate," I replied. "I've cried with worry about overdue VISA statements and a snarl of tax bills. That was humiliating, but what's worst is the distance between what I am and the person I wanted to become."

In the depths of the retreat, loved and forgiven, my tears began to free me of pressure and pain. As I wept, I began to forgive myself. I softened. Mom was wrong. Bawlin' and blattin' helped me much more than armoring up. Holding back the ceaseless tide had always been a fool's errand. It wasn't just okay to give up on the stupid side of a losing war. Surrender was the smart thing to do. I'd been fighting the wrong war a long time.

My parents had done the best they could with what they knew. Many of my wounds were self-inflicted. I'd spent too much time hating myself and blaming my mother and father. I'd known that before, but now I felt it. I thought embodiment would feel good. Not this part. These epiphanies were ugly. These patterns were the parts of me I had to shed if I was to come out clean.

I said nothing more to Rick and Rose and, true to their word, they asked nothing of me. After holding me a long time, they went back to rocking me slowly. Relief is too small a word for the enormity of emotion that washed through me.

Like a baby, I cried myself into a deep sleep.

19

A t dawn, I awoke in the recovery room. Forgetting where I was for an instant, I startled to full wakefulness. The hammock swung gently. I looked over my shoulder. The door was closed and I was alone. My body felt long and loose. As I tilted my head back and forth, the movement in my neck felt fluid. Tentatively, I touched the top of my shoulders. It was as if the muscle had turned to a gel. I experimented with taking a deep breath and found that I could take in more air than before.

Weirdest of all, I could still feel Rick's fingertip on the spot between my eyebrows. I didn't understand his work, but I knew it was profound and helpful. Rick had hypnotized me but I didn't worry about it. He wasn't going to give me a post-hypnotic suggestion to dance the funky chicken every time I needed to pee. I was safe with Rick and Rose.

Rick had carried me to an elevator, I remembered that. Call it a daze or a doze, I'd been aware of the trip to the recovery room but, wrung out like a wet rag, I didn't want to talk. I needed time to process and, when I was too tired for that, to sleep. Rick had lowered me into the hammock gently. Rose and Rick had floated away like angels leaving me to dream of a better life, to experience my renewed body and mind.

Now fully awake, I stayed in the hammock a little longer, snuggling under an afghan. My life in Vancouver was so hectic and harsh, I'd frequently suffered long sleepless vigils waiting for dawn. This wasn't like my chronic insomnia. We'd started the session in the Jasmine Room right after dinner. After sleeping much longer than I normally could, I was rested and excited to start the day. I couldn't remember the last time I woke up so refreshed.

As the sun rose slowly, the house was silent. I watched the sky as the wind pushed fluffy orange clouds away. As sunbeams grew in strength, I had to do something with all this newfound energy. I climbed out of the hammock and took my blanket with me to the rolltop desk. The light blue stationery was fine, heavy linen. The pen fit in my hand perfectly. The jet-black ink flowed smoothly across the page as I wrote: *It's not too late to change. Stop treating yourself like a robot. Live more. To live bigger, let go, let loose! Be as kind to yourself as two strangers were.*

Could I ever be as gentle with myself as my hosts had been? Family and some friends — people I'd depended on for support in tough times — had blamed and shamed me. I'd never forgiven anyone. Those who sided with my ex about any issue during the divorce were on my shit list. I'd never forgiven myself either, for anything. I remembered every mistake in microscopic detail: full color, stereo, and surround sound.

But Rick and Rose evoked a power I hadn't known was still there. I felt renewed physical, mental, and sexual energy. This state was oddly familiar. I'd had it when I was younger, before a series of disappointments made me cynical.

No. That's not right. Nothing *made* me cynical. Shit happened and I allowed myself the luxury of cynicism. Cynicism is easy. It let me give up when I should have been remembering my ambitions.

As the sun rose, the world didn't look like it was out to get me anymore.

20

W hen I emerged from the recovery room, I found a note
from Rose on my bedroom door asking me to meet her.
After a quick shower and changing clothes, I found her
in the kitchen. Without a word, she gave me a hug and a big smile.
"You okay?"

"Absolutely."

"Take it slow today. You released a lot last night and probably
need to process. The internal work keeps going."

"I feel fine...a little embarrassed."

"No need of that. I can't remember the last time I was embarrassed. I have had lots of opportunities to laugh at myself, but embarrassment isn't very useful. You know you never have to feel that way
with us, right?"

"I feel that from you both. Thank you. Why should I take it slow?"

"People have varied reactions. I got kind of volatile after my first
session with Rick."

"Volatile? Really?"

"Rick would tell you that we can become more reactive when
we're suddenly pulled from the groove of customary behavior."

"What would you say?"

"Something like that but not theoretical: Take a kid with raging hormones. Send them to university. That first week away from home they're out from under their parents' control. Out from under the thumb, people do things they wouldn't ordinarily do."

"So I'm like a preacher's kid thrown into Frosh Week?"

"Raising consciousness makes you more sensitive, but it's not all kumbaya and tie-dye shirts. When people get hip to life outside the system, they can get mad. When you're on the inside a long time, whether it's prison or a submarine, when you get out things can get a little wild, not necessarily in a good way. Be gentle with yourself."

"I can see that. I'm often pissed at what's happened to me. Life hasn't gone according to plan. This morning I was thinking more about the distance between what I am and what I'd like to be. Change feels more like a challenge than a hopeless shit job now."

"Good! Just know that when senses are heightened, emotions are, too. It's a natural process and it takes time to absorb the changes. Drink lots of water today and watch your reactions to things. Pay attention to how you feel and see if you notice anything different."

"I will."

She offered me a clear coffee cup. The steaming drink had white foam on top, a dark layer, and the bottom half was white. I took a sip and broke into a huge smile. "I love it. It's so sweet! What is this?"

"Cafe bombon," she said. "Espresso and sweet condensed milk. It was invented in Valencia, Spain. Why it isn't everywhere is one of the mysteries of the universe."

"Oh, my God! This is starting out to be the best day." I took another sip and let out a contented sigh. "This is mother's milk. I want to drink so much of this stuff it comes out of my nipples. Cafe bombon lactation!"

"Hungry?"

"Starved!"

"How about a strawberry smoothie?"

"Sounds like ice cream for breakfast."

"Is that a yes?"

"You bet it is."

"With added vegan protein? I've got chocolate."

"Better and better. Yes, please. What's the schedule today?"

Rose grinned. "Rick would like to get you back on the table. You up for some more bodywork? It'll be deep tissue massage this time."

"*Mm.* I do like this place."

"I'm glad. You did a lot of work last night, Savvy. Some people put up more resistance before they can let go like that. Be proud."

"You guys did all the work. All I had to do was lie there and take it. That, incidentally, is how my mom described sex."

"Sounds like your mom needs to come here."

I laughed. "If you managed to get my mom into the Jasmine Room, her emotional blast crater would wipe out the island."

"Poor thing."

I almost laughed again but I could see by the tilt of Rose's head that she really meant it. I got quiet and sipped my cafe bombon. I was too hard on my parents, especially my mom. Rose's first reaction was to feel sorry for my mother. My first inclination was to mock her. Maybe noticing how mean I could be was one of the differences I was supposed to be watching for.

21

I was nervous but more than ready to spend time alone with Rick. I sat at the edge of the fountain at the bottom of the stairs. Black Moor goldfish paddled in the pool at its base. They hovered just under the surface, looking up at me with huge googly eyes.

After a few minutes, Rick emerged from behind a sliding paper screen. He wore loose black pants and a white hemp shirt that reminded me of a martial arts gi. His three-quarter sleeves showed off the sinews in his muscled forearms. "Good morning! You're looking lovely. Did you have breakfast?"

"I've discovered the joy of cafe bombon and strawberry-chocolate smoothies. I may never have anything else for breakfast again...or lunch. That'll be an easy replacement for cooking turkeys at Christmas and Thanksgiving."

"You're feeling well, then?"

"Very good. Thanks for last night. I thought I'd get a massage so I didn't expect that. What do you call what you do?"

"It's bodywork that pulls from several approaches. Space and time are what we all need. When we step back into safety, emotions you usually keep down can come up."

"Like vomit? Scratch that. It was a happy release in the end, like getting the poison out of my system. I feel different."

"How so?"

"Slept well, for one thing. I've got more energy because of deep sleep, I guess."

"Notice anything else?"

"I want to do things."

"Like what?"

Sexual things, I thought. *I want to do you.*

I stared at the floor. "Normally I make fun of people who want to do stuff. You know, what's with all the mountain climbing when we've got Google Maps? Nobody has to go anywhere!" I was joking again, but his question had been serious. "Sorry, I'm being too glib. I guess if I have to boil it down to one thing — "

"You don't have to if you don't want to."

"I do! It's just...my life in Vancouver feels like I'm running a race I can't win. I'm going in circles and everybody else is actually headed somewhere. I always have a ton of shit to do but the view doesn't change. Right now I feel like I've got lots of energy. I want to use it for an ambition instead of...I don't know. I'm tired of not knowing."

"Instead of acting out of desperation, you want to take progressive action?"

"That's it, yeah."

"Would you like to go to the next phase? This part looks more like traditional massage."

"I'm ready and willing."

So willing.

Rick gave me another one of his sweet smiles. I wanted him to pick me up and rock me like a baby.

"Tell me something about you, Rick. I know you have this place and, I gotta say, it's pretty great. If I'm going to open up and be vulnerable, give me something. Tell me something about you that won't fit on the brochure for this place."

He took a moment. I thought he wasn't going to answer. Then, "In the South Pacific, there's a volcanic archipelago called the Republic of Vanuatu. Ever hear of it?"

"I'm a travel agent so you'd think I would know. I'm almost sure I've never heard of it."

"Don't feel bad, it's pretty remote. Anyway, in the Northern region of Vanuatu, wealth is determined by how much you can afford to give away. That's my measure of wealth. What else do you want to know?"

"I don't know. What's a guy like you afraid of? Anything?"

"Sure. Moray eels creep me out."

"Moray eels?"

"They have two jaws and the second set comes forward like the monster in *Alien*. They're called pharyngeal jaws, drags the prey right down the eel's throat. I just can't bring myself to dive around morays. I'd rather swim with sharks."

"Okay, strange choice. Keep going. Do you shave your chest?"

"No time and I can't imagine why I'd do that."

"Try again. C'mon. Something personal," I urged. "You're getting warmer...."

"I'm uncircumcised."

"Hot."

"There you go."

Rich, sexy, altruistic, smart, and funny. "If you weren't so modest, you'd be an easy guy to hate, Rick."

"Thanks, I think."

"Um...so...what do you have planned for me today?"

"Please come this way. It's time to show you Stage Two. Do you prefer light, moderate or deep pressure?"

I looked him up and down and pictured the bulge in his wetsuit again. I stared at his crotch meaningfully when I said, "I like it deep."

I blushed a little. I was sure Rick saw me as one of the poor help-less people who didn't dare reach out to grab some joy. Goddamn it, I didn't want to be one of those people. I wanted to be a bold and unselfconscious like Sabine and Rose. So far, my role in the movie of my life was low-level minion.

"When you get on the massage table, get under the sheet and

blanket." Rick reached for the door. "As we go, let me know if the depth is too much. I'll leave you to change."

"You want me naked?"

"And climb between the sheets, face down on the face cradle, please. There are a couple of heaters on the table. Tell me if you get too warm."

I'd come to a sex spa or so I was told. Now the sexy masseur was about to leave me alone. I was fourteen again. Andrew Feldman, a boy who walked me home from a school dance, was leaving me on my front step, too shy to kiss me goodnight.

"Rick?"

He paused at the door. "Questions?"

"You want me to undress on my own? I've been undressing myself for a long time. What if I told you I'm ready for more?"

"Let's take it slow. Call me a romantic fool but we haven't even had our first kiss yet."

"Sabine and Rose are so forward. I thought you'd be like that. I didn't expect 'the boyfriend experience.'"

"I'll start you off facedown, please."

"I like it facedown." That was supposed to be seductive. Damn, I was awkward.

"Rest your face on the face cradle and move the pillow under your hips. Make yourself more comfortable."

"I'm going to be honest with you — "

"I hope so."

"I haven't gotten laid in three years and now you're telling me — "

"You're in the right place, Savvy. You're on the right path, but it's not the right time."

His voice were so deep and seductive even as he turned me down. I wanted to fuck his voice. "Rick, when the anorexic girl asks for a ham sandwich, you give her a goddamn sandwich!"

"You want to scratch an itch. I love your enthusiasm, but I don't want to just scratch an itch. I want to bind your wounds."

"If I'd cried less on the table, would you be having sex with me now?"

"Probably. Some clients are ready right away. I don't think you are. Opinions differ, but I have to go by my judgment."

I needed satisfaction and my face must have told him I was fed up.

"You can get sex anywhere, Savvy. It takes great self-control for me to refuse your invitation. Your boldness is a good step, but I don't want you to have any regret afterward."

"Oh, for God's sake!"

"For *your* sake."

"This is so uncool, man."

"Holding back is for my sake, too," he said.

"What?"

"I'm not a sex robot, Savvy. I'm a human being. I'm part of the equation, too, and I'm not ready."

That shut me down hard. Heat rose in my cheeks. "I'm just trying to move on. I haven't had sex in so long my hymen has grown back. I'm a born-again virgin." I didn't mean to sound defensive, but of course, I did.

His smile was kind, but he didn't waver.

I could feel my frustration climbing into the range where I might start throwing things. "Rick, women make up their minds whether to say yes within seconds of meeting a man."

"Yup. Men make the same evaluation."

"I wanted you since the moment I met you in the library."

"Very flattering."

"Your wetsuit is very flattering. Sabine also gave you a high recommendation in the mind-blowing sex department."

"I'm concerned that rushing would not help you."

I flashed back to the night I asked my ex-husband to slam me from behind. He chose watching TV instead of having sex with me.

I threw down a challenge. "I need some love. Now."

"The greatest act of love I could give you at the moment is patience. I need the same from you. I'm not just a pump."

"I don't think you are."

"Then don't treat me like a dildo."

"Oh."

"Savvy," Rick said, "do you know what I love about Christmas? Opening the presents is fun. Discovering what's inside is fun. Anticipation is best of all. With you and me here, in this room, it's like Christmas Eve. I love anticipation, getting to know each other, learning from each other. I want what you want. That's what makes our time here so special. I want you, but I'll wait till we're on even ground. That's why I need to give you the boyfriend experience."

"Pretty shy boyfriend."

"I love your lust but I need to make sure it's coming from the right place."

"How?",

"The progression is compassion, passion, pleasure." He slipped out the door and closed it behind him. "I'll leave you to change."

I pulled off my clothes in a hurry and got under the covers, cursing Rick Barrister with every breath. One pillow was under my belly and the other was under my ankles. The table was comfortable and the moist heat began to seep into me immediately. The room was warm, too. It should have been nice. I wasn't any less mad.

After a moment's thought, I pulled the covers back so I was naked on the table. I pushed the belly pillow down so my ass was propped up. I spread my legs a little and waited for him to return. He'd said he wanted me. The way he looked at me, I was sure that was true. Time to test his resolve.

I'd never had sex on a first date but I was older now. Doug had already taken my best years and I was sick of waiting. Let Rick walk in and say no to what I offered. If he was going to tease me, I'd throw down a naked dare.

He knocked on the screen. "Ready?"

"Yes," I said. *Come and get it!*

Rick walked in and, without a word, covered me up from neck to toe.

"I'm going to ask you to breathe a little bit deeper and a little slower. That will give your nervous system the correct message. You aren't running from wolves. Doesn't it always feel like you're running from wolves?"

I let out an exasperated sigh. "I guess so."

"You'll know you're making progress when you're running toward something instead of running from something."

"Fine. Massage me."

I sounded petulant and I didn't care. He was so worried about my mindset. My mindset was a blistering combination: horny plus simmering rage. I was so angry, I almost called Rick by my ex-husband's name.

But I wasn't angry at Rick. I was angry at myself. I was a hiker at the bottom of a steep trail, looking up. The top of the mountain was obscured in mist. I didn't realize how much work I still had in front of me. Sometimes we have to cross a cliff sideways or retreat before we find the path to go higher. Fear and wallowing in anger froze me on my climb. I was the divorced woman cliché. I'd lost three years post-divorce moaning about losing "the best years of my life" to the wrong man. I could not fathom a world where the best years of my life could still be ahead of me. If there's nothing to look forward to but sadness, stress, and deeper debt, what's the point? Something had to change and that something was me.

22

I'd had massages before but nothing like Rick's deep tissue treatment. He began by touching the base of my spine and between my shoulder blades, rocking me gently. Next, his warm hands vibrated. I trembled in nervous anticipation. I felt the gentle ripples of his work all the way to my nipples.

Rick's work was methodical and unhurried. He kept me covered by the sheets. Instead of going straight to using massage oil as I expected, he employed the top sheet as a grip, pulling my muscles at all angles.

"Some people find this next part uncomfortable," he said. "Let me know if it's too much." His hands moved to my lower back. Rick rolled the skin between his fingers, pausing at several spots to lift the tissue straight up. As he moved down either side of my spine, I heard three crackly pops.

"Are you a chiropractor, too?"

"No, those sounds were not your vertebrae. That was your thoracolumbar fascia."

"My who?"

"It's a layer above the muscle. Those pops were the fascia separating from the subcutaneous tissue. You okay?"

"Yes. That...actually felt good. I was surprised, is all." I wiggled my butt a little. "Feels looser already."

"Cool."

"What are you doing to me now?"

"I'm doing it *with* you, not *to* you."

"*To* me comes later, right?"

"I'm stimulating your nervous system with a low vibration. Breathe a little deeper and a little slower. Feel it more than you think it. Let go of your expectations and stay in the moment."

"I've heard that staying in the moment is good for the brain but a lot of moments are boring or they suck."

"Not all moments are equal. How is this moment?"

Rick moved down my legs and uncovered my right foot, squeezing gently at first, then more firmly. His big hands were warm and sure. He pulled my toes one at a time. He got a gentle pop out of the joints in each one.

"This moment is good," I admitted.

He worked my foot without massage oil at first. When he was satisfied my foot muscles were as loose as they were going to get, he switched to using a heated gel. Between the warm gel and the moist heat cocooning my body, I began to melt into the pressure and pleasure.

"That's it," he said. "You're letting go."

"I might purr."

"Purr or sleep or talk, whatever you need to do. You decide. Don't feel you need to respond if you don't want to."

"I'm a talker," I said. "I've got questions."

"Sure."

"I won't distract you?"

"My hands know what to do."

"They sure do. I'm tingling. You know...in my conversation with Sabine, she called your sweet retreat here a fuck spa. Sabine does have a potty mouth, doesn't she?"

"She wouldn't mind me telling you, 'Fuck, yes.' Sabine enjoys dishing out shock value. In my experience, sapiosexuals are the most verbal during sex and massage."

"Loud?"

"That, and inventive. Spanish sapiosexuals are verbal and loud to the tenth power. This area is soundproofed, but still...wow."

I imagined Rick fucking a Latina on this table. Would she scream for a quick merciful orgasm or would she beg for an even harder fuck, telling him to keep going and going? Why not both? That's what I wanted: a rough pounding. My ex used to call it 'rogering' but I always hated that expression. I could use a slow, gentle, loving screw later. First, I needed my chimney thoroughly swept.

Rick uncovered my right leg and massaged the calf. He worked his way above the knee. I gasped as he found a knot in my hamstrings. He paused there and waited for the pain to ease.

"What's that?"

"Trigger point."

My discomfort eased and the muscle relaxed. After a moment, he continued kneading my thigh, moving higher and closer to my groin with each stroke.

As Rick massaged my thigh, I wished he'd get to work on those pesky vaginal trigger points. It wouldn't take much to trigger my first orgasm.

"Are you still angry with me for not jumping straight to sex?" Rick asked.

"The 'boyfriend experience' thing? I'm frustrated. I put myself out there. I'm put out that I would put out and you wouldn't put it in."

"I haven't heard the expression, 'put out,' in a long time," he said.

"If I talked dirty like Sabine, could we skip ahead?"

He was quiet for a moment, working my left thigh and apparently considering my suggestion. Finally, he said, "We should focus on enhancing your neuromuscular function today. Let's not skip steps."

"If you had any compassion, you'd move your hand north a few inches."

"Last night, we worked on your emotional body."

"It was gentle surgery. I felt like you and Rose really opened me up."

"You did that. We just gave you the opportunity to let go. Try to hold on to the gains you get from each session. People can receive life-changing epiphanies on the table, but if you don't hold on tight and act on them, miracles fade away. Everybody's monkey brain constantly tries to change the mind channel. Rushing to the next stimulant too quickly diminishes any profundity we discover. The next shiny thing distracts us before we deal with the last shiny thing."

"I've...uh...I've written a few things down, to remember."

"Good!"

"About last night, though, what was I supposed to get out of the Jasmine Room session?"

"We don't control how your body reacts. You react how you react."

"Please, skip the caring Zen master shit. Just tell me what I need to do to fix me."

"I'm not trying to be difficult," Rick said patiently. "From our conversations, I'd suggest you show yourself more compassion."

"If by compassion you mean masturbating right here, right now, I'm considering it."

"You're deflecting."

"Am I?"

"And pouting," he said

"If I wasn't pouting before, I am now."

"Think a happy thought." After a moment's silence, he added, "Happier than that."

I chuckled. "You're funny. I'm a whiner."

"It's not whining if you're honestly trying to deal with your issues. I understand you're feeling stuck."

"Sometimes my life feels like someone has sewn me into my sheets while I was sleeping. I try to find the way out but there's no escape. I'm flailing and the air is stale and I'm trapped. The sheets wrap around me, tighter and tighter. I have thought about giving up. I can't imagine what life would be like on the other side of declaring bankruptcy, though. What would I do next? Work in sales in the

Greasy Fries Department in the exciting fast food industry? I've always dreamt of independence, seeing the world, working for myself. I'm not living the dream but if I don't figure out how to be that, who am I?"

"Only you can answer that."

"Shit."

"You'll figure it out. What brings you happiness? Happiness comes first. Don't wait until you have everything."

He continued the deep tissue work without a word, giving me time to work it out for myself. His movements were confident and, slowly, I gave in to the pressure and pleasure of his work. My muscles softened. My heartbeat slowed.

Though I still wanted to come, for the moment I gave up hoping Rick would change his mind and start fingering and licking me. That didn't stop me from picturing him doing that. "Sometimes when I'm super stressed, the only way to get to sleep is to burn off the nervous energy by masturbating. I call it, 'taking a sedative.' I...uh...sorry. I'm not sure why I told you that."

"Walls fall. Stuff bubbles up. No need to be self-conscious."

"I'm not so sure taking a sedative is working for me, anyway. I feel like my head's in a vise all the time. The stress is constant. Even when things were going well with my ex, I usually had to try hard to relax enough for sex. I'd have a hot bath and some wine before coming to bed."

"When you start with 'trying hard' to relax, you're pushing a rope. These are common reactions to stress."

"I'm not a freak, huh? Good to know."

"Have you noticed that when you begin to relax you soon tense up again?"

"You see that?"

He slipped a hand to my right shoulder and gave a gentle squeeze. "I'm palpating it right now. You begin to let go and then tighten up. Your mind doesn't want to follow where your body is going. My aim is to make the soft tissue soft, the way it's supposed to be. You carry a lot of tension."

"Sexual tension."

"I look forward to releasing that, too. First, let's focus on your muscles."

I was about to say pussy muscles. Then I remembered what Rose had said about slowing down and savoring food. I yielded to Rick's hands and focused on the experience. Sometimes he used a lot of pressure. Other times he backed off and kneaded my body gently. He often used his forearms and elbows to go deeper. Mostly he worked in silence. Occasionally, he would ask me to tense a muscle before coaxing it to soften even more.

Throughout the session, Rick only uncovered the area he was working on. Even when he worked on my butt, he worked through the sheet with his elbow. His touch was always masterful and, to my taste, too respectful. I had to admit, despite the chunk of bad mood weighing on my brain, my body felt much better.

When I turned on my back, he lifted my legs for me and slipped a pillow beneath my knees. I was very aware of Rick as he moved around the table. Rick seemed fully engaged with each stroke. No one had ever paid this much caring attention to my body. He worked, talking with his hands, learning my body, and teaching it, too.

He pulled my fingers in a way that made my joints pop. Wringing my arms, they felt loose like cooked spaghetti. Next, he helped me stretch my neck. My eyes flew open when I felt a crunch and heard several pops in my neck.

"If you paralyze me for life," I said in my very best old British lady accent, "I must warn you, I shall be very cross." I giggled. Staying in character, I commanded, "As your queen, I must insist you tie me to a four-post bed with silk ropes. Forthwith, you shall slake the fuck out of me."

"Patience, my queen."

I broke character and the Alabama fell out. "Well, bless your heart. Goddamnit."

When I turned my head, I could put my chin on my shoulder with ease. Experimenting with bending sideways, I could bring my ear to my shoulder on each side. "Wow. You're making me a boneless chicken! Or an owl."

"When the tension eases around the spine, sometimes you get spontaneous spinal releases like that. I never set out to get those pops but they can come on their own as the muscles relax."

His work was so careful and thorough, I was sure Rick really cared for me. However, since he hadn't made it sexual, I still felt rejected.

"How long do you think we've been in here, Savvy?"

"Dunno. Almost an hour?"

"Almost two. That's how you know you've been in the moment: when the minutes don't matter, when you come up for air and a lot of time has passed. That's the time machine at work. It's meditative. When we are doing what we need to do, fully and sincerely, we step outside of time. Have you had that experience?"

"Not often. While reading a good book, I suppose."

"The problem is it tends to happen more when we are very young. Remember when summers seemed to last forever?"

"I do remember that feeling, yes. Where'd that go?"

"It gets beaten out of us. We run our lives by clocks too much. Time is the boss. If you want to feel free, find the thing that totally absorbs you. You can recapture that feeling of full engagement. What were you doing when you last felt fully engaged?"

"Last night and this morning."

"I mean in the world."

"I felt that way writing English papers and short stories. I used to get lost in books the same way. I loved to read and write."

"But you don't get lost in reading and writing so much anymore?"

"No time. I read Facebook."

"Doesn't Facebook take time?"

"Yeah, I lose time to Facebook. When I'm done, what I've looked at is mostly forgotten. I don't have a sense of accomplishment like when I devote time to a book. A whole book feels like a huge commitment, though."

"We all have the same twenty-four hours."

"Said the rich guy who works three hours a day."

"Granted, but if you aren't having a good time, one day all you'll have is a pile of to-do lists. You don't want to look back and realize you got the dishes done but never had fun. We're here for more than getting through the grind."

"Hard to argue with that," I said. "Sorry, I didn't mean to sound snarky about how much you work."

"I try to make all my work playful so really, I hardly work at all. Working on you isn't work. It's my pleasure. The privilege of working with you makes me feel very rich," he said.

I stopped breathing for a moment. "What a sweet thing to say."

"I mean it." He cupped my skull between his hands and gently turned my head again so my chin rested on my right shoulder. "Improved range of motion. And I see in you the potential for a great awakening that could help many."

"Yes! I haven't had sex in three years! I am a fiend! I'm ready to join your cult for world peace and multiple orgasms!"

He laughed.

"Sex, sex, sex!" I said. "That is what got me here. What's your position on love, smart guy?"

Rick sobered. "I'm for it. Everybody needs love."

I sighed. "We sure do."

I didn't want to talk anymore. The half-Samoan Adonis with Mahatma Gandhi's patience, gobs of money, and dreams of world peace had me naked but for a sheet and a blanket. I wanted Rick between my legs kissing my clitoris. I wanted to demand he give her a spit shine. The bodywork was great, but a good polish would really clear my head and ease my stress.

23

I lay face up. The light was dim. I figured I was as happy as I was going to be without a finger in my ass and Rick's tongue flicking fast and light over my vulva.

Would this be the moment Rick lowered his perfect mouth to my lips? Would we kiss first, for a timeless time, like in the romance novels? Would he knead my breasts as I moaned and shivered in trembling anticipation, wet and ready? Would he suck my erect nipples hard? I wanted to spread my legs wide, grab his hand and hurry him, make him reach for my slit. He'd stroke me, up and down, stirring me, teasing me, alternating between gentle and firm pressure.

Would he throw back the sheet, unable to contain his animal instincts? Or would he pull the sheet and blanket down inch by inch, the slow reveal? How long would I have to wait to rip off his shirt and feel his muscular chest against me? I wanted to lick him as he tongued me, to moan around his cock until he couldn't take my tender ministrations anymore.

I didn't want him to be gentle. I wanted him to plunge into me, impaling me, hammering me, and holding tight. Cuddling and ease were for later. I wanted to wrap my legs around him, locking him in. I'd squeeze his cock as tight as I could and I wouldn't release him.

Rick would call me a goddess and try to tease me again.

I'd growl, "Shut up and fuck me harder!"

Every move would be urgent, lust uncontained: Rick's head in my hands, his mouth on mine, his hips pistoning, driving into me. Breathing like we were in a race, we'd cross the finish line together.

He was young and strong and handsome. He'd keep going. I'd fuck him like I was mad because I was a little mad — mad as in angry, but crazed, too. It would be fucking awesome and awesome fucking.

That didn't happen. Not yet. Rick asked if I was comfortable under the sheet, the blanket, and the heating pad. With those barriers between us, I might as well have been wearing clothes.

Confused and blushing, I answered, "I'm comfy," and Rick returned to working on my feet.

Gee-zuzz! Who does a girl have to blow to get laid around here?

With a pillow under my head, I could see the muscles in his forearms bulge as he sent vibrations into my feet and up my legs. Watching those muscles and feeling those tremors kept my nerves firing sexy tingles.

"We are surrounded by distractions," Rick said. "You will progress once you focus on one thing."

"I am feeling very focused," I said.

"Really? I thought you spaced out for a moment."

"I heard Vancouver Island is full of flakes and nuts. Which are you?"

He smiled. "I'm not a flake but I do speak that language fluently."

"So you are a nut."

"The most interesting people I know are a little nutty. The trick is to be a little crazy but in a functional way."

"Fine. What do you suggest I focus on?"

"While I take a breath, join me. Pause a moment to check in with how your body feels."

The answer was: I felt amazing. It was as if he'd found a coiled spring around my spine and unwound it. The muscles in my arms and legs felt like they were filled with warm water.

"Try a visualization as you feel your body softening even more. Close your eyes and listen to the sound of my voice."

I could listen to his deep rumble forever, but I'd prefer to hear him groan as his lips and tongue massaged my twat. I'd just done a very thorough and effective visualization and the theoretical sex had been legendary. I wanted more of that but I wanted it to be real, and immediate.

"Let each breath become longer," Rick suggested, "but softly. Don't force it."

I nodded, trying to follow his lead.

"Your feet are warm and heavy and relaxed and soft."

"*Mm*," I agreed. But have you got a hard-on for me?

"Now think about the muscles in your calves," he said. "Allow them to soften and relax even further. Let those muscles get long...longer. You're more relaxed. Good. Allow the feeling of relaxation to deepen, nothing else to do now, nowhere else to be. Let that feeling of relaxation come up through your feet, your lower legs, up through your knees, and into your thighs."

Spread my thighs, I thought. *Let me feel your hot breath and molten kisses.*

"Stay with me," he said. "Relax your buttocks..."

Flip me over. Do me, do me, do me!

"Imagine your body getting heavier...warmer...more relaxed."

Dammit, Rick! How am I supposed to concentrate with you and your dick so close by?

"Remember these sensations of relaxation. Visualization takes practice. Don't worry if you don't feel the full effect right away. When you want to return to this feeling, to relax, to de-stress, or to sleep, remember this feeling. You can come back to the warmth of this room and this experience at any time...your body long and soft and relaxed."

Rick gave me a little bow and a smile before heading toward the door. At least he didn't say "Namaste."

"Wait."

"Yes?"

"Is this the end?"

"Typically, I'd give you more massages to deepen your relaxation. I want you to be able to take the stress-busting exercises with you when you leave. We'll have to see how you react to this session."

"So...no sex? Again? Really?"

"Anticipation heightens the senses."

"After getting on a seaplane to be here, I really want to be pissed at you. I do feel good but, seriously, seaplanes scare me. Coming here scared me — "

"Some come from the other side of the planet," Rick said. "No mercy for you tonight. I want to assure you that you have my full attention, good intentions, and compassion."

"Thank you, Rick. I do appreciate all you've done. That's the best massage I've ever had, better than I imagined it could be — "

"But you want more."

"I've never thrown myself at someone like I've been hitting on you."

"I'm looking forward to the next stage. Believe it."

"Why wait? If it's about dragging out the seduction and anticipation — "

"No, it's more than that."

"What else, then?"

"Do you know the term "avidya" from yoga?"

I shook my head.

"Yogis blame the lack of knowledge of the self for all human suffering."

I thought of a self-help book Kelly gave me for Christmas. It was supposed to help me get past my mental blocks, or as she put it, "Get over your divorce already!" I looked up at Rick and, I'm ashamed to say, pleaded a little. "I read somewhere that desire is the root of human suffering. I'm feeling a lot of desire and I am suffering!"

"Epicurus would agree with you. To deny desire is to deny what makes us human. Everyone desires things. You will get the pleasure, too."

"When you vibrate your arms and hands, all I can think of are the things I want you to do with those hands."

"I know."

The heaters on the table had warmed my body. The look in his eyes warmed me more. "Is it easy for you to turn me down? Are you getting off on saying no? Tell me it isn't easy for you."

"It isn't easy."

"At least there's that. You should know, when my husband refused to fuck me, it was the beginning of the end. I started throwing things, stuff broke. I don't know how well I'll handle rejection. Not here and not now. Not from you."

He stepped closer, trapping my palm between his hands and his chest. "Look in my eyes. I'm not blind. Feel my heartbeat. I am not heartless."

"Aren't you?" With my free hand, I threw back the sheet and blanket. I trembled and I could feel him trembling, too. "You want me? Prove it."

He guided my hand down his torso, over his strong chest, and across the deep lines of his tight abdominal muscles.

Still staring into his eyes, my palm found his hard cock. The long shirt and loose pants could not conceal his throbbing erection. I could feel his pulse. I rubbed slowly up and down, appreciating his warmth, his turgid length, and girth. I don't think all penises are beautiful. In fact, mostly they're ridiculous. But not in the heat of passion. Not when your heart pounds to the beat of pure animal drive. I'd forgotten how powerful lust could be. I would have done anything for the feel of it, for the taste of it, for the love of it. I was sure I'd love every inch of Rick's wonderful cock filling me, fucking me, pounding me. I couldn't wait.

"I want you, Savvy. Do you believe me?"

"Yes."

I should have known what would happen next. The bastard made me wait. Slowly, Rick pulled away. He stepped toward the door and slid back the shoji screen.

Incredulous, I asked, "You're leaving?"

"See you soon. We'll talk more."

"Damn it, Rick!"

"Maybe we'll do more than talk."

"You're not showing any compassion at all!" I pulled the pillow from under my head and threw it at him as hard as I could. Missed. Fuck!

"Sorry," he said.

"Compassion, passion, pleasure, my ass!"

"When the time comes, I'll pleasure your ass if you want — "

"Look at that, we're back to wordplay. That's not gonna do it, Rick. I want to come now!"

"I look forward to seeing you again." His gaze devoured my nude body. For a moment I thought he'd take me in his arms, French me, smother me in kisses, suckle me, lap at my vulva, devour me, impale me, fill me, fuck me, possess me. Instead, Rick moved to the doorway.

"I can't decide if I hate you or not. When's the next stage?"

"When you're ready. I take no pleasure in taking no pleasure."

I stood naked before him. My breasts tingled. My pussy ached. I wanted to come and come hard.

"You," he said, "are every man's fantasy. When we get together, it's going to be soon and it will be special. I promise." With that, Rick turned and walked away.

24

I owed Rick an apology for being such an ass.

Later, after I got dressed and settled down, I felt lighter. It wasn't just my mood that had swung back to bearable. I felt better physically. As I circled the room three times, I found that I moved with a newfound grace.

I allowed myself time to notice the differences Rick made in me. My feet were straighter. I stood taller. On impulse, I lay on a mat and experimented with a few stretches. That came easier than I expected, too. My shoulders were a little sore where Rick had worked those muscles deeply. However, the muscle was pliant. I breathed deeper than before. It was as if Rick had given me a good workout. I felt like I had done something physically challenging and came out of the experience better for it.

Calm. Softer. Longer. Relaxed. Deeper. Heavier. Warmer. More relaxed. Calmer. The mantra eased my embarrassment.

I began to forgive myself a little. Rick had made it clear he wanted me. There was lust in his eyes, but he'd refused me until I figured things out. His rule was reasonable and his way with me was like his massage: gentle yet firm. I'd panicked, treating Rick as if he were my ex-husband. I had projected my doubts about my self-worth on a relative stranger who owed me nothing.

That afternoon it was still a mystery to me what I would do after shutting down the travel agency. Maybe Rick would put me in touch with a good bankruptcy attorney. Whatever solutions might come, working out the answers was up to me.

Before I could face Rick or Rose, I needed a shower. As my mother would say, "Sin doesn't wash off in the bathtub no matter how hard you scrub. Sin stain sticks. If you want to be clean, don't get dirty in the first place."

My bathroom had a fancy Roman shower with a huge nozzle overhead. It was like standing in warm, heavy rain. Sprayers mounted on the wall gently caressed me with hot water from every angle. The cabinet offered an array of shampoos, conditioners and soaps: peach, tangerine, satsuma, goat milk and lime.

The water temperature climbed. One jet of water angled up in such a way that, if I squatted ever so slightly, it hit my pussy in a pleasant pulse. I smiled as I experimented with the pressure and heat. I bent farther. The water, gentle but firm, pressed at my anus. With a shower like this, it was tempting to think I wouldn't need Rick Barrister or Rose Sinclair. It wasn't enough, though. I was not one of those people who could fall in love with and sexualize an inanimate object — a computer, a toaster, the transmission from an old Ford pickup — and live a happy life. Yes, somewhere out there, some guy was fucking a radiator. That sort of thing really is on the continuum of human sexuality. Though a sex-positive affair with manufactured hardware sounds simpler, that sort of relationship wasn't for me. I needed warm flesh, hot hands, and willing tongues.

Human contact used to come so much easier. Somehow, I'd allowed my social life to slide from a wide circle to a narrow constrictive oval. Friends who got pregnant seemed to gravitate to other women with kids. I love children, but I felt like I was on the outside of that happy family aquarium. It didn't feel right, tapping the glass.

Every person I met was a potential client so I had to at least pretend at professionalism. I couldn't relax and be my usual sarcastic self. Doug's friends weren't really my friends, either. In all of Vancouver, I had Kelly and Doug. Kelly had Paul and eventually, Doug had Patsy (repeatedly, in the back of a Subaru Forrester). Fires left untended will die.

In the first couple years of my marriage, I wore lingerie to bed or nothing at all. At some point, I switched to flannel. I don't blame the failure of my marriage on comfortable pajamas or cold Canadian winters. However, I did wonder when Doug and I "allowed passion's flame to flicker," as they say in the sad parts of romance novels in which authors lament marriages gone lame. We couldn't keep our hands off each other for a chunk of our twenties. Doug and I had married young — too young as it turned out. We were certainly too young to act so old. Somehow, the lingerie got relegated to special occasions, like anniversaries, Doug's birthday, Christmas, and Valentine's Day. We didn't get dirty often enough.

I blamed work, mainly. We certainly did work too hard. After seven years, Doug started talking about Patsy as his "work wife." We laughed about it at first.

When Kelly heard me mention Patsy a bit too often, she made some comment about the infamous seven-year itch. I didn't take her warning seriously. Maybe I should have pulled my lingerie out of the back of the bottom drawer.

When we spoke our wedding vows, Doug and I never imagined a time when we would have to try to make our marriage work. I'd always thought that if a friendship or a marriage required effort, it wasn't much of a relationship. There's another reason I was divorced and had so few friends. Writing a confession with 20/20 hindsight is embarrassing. Truth is such a cold-hearted bitch.

Kelly saw my marital problems long before I did. When she pointed out Doug was "emotionally unavailable," I told her to butt out. I told myself she was projecting her relationship issues on my marriage. Kelly and Paul worked things out, though. I didn't know the details. By the time Doug and I were burning down, I didn't consult Kelly much. I didn't want to hear the key to someone else's happiness.

After I found out Doug had gone to work on Patsy, poking every hole plus the space between her tits, I almost wished Kelly's marriage had failed, too. We could have moved in together, sworn off all men, become lovers and saved money on rent.

As my marriage crumbled and the divorce proceedings stumbled forward, I often fantasized about taking Kelly to bed. My best friend was my work wife. It only seemed fair. I never told Kelly about those feelings.

Most of all, I longed for a time beyond worry. Rick would say that every day we chop wood and carry water. After achieving enlightenment, or failing miserably, chop wood and carry water. Keep going, working, living and loving, but do it better, with clarity of purpose.

That's Rick. I'd put it a different way. Stub a toe? I believe in TWAT: 'Twas Always Thus. Whenever anything goes wrong that's like the last something that went wrong, say it with me, "*TWAT!*" And keep rolling on.

During the divorce, I obsessed over apocalyptic movies. To avoid thinking about my return to the office each Monday morning, I watched *The Walking Dead* every Sunday night. The show pulled me into its mix of horror and soap opera. It was fun to imagine myself in the story: no rules, no credit card debt, no chasing money at all. As one of the last women on Earth, I'd have no time for petty regrets. If the world went zombie, and I was freed from debt and mundane concerns, I wondered what kind of person I could become.

Rick had made it clear I had to work on myself before we could have sex. I'd been so shitty to him, I had to apologize before we got naked together. I felt new pressure to rewire my brain and become a new person, preferably someone I liked more. Intellectually, I knew it was far past time I moved on. My time with Doug was dead. My marriage wasn't going to come back from the grave. Divorce was my zombie apocalypse. I had to accept that and find a way to thrive in the post-apocalypse. But how would I stop wallowing?

I often thought I had succeeded in letting go of Doug, but that was always temporary. I'd promised myself I would drop my old baggage to embrace the spa experience but, barring a concussion, memory is never far away. Unbidden thoughts bubbled up and I'd begin to obsess again and stalk his Facebook page for new photos. Any small reminder, such as a subject Doug had talked about in passing or a restaurant we'd visited together, triggered renewed self-loathing. Cold memories were brought back up to a simmering boil. Driving past his Subaru dealership could make me erupt in hot volcanic fury. Still, I drove miles out of my way to pass his car lot, swearing and waving a middle finger, safe in my car where no one could hear me. Divorce made me a lunatic. Anger held me back from moving forward with Rick, Rose or anyone else.

But there was more to it than simple infidelity. My rage boiled over when I pictured Doug fucking Patsy in my bed. However, that was not my worst moment. The crushing blow that finished me arrived when my ex apologized for cheating on me.

That sunny morning Doug dropped the bomb on me, birds sang lovely songs outside our kitchen window. Birds call out to check in with each other, to mate, to warn each other of danger. Trying to keep calm, I listened to their music: chickadees, song sparrows, a northern flicker. Every winged thing sounded pretty happy to be alive.

"I shouldn't have brought Patsy home," Doug began.

"To our bed."

"I don't know what difference that makes."

"If I hadn't caught you, how long would you have kept the affair going without telling me? You'd have us both. If you weren't caught, would you even be sorry? When were you going to tell me, Doug?"

"None of that matters anymore. You know about Patsy and me now. I should have told you the truth long ago, though."

"How long has this been going on, Doug? How many late nights and lies — "

"Not that long."

"Whatever that means."

"What I should have told you years ago isn't about Patsy. It's about you. I don't love you anymore, Savvy."

"Okay."

"We were kids when we married," Doug said. "Maybe I never really loved you at all."

I stopped and stared, forgetting the dishcloth in my hand. "N-never?"

"Don't look at me like that."

"Tell me how I should look. You're stabbing me in the chest and wiggling the blade around. Make sure you cut out my heart. Should I smile? You want me to smile, Doug? Why are you saying you never loved me? Why is that even necessary?"

"I don't know, Savvy. I'm trying to be honest. I'm saying this isn't the loss you think it is. It's just a change."

"You got a new couch. You're throwing out the old couch. Is that it? I'm disposable? If you never loved me, why are we married? Was that nothing?"

"We were young, Savvy. In hindsight, I guess I was just trying to get laid. Being with you, I got a steady supply. It's not a sin. It was a mistake. Sorry."

Silence opened between us. I held my breath for a moment. Doug stared down at his open hands, hands as empty as his heart. He sat at the same kitchen table where I'd prepared so many meals for us. He'd told me he loved me many times, so much I believed him. Doug said those three words so often, perhaps they lost all meaning. Maybe throughout our marriage, all he really meant was, "You make a hell of a fried chicken. Also, nice tits."

I sensed no real dejection in his face. He wanted me to think he was bewildered, but all I detected was smugness. He rejected me and enjoyed that power. I'd loved him, but he never loved me. He had someone new to go to and I had no one. He'd won.

Then he shrugged. In a single shrug, there went my late teens and twenties, flushed out to sea like so much shit. Since that day, despite numerous resolutions, my anger kept boomeranging and hitting me in the head. I had to find a way to make my ex disappear from my brain without digging around in my skull with a sharp stick.

After I moved out, I tried distractions to put Doug out of my mind: scrapbooking, knitting, Zumba. I'd signed up for those courses at a local community center. After my initial frenzy of activity died down, I quit going to classes or even giving those pastimes a thought.

I had to make Doug similarly irrelevant to my life, but how? How could I stop wallowing?

Rick's voice came into my head. "Reinvent yourself. Do it again until it sticks." That was the challenge I had to overcome before he'd let me get at his sweet dick. My psyche needed a fresh coat of paint. I needed a full ego renovation to bring me up to code. Since the divorce, I'd gone out of my way to avoid risk or change. I tried to be Mama's Good Girl, but life remained craptacular. Nothing wrong with being a good girl — whatever you think that is — as long as you choose it. I hadn't really chosen anything. Look beneath anger and you find fear.

Kelly tried to set me up on dates without my permission. For instance, she invited me over for a barbecue when one of Paul's single friends "happened to be in the neighborhood." Her setups never worked. I walked the line between cordial and aloof, asking polite questions, but giving nothing of myself. As soon as an exit seemed civil, I thanked Kelly and Paul for their hospitality before making excuses to leave early.

I feared strangers, commitments and complications. If the guy was cute, I went home for a date with my vibrator. I'd think of those swains as my robo-dick buzzed away — in, out, in, out, circle, circle, in, out, buzz, buzz, buzz, busy as a starved bee. After my orgasm, I'd soon forget their names and faces and go on about my day. I had no life and immersed myself in the mundanities of trying to make a living. Vibrators are notoriously undemanding. Give them fresh batteries and they'll leave you alone until you want them. Vibrators don't leave the toilet seat up. They don't mess the sink with beard hair. If peanut butter was left on the knife in the sink it was because I left it there.

I struggled on and the more miserable I felt, the harder Kelly pressed for me to "get out on the dating scene."

"'Scene?' Crimes have scenes."

"Savvy — "

"I don't need more drama."

"You're still young. You're not dead — "

"Only on the inside."

"What's wrong with getting out and having fun?"

"My father would say you really mean 'tomcatting around.'"

"That's a term reserved for guys, I think," she said. "Don't slut shame, Savvy. There are liars and cheaters and people having a good time with the gifts God gave them. No such thing as sluts."

"*Meh.* Tomcatting is an apt analogy. If I get out and have fun, one of those guys may will follow me home so I can pet him. Before you know it, I'm back to cooking and cleaning for another guy who says, 'I love you,' when he really means, 'Thanks for the blowjob.'"

"All men are not Doug," she said. "You sure you'll never even date? Maybe get remarried? Someday?"

"No way. Too risky. And a second marriage is like putting spoiled meat back in the fridge. It doesn't come back out better just because you cooled it off."

Fear was my default. That had to change. I had to change.

25

Life after divorce wasn't all D battery dildos and feeling sorry for myself over tubs of ice cream. I worked hard to drum up new business: expensive Facebook ads, useless newspaper ads, humiliating cold calls. I couldn't afford to pay the post office to deliver junk mail to potential customers. Instead, I walked around nice neighborhoods to leave door hanger ads on doorknobs until it got dark. With Doug gone, I told myself I had to pour all my energy into making my business a success.

When I wasn't working, I slept more than usual. I went to bed early, retreating into sleep to avoid feeling. Soon depression and insomnia dug in. To avoid thinking, I lost myself in late night marathons of George Romero and John Carpenter movies. I studiously avoided anything romantic. No Nicholas Sparks movies for me!

I've known several divorced women and men. Most went on a tear after they threw off the marital anchor. They met people online and had a run of one-night stands. Older women lamented that available men were typically fat, weird, or gay. Suitable men do exist, but some chicks don't mind sampling a few unsuitable guys, kissing lots of frogs to get to one prince. They talked with some glee about getting plowed to make up for misspent years. Lost time really has a knack for staying lost, though, doesn't it?

Eventually, some of those same women confessed that they got fed up with dating: "Too hard," "Not worth it," and "I have to move far away to a different city to get away from that controlling maniac."

Some remarried only to divorce again. The odds for one secure and lasting marriage aren't good. The odds on follow-up marriages are worse. Once you loosen the lid on that pickle jar, it's easier to open.

I stayed out of bars and off Tinder. When Kelly asked if I was lonely, I deflected with jokes. "I prefer to keep my snatch STD-free. It's my precious. I keep it away from filthy hobbitzes and their hairy dicks."

It wasn't all a joke. I got tested after I caught Doug with Patsy. Waiting for the results scared the living shit out of me. I was relieved to test negative, but my fear stayed fresh. Memory is the best preservative. Soon after the break up/blow up, I returned home from work to find Doug in the bedroom packing his suitcase.

"I'm going to live at Patsy's for a while," he told me, "until things settle down a bit and we work out the details."

"Settle down a bit? How long will that be? You mean, like, after the heat death of the universe?"

"Selling the house, splitting the assets. You know what I mean. Don't be obtuse."

"There's really not much to split, is there? You've got a few old records in your collection, but I've got Spotify. I don't want your autographed Phil Collins album. *No Jacket Required* is a classic but — "

"I'm not here to fight, Savvy."

"About Phil Collins?"

"About anything."

"Why are you here?"

"To pack my things. I'm just saying there's a lot of stuff to figure out, like who gets what — "

"No, I mean why are you here when I'm here?"

"I don't set my own hours like you can, Savvy. I had to wait until after work." He kept talking as he packed socks and underwear, never looking me in the eye. I have no idea what he said. I wasn't really hearing anything, just muffled words from far away. I felt as if I was the victim of an explosion, ears ringing, senses reeling.

Anger building, I cut through the noise. "Have you been tested yet?"

"Tested?"

"HIV, AIDS, chlamydia, yeast, Rotten Smelly Dick Syndrome — "

"I'm fine. We're fine."

"You sure? How many other salesmen has Patsy taken into the back lot after hours before she set her sights on you?"

"Shut up, Savvy."

"Just saying," I said.

"Don't."

I knew my test results were negative but I didn't try to reassure Doug he was probably free of STDs. He was sweating and looking less smug. If he was going to stay with Patsy, I wanted him to wait and wonder in fear just as I had. It was mean but Doug had made me mean.

"Call me first, before you come back for anything," I said. "I don't want to be here alone with you."

"You don't have to be scared of me."

"Scared of you? I'm not scared of you, Doug. I'm scared for you."

"Huh?"

"What if your dick rots off while you're here? You could be bawling about that, rolling around on the floor bleeding and begging me to call for an ambulance. I'd have to sit down and have a long think before I called an ambulance. Sorry." Eloquent shrug.

"Fuck you, Savvy."

"Fucking me is off the table. You didn't do that enough. Now you won't at all."

"You always have to have the last word!" He slammed his suitcase shut and headed for the bedroom door. "Here's my last word: Good-bye, Savvy."

"That's two words. And Doug? Don't call me Savvy again. It turns out I've been sleeping with a stranger. I thought I knew you. I trusted you, past tense. Only my friends call me Savvy. You can call me Savannah."

"I'll call you Bitch."

"Miss Savannah Bitch, then. As long as I'm not your bitch, sounds peachy."

Marriage is a plane that feels reliable and safe on takeoff. As the flight goes on, the fuel doesn't burn so hot. Cracks may appear in the engine blocks. If the wings fall off, you find yourself in freefall. After Doug walked out and we put the house up for sale, I was crashing at high velocity. Holes riddled my parachute.

I traveled more for work, trying to make the agency succeed in new ways. I tried to establish deals with hoteliers and courted corporate clients. Kelly enjoyed that part of the work more than I did. I should have sent her in my stead, but she had her husband for financial backup. The agency was supposed to be my livelihood. I pulled on a brave and friendly mask each day and reverted to resting bitch face each night. I knocked back umbrella drinks in a lot of hotel bars. Strange men offered to buy me drinks. I politely refused and told them I was married. I often spotted fresh tan lines where wedding rings were supposed to be.

A couple of strangers had a serial killer vibe. Those guys made me wonder if I'd end the night running for my life down a hallway. Would I be another statistic? Or would I be up all night explaining to a cop why I stabbed my pursuer in the throat with car keys? I don't much care for guns but every woman should be awarded a sword at the onset of puberty. That would make that first trip to the drugstore for feminine hygiene projects momentous in a fun way.

Some passes thrown my way were amusing. I told one guy I was a nun. That did not deter him from asking if I wore a habit, and if so, would I be up for a tongue job? And people wonder why divorced women have a hard time finding the right guy past thirty. I had my pick when I was in university but I'd stuck with Doug since high school.

Actually, there are single, available and lovely men in hotel bars.

Such men are everywhere. I could have invited those strangers up to my room for some sport sex and disappeared in the morning — any of them except for the guy with the nun fetish. I would have had no commitments, plus I'd get a few fresh memories to review when I was back home pulling my robo-dick from my nightstand. I refrained.

Staying single was easy and safe so I remained unfettered by new dick. No new vulvas, either. Instead, I went back to taking people on charters — no drunk groping businessmen touring Tokyo, though. I took elderly couples on bus tours through the Rockies to sew patches in my financial parachute. It paid, but not enough and not consistently.

I took pictures and made idle conversation with octogenarians who sat beside me on the tour bus. I ate alone and stewed a lot. I began and ended each day dealing with work email while Kelly held the fort. Our pricey little office in the mall ate a lot of profit. The harder I worked, the more my business morphed into an expensive hobby. Maybe potential customers sensed my Gremlins of Sadness. Maybe they picked up on my farty Pheromones of Desperation. Simpler explanation: the internet killed the travel business.

I told myself I needed more time to grieve the death of my marriage. That's what my photos looked like on Facebook: a funeral planning brochure. I created collages of pastel sunsets. I took endless pictures of mountains. The northern lights over Jasper and Banff are amazing cosmic displays, but all I felt then was the lonely cold indifference of space. The light show would go on forever without me. Even the beauty of the Rockies can take on a depressing sameness. My empty landscapes were vaguely sterile views, nature without warmth. There were no people or animals in those old pictures. I even lost myself for a time. I didn't want to see pictures of myself. Even looking in the mirror came too close to introspection to feel comfortable.

It's fashionable to complain about selfies. The worst snark is aimed at the cliched solo shot in the bathroom mirror — butt stuck out, duck lips pursed in vainglory. We're told that shot says, "I'm alone and I don't even have a friend to take my picture." Conventional wisdom says, "There's a psychopath demanding worship." No one wins the media battle of selfie subtext. There is even a study by psychologists telling us people who take selfies are narcissists. But maybe that's all memes, junk science, and hack comedy bullshit. They couldn't possibly all be bad, could they? I mean, I wish I had the confidence to take a selfie.

On a visit to a resort in Lake Louise, I looked a little too long at a lean handsome bartender. With his long black hair swept back, he looked like a cross between an athletic Jesus and a hipster dickslinger. He noticed me noticing him and blessed me with a bright smile. He was definite one-night stand material. His wide grin shot me a clear message: Hell, yes. I'll lick the maple syrup off you until you aren't sticky anymore.

I could have him, I thought. *Tonight. This could happen.*

Instead of moving to a chair by the bar, striking up a conversation and flirting, I finished my drink on the patio outside. I did not inquire if he could locate some maple syrup and bring it to my room. I watched the wind whip the lake as the pines waved goodbye.

If I had a time machine, I'd go back to kill baby Hitler. By law, this is required of the first person to master Time. After the Nazi baby slaughter, I would warn myself not to marry Doug. I'd work on keeping more friends instead of letting them drift away. I'd blow a few handsome strangers and let them get me off. I'd have more screaming orgasms. Vibrators are good and reliable, but unfortunately mastur-bation machines have rarely made me rise above a low moan.

With a time machine, I'd go back and fuck the bartender from Lake Louise. I'd ride hipster Jesus like a horse at the rodeo. I'd do him as if he was the last man on Earth and it was up to us to repopulate the planet.

Stepping back from my life and seeing my biography as Rick saw it, embarrassment washed over me. However, by the time I stepped out of the shower and wiped the steam from the mirror, I could look at my reflection without flinching. I stared at my reflection, peering in my eyes for a full minute. In the past, I'd let a lot of chances slide by. Emotions pack a punch. Embarrassment can be a big haymaker to one's self-esteem. However, Rick and Rose had remained so kind and treated me without judgment that I got a new sensation at the far end of embarrassment. I received the gift of clarity.

"Well?" my reflection asked me. "It's a new day. Time to let go of the old bullshit, right? This is your apocalypse. What kind of bitch are you going to be?"

I looked my reflection up and down, straightened up, pulled my shoulders back, pushed my tits out, and smiled. "I'm a badass bitch. From this day forward my secret superhero identity shall be...Thunderpussy? How's Thunderpussy?"

"Awful. Sounds like you fart hard from a place you shouldn't."

"Thundertwat?"

"Hell, no, same anatomical anomaly."

"But I'm feeling motivated and I'm in charge so — "

"That won't last," my reflection replied. "Just this morning you were full of yourself. Then you fell apart. Again. You think all those kids who go to fat camp are lean and long now? No. Wherever they are, they are sitting down, drinking the soda with all the sugar and avoiding mirrors and pictures. Failure is your sugar, Savvy. You'll go back to it."

"Reflection, you can be a real cunt."

"You know we don't like that word."

"I meant it in a friendly way, like the Scottish and Australians use it. But still scolding."

"Savvy, you're feeling young and full of blue piss at the moment but save time now and avoid even more disappointment later. You're only here for a few days. This will not last. You want to change, but everybody wants to change. You do plenty of things, Savvy, but you don't accomplish things. Your follow-through sucks."

"You sound like Mom."

"Criticism is love."

"Is it? People can change."

"They can, but do they?"

"I've seen inspirational stories on Facebook, sure. Why can't I? I'm people...technically."

"It thinks it's people. That's adorable. Savvy, if you were going to turn your life around, wouldn't you have done it by now?"[2]

My suspicion is that somewhere, hidden in the wrinkles of my brain (beyond the Warehouse of Painful Memories off Disappointment Avenue on the shores of Behavioral Replay Bay) there was a hidden hatch in my neocortex. Climb down that synaptic ladder, go deep into the darkness of my limbic system and you'd find a secret thought factory. In the control room at the heart of that neurological complex, my mother was still pulling the levers, spinning gears, turning my subconscious against me.

I smiled at my reflection. "I'm on to you now. I'd promised myself not to swell on my ex-husband and I slipped back into that old habit too easily. You're not wrong about my lack of follow-through and propensity for backsliding. I'll just have to be more on guard. Now that I know the danger, I'll stay away from the cliff. I think I've had quite enough self-loathing. It's finally time to move on and stop looking backward."

C offee's rich aroma drew me to the kitchen. Rose swam laps in the pool. As she paused to tread water she spotted me through the glass and waved.

What would I say when she asked how my deep tissue massage went? "It was great but I embarrassed myself when I begged for Rick to massage intimate deep tissue." A slightly better alternative might be, "Great, except that I threw a temper tantrum."

Rose swam to the near edge of the pool and walked up the under-water stairs. She emerged from the water, gorgeous and naked. I felt like I was watching a slow-mo shot in an R-rated movie. The sun was high and Rose glistened. She reached for a fluffy towel and dried her short red hair. Though her long limbs were festooned with roses and vines, the front of her torso was tattoo-free. Her pubic hair was trimmed to a slim vertical band. As she turned to the side to dry her hair, I felt more comfortable gawking. Her skin was so smooth, she looked airbrushed.

Rose's tattoos were not the usual blue. There were no extraneous, one-off tattoos on her body, either. Her back was her canvas. The roses down her arms and up her legs reached to gather in a garden across her shoulder blades. A green dragon and a yellow lioness twisted around a column of flowers spreading up her spine. Her slim, muscled body was a fine canvas, her tattoos a living mural.

She turned quicker than I expected and smiled when she caught me staring. I could pretend to search urgently for a coffee cup. However, tattoos are meant to be seen and I wanted to look. Rose surely didn't mind. I wondered if she'd been an exhibitionist before she came to work at the retreat. I decided she must have been comfortable showing off before she met Rick. I couldn't imagine Rose was ever a wallflower.

When she was dry, Rose wrapped the towel around her waist and knotted it in front. I slid the door aside for her and she walked in holding a big water bottle.

"Good afternoon," I said.

"Great afternoon! Did you fall asleep on the massage table?"

"I got off eventually."

"*Mm.* Rick worked on your shoulders a lot, didn't he? They've dropped. You were holding your shoulders high before, up around your ears. Rick calls it turtle syndrome. It's a defensive postural distortion."

"Huh?"

"You carried a lot of stress in your shoulders. Don't be self-conscious. Lots of people have the same issue. Now that your shoulders are down, you have a nice, long neck."

"Like a giraffe?"

"Like a model. No woman with a short neck ever rocks a runway. Check any magazine. You'll see, guaranteed."

"I never thought about it."

"You look wonderful."

"You look great, too," I admitted. My comfort level didn't match hers. I made a point of staring in her eyes even though her bare breasts were on display.

"Thanks!" she said. "I used to want bigger tits. I eventually accepted that I pretty much look like a fourteen-year-old boy from behind."

"Except for the art."

She grinned. "You got something good out of your massage, I hope?"

"I did. Not what I expected, but useful."

"You sound surprised."

"I was surprised by a lot of things." I wondered if she knew what happened between Rick and me. I asked myself what Rose or Rick would do in my situation. I suspected they would be honest and simply ask for answers. I took a deep breath. "Did you hear what happened with my massage this morning?"

"Nope. Confidential. Rick leaves disclosures to clients. Are you sore?"

"Not especially, a little around the shoulders, I guess."

"Every session is different depending on the client. If you're sore, try a little heat. We've got hot packs. If you're really sore, try an ice pack for no more than ten minutes. They're in the fridge freezer. Massage acts as biofeedback. Your body tells you the next day where it wants stretching."

"I need to stretch my neck and shoulders then. You sound like Rick."

"I've heard the heat or ice speech before."

"What was your first massage with Rick like? Or should I ask?"

"Coffee, first. Want some? I've been planting petunias by the tennis court. I took a couple of breaks, but I wanted to get the planting done before it got too hot. I got very warm but that made the swim even more refreshing."

Rose pulled a silver tray from the fridge and set it on the table. She pointed to two small canisters. "Cream. Soy milk. Honey, if you want. We have stevia." She poured two cups of coffee. I added some cream to mine. Rose took hers black. She took a moment to inhale the aroma wafting from the steaming cup before she set it down to cool. "Fire roasted coffee. These beans are called Esmeralda. It's so rich, I love it."

"Sorry I missed lunch. After my massage, I had some things to work out."

"Meals are what you want when you want them. What would you like?"

I didn't want to be a bother. "What do you usually have?"

"I can make anything, really."

"After seeing your body, I should eat what you eat."

She smiled. "You're lovely. You know that's so, right?"

I shrugged. "Sometimes I feel that way. Most days, less so."

"You can turn that ratio upside down. For now, how about an omelet?"

I nodded, relieved to be free of making decisions. Every day was a thousand decisions and I was glad to be off that hamster wheel for a few days.

Rose turned on the stove and pulled a couple of pans from a cupboard. "How's your geographic cure going so far, Savvy?"

"My what?"

"We aren't far from Vancouver, but the theory goes, to make changes, you have to escape your normal environment. Like learning a different language, you immerse yourself in the new language. When you change your location, you free yourself up to think differently. Here you have none of the usual cues and surroundings which trigger old patterns."

"You mean like all those guys who figure they aren't cheating on their wives if they're traveling in a foreign country?"

Rose laughed. "Something like that, maybe."

My place in Vancouver's rat race did seem a world away. I saw how I'd been running fast, wasting energy, and spinning in my little hamster wheel. I'd had to get away from my desk to see I didn't belong at that desk.

I don't think it's imperative that anyone run far away to see their lives from a new perspective. However, we have to be objective to see what we're doing. The geographic cure was taking hold of me. I didn't have everything figured out. I wasn't even sure I was on the right track. I was grateful to be on a new path.

Rose pulled several containers from the refrigerator.

"What've you got there?" I asked.

"Veggies for the omelet. Rick cuts up a lot of vegetables so they are always ready."

"I tried that a few times, but my veggies always got brown and rotten before I got to them."

"We eat a lot of food. It never gets a chance to spoil."

"You guys are so thin, how is that possible?"

"Most of what we eat are greens and vegetables. I don't count calories. I fill up on salad and, if I'm still hungry, I eat more."

She heated two frying pans, added mushrooms, red and yellow peppers and broccoli florets. She cooked the onions separately and added spices.

Rose measured nothing and cooked by instinct. That detail would have driven my mother crazy. Mom treated the preparation of every meal like she was building nuclear explosives. I preferred Rose's relaxed way. Watching her, I relaxed, too. After a bit, it didn't seem quite so strange that she cooked wearing nothing but a towel around her waist.

Rose caught my eye. "When I cook with oil, I wear an apron. Hot grease bites the nipples in a way I don't enjoy."

I sipped my drink and tried to remember the last time I lingered over coffee. Usually, I grabbed a huge cup in the food court for the adrenal kick to get me through the day. Stress and constant exhaustion made me crave caffeine, not coffee. The whole coffee culture thing was for people who loved the taste of hot bean juice. I guzzled and buzzed my way to the end of each work day. Burnt fast food coffee was for the hurried vulgar masses. Some people talk about coffee the way connoisseurs worship wine. True coffee devotees lounge as they savor. It's a sacred ritual in which the act of consumption only plays one part.

Spicy aromas soon filled the kitchen. Rose had mentioned their homegrown eggs would be different. I was amazed how orange the yolk of a really fresh egg could be. As the mixture on the stove finished cooking, Rose pulled a bowl of assorted nuts from a cupboard and a bowl of berries from the fridge. As she placed them on the table, she looked me up and down slowly and gave a lascivious grin. "Mix and match, whatever you like, same as my policy with sex partners."

I blushed. Then I was embarrassed that I had blushed. Therefore, I blushed some more.

"You're cute. You go pink!"

"Yeah, great...great. May I ask you a question?"

"Of course. Maybe I won't even make up my answer. Try me."

"You and Rick seem so...together. I mean, you seem to have things figured out."

A hundred people would have denied it reflexively. Rose knew how to take a compliment. "Thank you."

"Were you always so confident and...I don't know...help me — "

"Did I come out of the womb the way I am? No."

"You seem like you know yourself. I hate the phrase, 'comfortable in your own skin.' I don't think I really knew what it meant before, but it does seem to apply to you."

"When you're in the right place, you don't worry so much. I doubt I'd be so relaxed if my circumstances were different."

"What changed? What has the retreat done for you exactly?"

Rose did not hesitate. "I used to be a procrastinator. It took me longer to get my degree than it should have, took me longer to do everything."

"Hard to imagine."

"Don't put us on pedestals. We might fall and hurt ourselves."

I looked away. "I wish I had a tenth of your confidence. Even alone in my apartment, I'm self-conscious walking around naked."

"Confidence is easy when you know you're doing the right thing. My trouble was anxiety. I was a raging perfectionist."

"This, coming from the perfect woman."

"Perfect is the enemy. We can settle for personal excellence, though."

"Still sounds like a pretty high standard."

"I started to manage my anxiety when I realized I was putting more energy into not doing the things I wanted to accomplish. I'd think about my problems obsessively."

"I do that, too."

"Focusing on solutions moves things forward, but it's hard to keep that focus isn't it?"

"Darn straight and damn skippy."

"I have to get up early every morning. It's part of my therapy. If I think about doing things for too long, I get anxious and I don't do them."

"That was your answer?"

"It was part of my answer. I do take anxiety medication. I manage it. I don't know if there's a cure for whatever quirk is in my brain. Meds plus behavior management worked better than one tactic alone."

"I see." I didn't know what else to say.

Rose must have sensed my discomfort. "I'm telling you this because I don't want you to feel less than anyone. We found how to make ourselves happier but, like massage, it's different for each person. We aren't trying to remake you so you become one of us."

I stretched my arms out in front of me, gave her a blank stare and my best zombie moan, "One of us! One of us!"

She slapped my hands, but she was laughing when she did it. "We want to help you take a breath and step back so you can be your best. We won't try to convince you of anything. I can only show you something different from what you see everywhere else. Are you excited about doing different?"

"Yes."

Before coming to the island, I would have denied that I should change anything. That was The Savannah Way: head down, try the same shit over and over, grit teeth, hate myself, spend too much, owe too much, curse life, despise people, sublimate my existential rage with humor, bull through, drink too much bad coffee, lose sleep, never dare look up from my useless work and fail. Repeatedly.

"Rose?"

"Yes?"

"So...this might sound silly."

"Silly is okay. Don't underestimate the power of silly."

"Do you guys consider yourselves enlightened?"

"Fuck, no. That term has too much baggage. I'm not even sure what it's supposed to mean. Enjoying work, sex and play is enlightened, I guess. There are monks and nuns who deny themselves hoping to achieve it. Maybe some of them do reach a higher plane of consciousness or some shit, I don't know. Denying pleasure doesn't sound smart or compassionate to me. Sounds like they're scared to live. Sex scares the extremely religious. Women who enjoy sex scare them the most."

"You could be talking about my mother. When I got my first period she forbid me to let boys, 'pet the pussycat.'"

"The pussycat? That's adorable!"

"Mom told me, 'They all have dirty fingernails. You'll get an infection. Then you'll have to go to Dr. McKenzie. He'll know how you got it and Dr. McKenzie goes to our church!' Then she went on about flesh-eating bacteria."

"Your mom sounds hilarious."

"Never intentionally. Mom also told me the definition of promiscuous was having any premarital sex, even if it was with my one special fella."

"Not much for dictionaries, huh?"

"I'd forgotten that detail. No wonder I married too young."

"In talk therapy, I believe that's considered a breakthrough." She quirked an eyebrow my way. "Therapists would save a lot of time if they told everybody, 'Just blame your mother.'"

I burst out laughing. "I get it. I should take responsibility and — "

"Yeah, yeah, you're old enough to own your shit. Forget it. There's a theory the past doesn't even exist. That's why memories are so faulty. We think we're accessing memories, but we're really making them up. If you want to talk about human perception and time, talk to Rick. He's the sci-fi psychology fan. Sounds like bullshit to me, but whatever."

"What do you believe in, Rose?"

"Compassion, kindness, and pleasure. That's my religion. Sex feels divine. Even when it's not so good it can be pretty damn awesome. I figure my sexuality is god-given, holy and deity-approved. It's bad manners to refuse a gift so, you know...rock on."

I tried to picture my parents stuck in an elevator with my hosts. Somebody would have to crawl out of that roof hatch in a hurry.

"After aligning your words, thoughts, and deeds you get the rewards of passion and pleasure. I don't know why people have to take ethics and philosophy courses to figure that shit out. They'd arrive at the same place if they listened to kindly grandmas."

"That only works if you've got a kindly grandma handy."

"People come up with a bunch of rules for living. The more complicated the rules, the fewer people will follow them. But, that's me. Rick has to intellectualize because that's the way he is. I'm all about free love for everybody. Rule number one is simple: Don't be an asshole. If I can manage that feat consistently, I'll stand out in any crowd."

I lusted for Rick but I was falling in love with Rose. "I do feel your compassion. And I like your coffee."

"Cool."

I'd finally relaxed about Rose being half naked. I wasn't so self-conscious anymore. I added, "You're beautiful."

Rose stared deep in my eyes, earnestly. "You don't have to be afraid, Savvy. You know that, right?"

"I go back and forth so much. After the Jasmine Room, I thought I had all the answers. I woke up early and felt great. I was motivated, ready to take on the goddamn world. Then I had my bodywork session with Rick and I fucked up. I was a shit to him and my confidence fell apart again."

"Energy comes and goes and you can fall out of focus. That's normal."

"Is it? I have glimpses of clarity and optimism and, somehow, it slips away."

"Struggle to change is normal. You're hanging yourself from those high expectations. Detours and speed bumps are normal."

"I was picturing more of a relatively short training montage. I'd do something big and then I'd get standing Os, adulation, and checks in the mail."

"Just do you, boo. Don't hold yourself to someone else's standards and take it easy on yourself. You will figure what to do and stick to it. You want to get a car out the mud, you gotta rock it back and forth a bit before you can rocket away."

"And I won't fall back into self-doubt?"

"Why wouldn't you? Anybody with a functioning brain has doubt. But, you're here. We're together. Everything is going to work out okay."

I'd been alone for too long. I'd yearned for someone to lay beside me, to hold me at night when storms thundered overhead, to reassure me with confidence and care. Tears welled in my eyes and slipped down my cheeks. "Thank you for that, Rose. You've got a big heart."

She smiled as she gently wiped my tears away. "You know what? You need to have more fun! We're going to have a lot of fun together. Would that be okay?"

I thought about the kind of fun she'd offered since I arrived at the spa. My nerves were alive, electric with anticipation. "That would be much better than okay."

27

B efore Rose brought the omelets to the table, she placed a sprig of parsley on each plate. She put a single rose in a tall vase next to the tray of condiments. The cutlery and plates looked expensive. The table was a presentation worthy of any of the finest restaurants.

"Wow," I said. "You go all out."

"Bon appetit!"

Rose took a seat and ate in tiny bites. She frequently put her fork down to sip her coffee and pluck a raspberry from the bowl between us.

From the first bite, the meal was heaven on my tongue. To enjoy eggs, I usually required toast laden with pats of melting butter. With the added spices, onions and mushrooms, nothing else was needed.

"Tastes great!" The clock on the stove told me it was 2 p.m. "Feels like breakfast in the afternoon."

"I don't usually eat much until about now, anyway, so this is breakfast," Rose said. "The wake-up protein shake lasts me until I can stop to make something more substantial."

"You shouldn't have gone to so much trouble, though."

"No trouble. I do the same for myself when I'm alone."

"All this? The fine china and fancy omelette?"

"We're worth treating ourselves well. It's not only about the food. Relaxation is good for digestion."

"I gobble down breakfast over the sink or pick up a bagel at a drive-through in the rush to work. I eat too much fast food, I know, but with the slowdown over the bridges and people packed in so tight, city traffic doesn't have a rush hour. Every hour is crush hour."

"Most people complain about Vancouver's rain," Rose observed.

"I do that, too, but I deal with it by imagining I'm in a French art film set in Paris shortly after World War II. The rain is a metaphor for the short pointless horror that is our lives."

"Ooh, tell me more."

I'd just been fooling around. However, her question sounded like a fun challenge. "Um...I am Lisette, a poor misunderstood painter on the verge of greatness, if only I could afford to buy more canvas, oils, and brushes. My movie's in black and white so, naturally, all the paintings are drab expressions of existential angst...just like life." I winked to make sure she knew I was mostly kidding.

"Very French, Lisette. How does your movie work out?"

I stared into my coffee cup for an answer. "To get a show in a prestigious gallery, a villainous art dealer insists I sleep with him. I refuse his ultimatum. Lisette has dignity and a code."

"Admirable."

"Nah, Lisette ends up on the streets," I improvised, "painting with her own blood."

"Yikes. She's Goth. How does Lisette's story end?"

"Homeless, wandering, begging for small change and trying to sell her art. One day I plan to commit suicide by throwing myself off a bridge — "

"You mean Lisette plans to take her life?"

"Uh, right. But first, she draws her pain in chalk on the sidewalk along the Champs-Élysées. The rain begins to fall and the camera lingers on the beautiful horror she's drawn. It is washed away like all her dreams but, just then, an art connoisseur comes along. She sees Lisette weeping over a disintegrating masterpiece. The kind patron gives Lisette enough money for a bit of bread and wine and cheese."

"So Lisette is saved."

"Mm...no. Maybe. I don't know. Nobody knows."

"Huh?"

"In the final shot, you see Lisette walking away toward the bridge suffused in fog. The question left in the audience's mind is, to be or not to be? Will Lisette persist or is she headed to the bridge to end it all? Has she peaked or will she try again? Most of the evidence tells her, 'Just give the fuck up.'"

"What do you think happens, Savvy?"

I shrugged. "Needs a subplot early on where Lisette is misunderstood by a young lover who betrays her to marry a wealthy debutante or something. I haven't given that enough thought to fill out a solid two or three hours of depression. French art movies are super long...or at least they all feel that way. I haven't watched art cinema since I was pretentious and pretending I wasn't from Alabama."

"Did you really?"

"Yeah. When I went away to college, I figured I could pretend to be somebody else. I even considered going with a French or British accent. I kept up a Transatlantic accent for the first few days of frosh Week. That experiment failed."

"Transatlantic accent? What's that?"

"Me doing a Katherine Hepburn impression. It was exhausting. I settled for flushing the Alabama out of my speech."

"How'd that work out?"

"Still working on it. I'm embarrassed to admit it, but I committed to wearing a beret for a few months. I gave it up when I went home for Thanksgiving."

"Sounds serious."

"It was. In my freshman year, I had everybody convinced I was from New Hampshire. Doug was still South in the mouth so I had to pretend we'd just met at college. He went along with it for the blowjobs, I guess. I had to hang out with a different crowd from my second year on."

"Seems pretty elaborate."

"I was trying new things, away from home for the first time. I probably wasn't the only one pretending, trying on my new adult suit, figuring out how to be and how to be different. I'd watched Holly Golightly pretend to be someone else in *Breakfast at Tiffany's*. I figured I could do that."

"Reinvention is one thing, but you were running away from yourself, weren't you?"

"I can't believe I did that now. I rewatched *Manon of the Spring* recently and had to flush out the boredom with a *Fast & Furious* marathon."

When I looked up from my coffee cup Rose was staring and wide-eyed. "Lisette's story...is that a real movie?"

"Not that I know of. I make shit up."

"It sure was vivid and grim. Ever think of — "

Suicide, I thought.

"Acting?" Rose asked.

I let out a long sigh. "Nah, I freeze up when I talk in front of groups. When I was a tour guide, just talking over a speaker on a bus, my voice shook so much everybody got nervous. My knees knock. If I could speak in public, I might have become a lawyer."

"I have to ask, you aren't from New Hampshire but, are you Lisette?"

Rose's implicit question: Had I thought of harming myself?

I played dumb and stumbled on in a rush. "For some reason, in English lit classes, they call it pathetic fallacy, to use of the weather to set a mood, I mean. Rain means tears, dark clouds suggest looming gloom and if a storm's coming, it's not just about the weather. Somebody's gonna get fucked up."

Not wanting to be too much of a downer, I hastened to add, "Sometimes I pretend I'm in a black and white Bogey and Bacall. I love stories about solving murders where the hero wears a trench coat. Film noir is so cool. It's all about the trench coats, deception, guns, and snappy dialogue. Plus, back then, nobody worried about cigarettes causing cancer. They had jackets they wore just for smoking. Good times."

"For the rain, all I can suggest is a bigger umbrella," Rose said, "but have you ever thought seriously about — "

Suicide, I thought.

"Screenwriting?" she asked.

"Movies are all just superheroes now, right? Not sure where I'd fit into the Hollywood ecosystem. Maybe I should be more realistic, follow your example and start with eating better. Slow food sounds like it could be my speed. There's no one to say no to that ambition...but do you know what they used to call the slow food movement?"

"What?"

"Cooking."

"If taking the time to cook doesn't grab you, I have some killer slow cooker recipes. Put it in when you get up, set it and forget it. Eat it when you come back home at the end of the day."

"I've tried eating better in fits and starts. It makes me feel like an algae eater, sucking green fuzz off river rocks."

"Everything I eat is easy, healthy and tastes good. I'll give you some recipes to try."

Rose was a positive force in the universe, looking for the good in me instead of my inner goof. She offered ideas, alternatives, and solutions while I stood under a perpetual raincloud. It occurred to me then that I had a choice about what I gave voice to. I could do better so I promised myself I would.

"I bake a mean Black Forest cake. The recipe comes straight from the Black Forest. Once you eat mine, you'll realize every other black forest cake is an imitation that uses glue. Ooh! Have you been to the Granville Island Pie Company?"

I shook my head.

"We have to go! Their pie is the next best thing to Y pie."

"Why pie?"

"No, *Y* pie. Heh. Sorry, cunnilingus joke. You know? Dining at the Y? Me, having you for dessert?"

I smiled. That was going to happen. All I had to do was reinvent myself. I wasn't running away this time. I was running toward myself. I looked forward to finally getting aligned in word, thought and deed. I was genuinely thirsty for pussy and hard cock, too.

28

"Life is a smorgasbord and I'm here to sample everything before I die," Rose said. "I'd love to sample you, for instance."

Squirming, I pretended I didn't hear that last part. "Is that your secret? Eating badly only once in a while and learning to love salad?"

"I do have a trick. Living a long and healthy life is nice but I need a more immediate reason to eat well."

"Which is?"

"I'm an exhibitionist who loves to entertain guests at a sex spa. I feel good about being naked. I don't want to emerge from the pool and have you scream, 'Put it on! Put it on!' I want you to look at me the way you did when I got out of the pool. I don't have big tits but they are titillating."

I almost choked on my vegetable omelet. "Great. Now I know the secret: walk around naked a lot. I'll be sure to mention that next time I'm at a Weight Watchers meeting. That will go over well with the ladies in the church basement."

She giggled. I thought again how girlish, free, and easy Rose was with her laughter. I spent too many days straining to fake a laugh. I cleared my throat and tried not to think about what she said about me looking at her emerging from the pool. Naturally, I deflected with a joke. "How do you know someone is a vegan who does CrossFit? Don't worry. They'll tell you."

We laughed. We ate. I didn't reach for my phone to check for messages. I didn't wonder about the emails or Facebook updates I might be missing. I had no chores or appointments. Instead, I enjoyed our meal. I watched Rose as she breathed in the smells of the food. She ate slowly, savoring every bite and each sip of coffee. My gaze was drawn to her breasts. I wondered what it would be like to take a long sip of hot coffee and immediately take one of her hard nipples in my mouth? Would it get harder? Would she moan? Would she make me moan?

I dragged my eyes back up to meet hers and tried to maintain eye contact. "Most nights I eat a frozen dinner," I said. "I eat in front of the TV if I'm feeling fancy. This meal is fantastic, but I don't see myself digging fresh parsley out of the fridge every time I crack an egg. I admire you for it, though."

"Something else on your mind besides food and slow cooker recipes, Savvy?"

She was probably picking up on how I kept looking down at her breasts and taut abdomen. "Will you tell me about your first massage session with Rick?"

"You want to know if your experience was typical?"

"How do you know it wasn't?"

"Most guests go on and on about his magic hands. You haven't done that so I'm guessing you're questioning your experience."

"The massage was excellent. I have no complaints about his work on me...but it brought something out of me I'm not proud of."

"Sounds juicy. I'll show you mine if you show me yours."

I hesitated. I'd wanted to know if Rick had told her everything about my session. It was obvious he hadn't. Now she wanted me to tell her every embarrassing detail.

"C'mon, Savvy. Girl talk is good for the soul."

"I thought the expression was confession is good for the soul."

"Fine," she said. "I'll be pleased to confess."

"What if my story is more embarrassing than yours?"

"Then I'll tell you embarrassing things about me until you decide we're even. I don't embarrass easily. I could tell you about the shit most people would think I should be ashamed of. Deal?"

"I was taught to shut up and keep embarrassing things a secret."

"Me, too, back when I believed in that crap."

"You first," I said.

"Pain turns me on," she said.

I could hear my mother's voice screaming from the back of my brain already: *She's a dirty girl! A dirty girl! Run away!*

"Pain?" I looked at her wondering how much my face changed as I said it. I didn't know what to say. "You like it when people hurt you?"

"Hurt? No. I don't want anyone to damage me, but I do get off on pain when it's applied just so."

"How did you find out you were into that? I mean, did you have a bad boyfriend or something? Was it from getting spanked as a child?"

"Maybe some people do find out that way. For me, two things let me know I got turned on when it hurt a little. The first was the tattoos. I never had an orgasm while I got inked, but afterward? Oh, man. I'd fuck like, if I fucked hard enough, I might save the baby Jesus from the cross and cure cancer. I got so hot, no wonder some people go wild with tattoos. You see somebody with a lot of tattoos, nine times out of ten, they're a freak in bed. I'm not counting girls with a tat of a tiny flower on their back. I'm talking about the chicks where you can see their art from a block away. You bed one of them, you aren't sleeping that night, guaranteed."

"You said there were two things? What's the other?"

"Watching porn was the other big clue. I don't know how long it would have taken me to find the pleasure of BDSM without porn."

"My ex-husband used to tie me to the bed and blindfold me once in a while," I said. "I liked it a lot, but I have to tell you something. Don't laugh, but I can never even remember what BDSM stands for. Bondage...something with a D and Sadomasochism? Is the D for dominance?"

She laughed. "BDSM. Bible Discussion and Study Meeting."

I gave her my most withering look. "I said, 'Don't laugh.'"

"I didn't guarantee I wouldn't giggle. BDSM: Bondage, Discipline, Sadism and Masochism."

"Oh. Okay. My ignorance gets worse. After Sabine told me she was a sapiosexual, I had to google it to make sure I knew what she meant. Around her, I felt like I was way too dumb for her to be attracted to me."

"Dumb can't be fixed. Ignorance is quite easy to remedy. I love Sabine but she hits that sapiosexual button too hard sometimes. Smart is sexy to a lot of people. I suspect she still harbors some need for approval from others so she broadcasts her sapiosexual preference. It sounds more impressive than telling everyone you're a pretentious snob."

"My sexual experiences have been pretty vanilla," I said. "I like doggie, but I mostly got missionary and woman on top. Coming here, I feel like I've got a passport to a strange new country. I don't know what the local customs are or where to start the tour."

"Relax. Sex is a complex spectrum and we're all on that rainbow somewhere. Some people are into feet. Others can't have an erection if someone else is in the room. You can play anywhere you like on the continuum without going all in. Admitting you're interested in experimenting with BDSM — with me, for instance — doesn't mean you'll be screaming and begging me to shit on your tits five minutes from now."

I burst out laughing. I kept laughing until my sides hurt. "You were the girl in high school the other girls were warned about!"

"We are drawn to what we're told to reject. However, I'll have you know I was a sweet honors student and a late bloomer."

"What changed? I mean, how did you bloom?"

"Everything got easier when I decided to stop outsourcing my emotional state to strangers."

"What do you mean?"

"That's one of Rick's lines. When you surrender to the judgment of the mob, they get to determine how you feel about yourself. Ever read a mean review of a restaurant? Some can be legitimate, but a lot of people get off on snarky condemnation. The internet is anonymous so ordinary people let their inner monster out. It can feel good to let impotent rage out of its cage, I guess. I prefer a dom who is potent. I enjoy some pain but still," Rose tapped her bare sternum, "I'm nobody's bitch."

"Nobody's bitch," I echoed. "Heh. I was asking myself this morning what kind of bitch I was going to be. I want to be the badass kind. Teach me, Master."

She chuckled. "Badass bitches teach themselves. You'll know you've got it when you stop walking and start swaggering."

"I'm not sure I've ever swaggered."

"You will."

"Current status: Experiencing heavy doubt."

"Savvy, you're funny, but you also seem so innocent. I want to tie you down and eat you up. Would you like to do that? Would you like me to eat you up, like a kitten lapping up cream?"

Rose lifted my hand to her cheek. She leaned closer and ran her fingers through my hair, brushing it back from my face. Then she held my face in her hands. Her hands were soft and warm.

I stared back, bewildered, wide-eyed and as innocent as a Disney deer.

"I think you want to, Savvy. You want me between your legs, licking you...sucking your clit. I won't tease you like Rick does. I want to watch you come. I want to hear you moan. I want to feel you moan."

"I...*uh...oh...oooh*." I was wet.

"I want you to pull my hair, to pull me into you when you come. That's the other secret of healthy living. Replace the sugary desserts with lapping at a friend's pussy. Feed me, Savvy."

I could have reached down and unknotted the towel around Rose's waist. I could have sucked her nipples and let her suck mine. I wanted to grab her hair and pull her face — her mischievous, angelic face! — between my thighs. She could kiss my clit while I pinched her nipples and made her moan with the mix of pain and pleasure I knew she loved.

But I wasn't ready.

"Ahem. You were going to tell me about what your first massage was like. You...I got derailed there for a minute."

"Is derailed the verb you want? Turned on, maybe?"

"Yes."

Rose unknotted her towel and let it fall aside. She leaned back and stretched with her hands behind her head. Her nude body looked so long and inviting, I gaped at her, relishing the sensuous moment.

"I'm here to get to know you," she said. "I feel like we're already friends and I'm very attracted to you."

"Oh, I'm clear on that." I looked down at her bush and not just a glance this time. I stared.

"I like to be...open."

I could sink to my knees and tongue her relentlessly. We could have each other. I salivated. I almost drooled. I wanted her perfect box pressed to my mouth. I wanted what she wanted. I could hold her head, feel her short hair between my fingers and demand she fuck me with her tongue. No more teasing.

Rose parted her legs a little as she reached for her coffee cup. She brought the mug to her lips and sipped. Then she placed it in her lap. "Still very warm," she sighed.

I took a long slow breath. I imagined what it would be like to say yes to life instead of no. I imagined pressing my lips against hers, her mouth on my clit, her tongue "parting my nether lips," like in the books of historical erotic romance I kept hidden in my night table.

Even though I lived alone, I kept my naughty books hidden in case I died or something. I didn't want paramedics, firefighters, or burglars to surmise that all I did day and night was read smut and masturbate with an industrial-sized tub of Astroglide.

I wanted Rose so much. But I wanted Rick to do me, too. I wanted a deep pussy pounding. I needed it. I wanted to be taken. With Rose, sex would be soft and timeless. I wanted Rick to do me hard and fast.

"I-I'm not ready, Rose — " I began. "It doesn't feel quite right yet, not in the kitchen and not for my first time with a woman."

"You don't have to explain. I will answer your questions to the best of my ability. And do whatever else you want or need. I love it when a busty woman tells me what to do."

Rose pulled the towel back around her waist and stood to pour me another cup of coffee. "I told you I came here first for the gardens. After I found out a bit of what Rick was up to, I talked to a woman who was a guest at the time. She was a famous actress, blonde bombshell-type. I'd never break a confidence, but trust me, you'd know the name. I asked her what you asked me. She said Rick was the first man in a long time who touched her without caring that she was in movies. Other men made her feel like a doll or a tool or a pawn or a stepping stone or a bank account. Men chased, used, and idolized her. Rick's massage made her feel human. On his table, she was not a name or a celebrity. She was no less special, but he treated her like a real person. "

"I can see how that would be very different for her."

"Rick's rich. He's got his life together and that takes a lot of pressure off. He didn't need or want a single thing from her. When we make people into idols, we take away their humanity. That's why the same people who say they love celebrities are so terrible to them when they dare to age or fail or fall out of the limelight."

"That was her experience. What about yours?" I reddened again, embarrassed at my impatience.

"Sorry. Almost there. What I was going to say was, Rick can't control how your body and mind will react to any session. An ordinary massage treats our hardware. Rick taps into our software. What the actress said made me curious about what he could do for me. I went to Rick and requested a massage. I said something like, 'Gimme some of that or find someone else to weed your gardens.' I skipped the usual screening protocols for guests. He complied."

"Ha! If you were some grumpy old guy, he'd have found somebody else to take care of the flowers. He must have been attracted to you. And why wouldn't he be?"

"I'd like to think so, but I wasn't as happy then as I am now. I didn't feel attractive. I pushed a lot of people away and I could be abrasive.

Rick saw my sadness and answered the call. I didn't have to blackmail or bully him into it. Rick's the most generous guy I know, and trust me, a lot of rich people aren't."

"What happened to you on the table?"

"What I remember most vividly is the trigger point work. With Rick using his hands and elbows on me, I found a way to get some of the joy of tattooing without the ink. I really got into the range of pain he could put me through without leaving a bruise. His hands are so strong! Each muscle release left me looser and more relaxed. Trigger point therapy can give the receiver a little discomfort or the pain can be exquisite. He sure got me wet and moaning. Rick saw how I responded to heavy pressure so he kept going."

"Kept going? As in — " I almost said fucking.

"Trigger point marathon," Rose said.

"He did some of that work on me, too."

"The knots can be bands of tight muscle or localized spots of tension. Rick describes what he feels as the end of a pencil eraser, a spot a little harder than the surrounding muscle. He has amazing palpation skills."

"Yeah, I felt that."

"Okay, what's up, Savvy?"

My defenses crumbled a little and I admitted, "I got really turned on when I was on the table."

"That's okay. I got hot and bothered my first time, too. Every time, actually."

"But, I got...handsy."

"Oh," she said. "That's against Rick's rules for the first deep tissue massage."

"I got mad and said some things I shouldn't have. Since I cooled down, well...."

"I'm sure Rick was the perfect gentleman."

"That's the problem. I didn't want him to be able to resist me."

She took a sip of coffee and looked thoughtful. "I've debated this issue with Rick — "

I almost spit out my coffee. "Debated? Me?"

"No, no. Not you!" She gripped my hand. "I've debated with Rick about the issue of denying sex in the first session. If every bodywork session is unique, why stick to a set of rules that applies to everybody in just one regard?"

"I'm not the only one where this issue has come up, then?"

"Nah. Look at him. He's Rick Barrister. If you're a reasonable woman with a pulse, you've got a serious twat tingle for him. He's like Dwayne Johnson with hair. The Rock without hair is hella hot, too. I'd do him."

"So maybe Rick should change his policy."

"Maybe he will. You should have seen me on his table for my first time. I begged him to fuck me."

"Begged?" I reddened.

"Oh, yeah," she said. "Threw off the blanket and made it clear he should do me then and there while he worked the trigger points in my neck and pulled my hair."

"*Heh.* Crazy," I said weakly.

Rose sat up straight in her chair, her inner lie detector buzzing. "You, too?"

"Yeah," I said miserably. "Maybe those first massages aren't all quite so unique as you think."

"We have so much in common, Savvy. We're going to end up fucking Rick and each other, all of us together."

"Ah. Uh...."

"Am I wrong?"

I brightened. "I was thinking the same thing, actually."

29

I thanked Rose for the meal and offered to do the dishes.

"Nope. Sheila will be in soon."

"Who's that?"

"Sheila takes care of the inside of the house and cooks the big meals when we're hosting more people. An excellent vegetarian chef, self-taught. This Christmas we're hosting a returning guest who is a master baker. Sheila and I are going to take lessons during her visit. Sheila wants to do fancy things with fondant. I just like chocolate cake."

I wondered about the women Rick surrounded himself with. "What's Sheila like?"

"Kind and sweet. She's a minimalist so she doesn't have a single extra thing. Used to live on a houseboat so she's very particular about what goes where. If she buys a new item she gives away something old. When she came here she fell in love with shoji screens so she redecorated her cabin to that taste. Her place looks ordinary and rustic on the outside. Inside, you'd swear you'd stepped into a traditional Japanese house, right down to the tatami mats."

"What did she do before she came here?"

"Corporate law. Worked for oil companies or some shit."

"A lawyer? Really? I better do the dishes, at least."

"You've got other things to do today."

"I don't think a lawyer should be washing my dishes."

"That sounds funny."

"I didn't mean it to be. There's rules — "

"What rules?"

"I mean — "

"Are you a reverse snob, Savvy?"

"Uh...maybe. Let me think that through."

"Do you think a life of service deserves a lower rank in some arbitrary hierarchy?"

"Well, not when you put it like that." Rose had posed a question instead of making an accusation. I was used to accusations so I was put off guard. I felt witless.

"We're all here to serve each other," she said.

"Yeah, but the hierarchy isn't arbitrary, though. There are high-priced professionals and there's people like me. She should be off earning money and defending Exxon or something, right? Her time is worth more. That's math. She really gave up billable hours to cook and clean?"

"She gave up her old life for happiness."

"Oh."

"You okay?"

"In the main, mystified is more like it. I hear what you're saying, but I'm guessing her parents killed themselves when she gave up all that money. How does a lawyer end up working here? Mental breakdown? Burn out?"

"Legal stuff can go on for years. Sheila's senior partners pushed her to land new clients, make bigger deals and chase more retainers. Not everyone she worked with was nice. She often had to defend things she didn't believe in. Her life looked great from the outside, but her hair was falling out. Sheila's heart started racing as soon as she sat at her desk. She dreaded Monday mornings so much, Sunday nights were for crying."

"I know that feeling. Good for her, I guess. I just can't imagine going through law school and dumping it all in the end."

"Dumping it all was the beginning of her new life, not the end."

"Sure, sure, but the power suits! She gave up pinstripe power suits, didn't she?"

"Sheila had quite a career going, it's true. I think she'd paid off most of her student loans by the time she pulled the ripcord. She got to a place where she could see how the rest of her life would unfold: senior partner someday, eventually retire and do whatever it is old lawyers do. Her path was set as long as she didn't have a heart attack from the stress. There's a strong allure to imagining the life you might have lived. Switching tracks so you try out that life is very brave."

"But what if it's dumb?"

"You make it work or you make something else work. You've got to let go of the first trapeze swing to get to the next trapeze swing."

"But how do you know the gamble will pay off, that you'll go anywhere?"

"You don't. Rick would do a cost-benefit analysis. I'd say listen to your heart and grab the swing. The experiment can be undone if it gets all fucked up. It's worked out for Sheila. She made an unconventional choice to see where it would lead. It led her here."

"I guess knowing the way ahead too well would be like watching a movie where you already know the ending."

"Sheila has a home she loves, friends who love her and work that offers comfort and variety. She got a sense of accomplishment that constant paperwork and arguing in court could not provide. She calls our retreat experience, 'Going sane.'"

"*Hmph.* I have no clue what that would feel like."

"I hope you find out. You've got a mission that may help you with that."

"Mission?"

"Sheila's place is the first cabin up the way, the one with the red door. I'm going to suggest you go for a walk, out the back and take a left through the gate. Say hi if you see Sheila. Explore your options farther along that path."

"What does 'explore my options' mean?"

"You know, just go for a walk, get close to nature."

"I have mixed feelings about nature. It's where they keep the ticks and Lyme disease. It should be paved."

I imagined Rick waiting for me in a cabin wearing a tuxedo. I'd open the door. He'd stand next to a round bed with satin sheets covered in rose petals. He'd offer me champagne. The tux would be a stripper's suit with rip away velcro tabs. He could be out of the tux in a second and give me a lap dance. I'd pour the bubbly over my naked body and let him lick it off me.

Spotting my smirk, Rose asked, "What did I miss?"

"I'm being silly. This place isn't what I expected. I thought the retreat would be more sad or funny or something. Ignore me. You guys have created a profound place. You're trying to do important things. I pictured...well, it doesn't matter. This place has more dignity than I expected."

"You thought we'd be more like Vegas in the '70s, didn't you? Sleazy? Greasy? Velvet Elvises on the walls?"

"If you have multiple paintings of Elvis, the plural should be, 'velvet Elvi,'" I said.

Rose giggled.

"I'm sorry about my shitty prejudices. This trip is a little like showing up to a porno shoot and discovering that the stars aren't just bodies with big dongs and mouths with vacuum suction. They're real people with high ideals to match their high heels, big-ass aspirations, and a burning interest in C-SPAN. This is going to sound bad, but I just noticed I had a blind spot. I fucked up."

"That's why they call it a blind spot. What do you see, now that you've looked?"

Blushing, I admitted, "I equated higher sex drive with lower IQ. That was stupid."

Rose frowned. "I understand, but don't tell Sabine. She'll bore you for an hour with how well she scored on the MCATS and LSATs.. She takes advanced math classes for fun. One of these days, I'm going to take Sabine aside and tell her straight, 'Okay, we get it. We love you! Stop trying so hard!'"

I loved Rose for that joke. She let me off the hook, deftly and effortlessly.

"You are Renaissance people," I said.

Rose blew a raspberry. "Our retreat is an ambitious experiment, difficult to do well. Still, Rick's got the mojo to make it work."

"Is Rick waiting for me in that cabin at the end of the path?" I asked.

"He went out to get a new part for the motor on his boat. He'll be back late this afternoon. In the meantime, there's plenty to do with just us girls. What do you say? Do you want me to sex you up now or later?"

I blushed and squirmed.

"Later, it is." Rose leaned in and gave me a quick sisterly kiss on the cheek.

"If a guy said that...if anybody else came on to me like that — "

"They'd be an asshole." Rose looked so relaxed, I relaxed, too. She reminded me of my father's dad. Granddad could say just about anything yet he always failed to offend.

The conversation took a sharp turn and Rose looked at me earnestly. "Have I misread you, Savvy? If you're not interested, it's cool. Honesty won't hurt. I don't want to be an asshole."

I took a deep breath and let it out slowly. "You didn't misread me."

"I'm getting mixed signals. You afraid of the pussy? I purr if you pet her."

"You are...exciting. Exciting is a little scary."

She chuckled. "So we're good? May I keep putting myself out there? I put out. Hard."

"I do want you."

"But it's a process. I get it. Take all the time you need. If Rick were here, he'd talk about neuroplasticity and rewiring our automatic responses and I'd need a nap. It's a good thing he's such a sexy brainiac. And a great thing he's not here."

"Rewiring my brain? Is that what we're doing?"

"You are. Something on your mind, Savvy?"

"Just wondering what I'll be like when I leave."

"Depends on you," Rose replied. "I've found guests from conservative backgrounds tend to embrace our ideas very quickly. The ones who arrive here thinking of themselves as libertines are slower to make small changes. You might even reinvent yourself."

"Overnight? I am in a hurry. I've already lost so much time."

"It's the conversion experience. People who push their real feelings down for a long time experience a huge pressure release when you finally shake the bottle and let the cork pop. That's why the sex button is so powerful. People are too dammed up."

"I do keep telling myself I need to start over."

"But do you want to?"

"I've made a mess of my life."

"Not what I asked."

"I'm a wallflower and a wallower."

"I'm a swallower."

"Touché."

"You sell yourself short."

"I'm five foot, five inches."

"You have such potential. Don't you see it? Sabine saw it in you."

"She wants to get me into bed."

"Who doesn't?" Rose gave me a warm smile and, for a change, I didn't even blush or stammer. I thanked her for the compliment. That's a buttload of progress, isn't it?

30

"Take the path to the left," Rose reminded me.

"Can you give me a hint? Is this a test? Am I going to have to steal treasure from a dragon? Chat with a burning bush? Fight ninjas?"

"What?"

"That's what secret societies do, right? Some kind of test or hazing...spanking, maybe? Well, paddling, obviously."

"Paddling, huh? I'll be sure to bring that up at the next meeting with the inner circle. When you come back, we could do something fun, too. How about a trip into Victoria? I want to show you my favorite bookstore. It's awesome. I want to show you all sorts of things. In the meantime, wander and explore as much as you want. You get there when you get there. There is no appointment time. It's all up to you, no pressure."

My mind raced. *Up to me. Take the path or not. Go home or not. No one is coming to save you. No pressure, but your life all depends on what you choose. And don't assume it's all going to magically work out well. Just make good things happen!*

I doubted my capacity to make good choices. I had created a desolate social life in Vancouver. I'd piloted my failing business into the ground. My life was all nouns: divorcee, loser, lost soul, future old cat lady. I needed to get some verbs in my life: like, love, do, achieve! *Rah, rah, fuckin' rah.*

I walked out into the afternoon sunshine, past the pool, and through the gate. Beech trees, flower boxes, and birches lined the path. A couple of hundred feet on, I looked back. The thick foliage closed around me. I couldn't see the house. White wooden archways marked the path at twenty-five-yard intervals. If caught in a sudden cloudburst, I wouldn't be far from the protection of thick ivy.

I imagined Rick and me caught out here in the rain, under those arches. My dress would cling to me. I'd pull off his wet clothes and throw them aside. He'd pick me up and I'd wrap my legs around him.

The arches. I blanched. "Going back home to the golden arches of McDonald's is going to suck ass," I said aloud.

Up the path, I came upon a picket fence of distressed wood. Covered by thick vines, I guessed the wood was probably reclaimed from an old barn. Beyond the gate, a quaint log cabin sat in a small clearing. The front door was bright red: Sheila's cabin. A small hand-painted sign told me so.

Wash hung on a line between the cabin and an outbuilding. An impressive woodpile was stacked to dry under a long shelter. The roof was made of solar panels and a small satellite dish sat atop the outbuilding. I guessed that building housed batteries for the solar panels. A large hammock stretched between two beeches.

I imagined a lazy afternoon in the hammock, reading, and napping. I'd only get up to pee and to drink fresh pink lemonade. Cherry Kool-Aid is best after a workout or as an evening aperitif.

An empty rocking chair sat on the small porch beside a hummingbird feeder. A weather vane was perched beside the red brick chimney. Despite the solar panels and satellite dish, the log cabin had a rustic aesthetic fitting its surroundings. It looked like such a cozy place to live, safe and tucked away from the worries of the world.

The Pacific's surf pounded down the hill behind me. In the

distance, the Rockies stood against a blue sky. It was as if I had stepped into a fairy tale.

I wanted to climb into Sheila's hammock. I wanted to pause to explore the unfamiliar feeling of not having to be somewhere else. During my massage, I'd felt that sensation: The clock didn't matter. In my regular life, I was always out of time. Here, the phrase meant something else. At the retreat, "out of time" meant outside of Time.

Savoring that moment reminded me I'd feel shitty later. When I contemplated my return to real life, I dreaded my desk and my dreary apartment. Vancouver meant rain, deadlines, more rain, overdue bills, and disappointment. Soon, I wouldn't be able to afford to stay in the city. Then what? I couldn't seem to allow myself to enjoy anything.

From the cabin, a woman yelled, "Stop!"

I looked around, worried I'd dawdled too long and someone thought I was a trespasser.

"You're not done, Ryan!" The woman sounded angry. "Come back here, you bastard!"

I retreated behind the ivy at the gate, anticipating trouble. Instinctively, I reached for my phone. I patted my pockets. My phone was charging on my nightstand.

The red door popped open. A shirtless young man who looked about twenty almost fell as he stumbled from the porch and down the steps. "Take it easy, Sheila!"

A pretty Indian woman followed, quick on his heels. Her breasts were bare. She wore a hip-hugging sarong. "Come back inside!"

"I'm late for work!" His shirt was balled in his fist. He shook it out and began to pull it on hurriedly.

As he reached for the buttons, she grabbed his hands and pressed his palms to her breasts. "Work will always be. We will not always be."

Ryan seemed to consider this and capitulated. Slowly, he kneaded her breasts.

Her hands slipped down to his belt as she sank to her knees in front of him. So this was the housekeeper/lawyer who was so strict about putting things where they belonged? She pulled out Ryan's dick and brought it to her lips. She looked like she was shaking her head no in an exaggerated way as she slid her mouth across his shaft.

Ryan took in a sharp breath and let out a long groan.

Sheila paused and Ryan groaned louder. "Don't stop now!"

I sympathized. I knew the frustration of being denied pleasure. As she looked up at him, I was sure he wouldn't have to wait long for satisfaction.

I heard her say something with her mouth full. I'm pretty sure it was, "You're going to be a little late for work."

Sheila sucked him down greedily, pushing her nose to his taut belly.

I gasped. I watched, frozen in place. This was a different kind of fairy tale. It was an improvement on the story of the three bears or Alice in Wonderland.

I watched the pair, riveted, as her head bobbed up and down on his cock. I thought I should go, but what if they heard me? They'd know they'd been seen. Worse, I'd be caught peeping. Even worse, I'd miss the show. I wasn't going anywhere. Nothing could make me stop watching.

Moaning, Sheila grabbed Ryan's hips, urging him to fuck her mouth.

The young man tipped his head back and surrendered to her lips and tongue. "Oh, yes...yes...Sheila! *Yes!*"

The spit-smack sounds of a juicy blowjob gave me a sweet ache. The last time something like this had happened, it was me walking in on Doug and Patsy. This time it was two strangers having sex in front of me. I could see this scene objectively. With the gut-punch of betrayal drained from the act, I could enjoy watching this pair without complications.

She pulled back suddenly and smiled up at him. "Are you going to do me right or what?"

"Whatever you want, but don't stop yet!"

Careful to be quiet, I took a step behind the cover of the ivy. I worried if I moved too quickly, they would spot me. Who would believe I had simply paused to admire the cabin?

This was so much different from watching porn. This was intense, immediate, and strangely life-affirming in a way professional pornography rarely seemed to manage. Few of those actresses seemed to have any fun. So many of the men in those movies seemed angry. Sheila and Ryan obviously had some kind of history, a relationship, and a story. They liked each other. She was older than Ryan — a streak of gray shot through her widow's peak — but I couldn't guess how much older.

Ryan fell into a rhythm fucking her mouth. She moaned and her enthusiasm seemed to pull him closer to the edge. He stopped bucking his hips abruptly. "Ooh, Sheila, I'm going to come!"

She pulled back and gripped the base of his penis. "Oh, no you don't."

"*Gah!*"

"Please!"

"No."

"Ooh."

When she was satisfied his peak had passed, she began jacking him in her fist again. Then she took him in her mouth again and pumped him furiously.

I felt a warmth gather in my belly. I looked around nervously, still scared of getting caught. My apprehension — no, fear — intensified my excitement. Watching two strangers fuck in real life made me hot and wet.

Sheila grabbed the base of her partner's cock again. He moaned for more. She just looked up at him and smiled, completely in control. She flicked her tongue over the head of Ryan's cock.

"Finish me! Finish me in your mouth, please!"

"Uh-uh. I told you, you do me right or you don't get anything more for a week."

"C'mon!"

"Make it two weeks for whining."

"What do you want?"

"You know what I want." She stood and, with one hand wrapped around his rigid dick, led him back to the porch. Sheila sat in the rocker and put her knees up on the arms of the chair. She pulled her sarong aside and commanded him, "Go for it."

Ryan knelt in front of her and buried his face between her legs.

"Ooh, Ryan! Your tongue! Your tongue is so fast and hot, baby!"

Three years had passed since I caught my ex cheating with Patsy in my bed. This time, my feelings weren't complicated. I was surprised to find the memory of Doug and Patsy had no power now. The situation was similar enough to be a reminder, but I felt no pain. All I felt was the need to come.

My clit ached for attention. Already wet, I slipped my hands under my shorts. I imagined myself in a sarong, enjoying sunlight's warmth on my bare breasts, the wind caressing me. As Sheila's sensations built to a crescendo, I pretended I was her. I imagined myself rocking and wriggling beneath a hot man's tongue. I love having my clit sucked. I love getting teased with gentle circles all around the clitoris but not quite on it. I love it when my clit is lapped to the point of climax. I wanted to be Sheila, in control and demanding satisfaction.

I wanted to be Ryan, too, commanded and subservient and helpless in the shadow of irrepressible desire. Sheila and Ryan had passion. I wanted passion like that. Instead of being dictated to by bill collectors, I wanted to be governed by pleasure and primal need.

Sheila panted, "Play with my ass, baby! Ah. Ah, yes! There! Yeah!" She grabbed a hunk of his long hair in her fist, pulling him closer, deeper.

I plunged my left hand down the back of my shorts. I could feel my rosebud open slightly, accepting my probing fingers and igniting my nerves. I rocked my hips and pushed at my anus while my right hand worked my clit.

"Do your duty," Sheila said, raising her pelvis and pulling the sarong back farther. "Do me now! Serve and service me! Shove that rod in my hot pocket or I'll give you blue balls for a month!"

Ryan obeyed. He pulled the whole chair closer and slipped his arms beneath Sheila's calves. She wiggled down farther toward the edge of the seat. She threw her head back and her jaw dropped open as he entered her. He began to rock her in the chair, up and down his cock, making her ride him. His strong ass muscles flexed with the effort of driving into her.

I glanced around again to make sure no one was coming along the path. My excitement heightened. I wanted a dick and not just any dick. I didn't want Ryan's dick. I wanted Rick Barrister to plow me in a rocking chair just like that. I needed relief. I moved my fingers faster, making myself come, quick and easy. I tried not to make a sound as I came. I bit my lip. Stifling my moan intensified the arrival of my orgasm.

In porn videos I'd seen, men didn't come in women. They came on them, shooting a sticky load across their face or on their backs. There was something sweet about a man coming inside a woman. Despite Sheila's demands, Ryan's begging, and the height of their mutual need, it was romantic, too. They needed each other equally.

They needed each other equally. I wanted that. We want most what is denied us.

As the pair's passion built to their crescendo, I started back toward the house on rubbery legs and weak knees. I wondered, why the fuck did I say no to Rose's offer? Why wait for Rick? I could have had Rose's hot tongue servicing me the same way Ryan had serviced Sheila.

I was lonely. I had chosen loneliness for reasons which now seemed both staid and increasingly mysterious. I didn't have to be alone. I often said I wasn't a prude, but I was. Fear held me back, but fear of what, exactly?

I didn't have the pleasure of Rose's tongue because I was still acting on rules set by my mother. I was stuck with one image of who I could be, clinging to it. I acted like a robot whose behavior was programmed by arbitrary rules. Having sex with Rose didn't mean I couldn't have Rick later. What the hell was wrong with me? Did I think I was going to live forever? I wanted to try sex with a woman. A beautiful woman had offered and, still, I had refused.

Stupid! I was too cautious. In business or in my personal life, I was too slow to act and too long on regret.

"Say hi if you see Sheila," Rose had suggested. *Ha!* No way, but even if they had heard me, Sheila and Ryan were past caring.

I heard Sheila come, long and loud. I tucked in my shirt as I tiptoed up the path. Sheila and Ryan were still in the throes of orgasm as I slipped away.

On the trajectory I was flying, the best I could claim at my death was that I survived a bunch of days. I managed to sleep indoors each night. Any dumb dog could claim the same. That would make a grim eulogy.

My life was pretty fucked up, that's been established. It was time to unfuck it. Thus my newfound commitment to becoming unfucked up was born. I would explore my darkness, flail proudly, drown publicly, and — maybe — walk away from the public pool with the magic word: transcendence.

I finally knew what I wanted to do. I wanted to have a lot of sex and write about it.

31

U pon my return to Rick's house, I went up to my room and slept a while. I felt like I'd been pent up for so long, releasing my body's tension made me feel like a rag doll. Later, I went down to the kitchen. Rose was working down by the dock so I fixed myself a small salad and lounged in the library, perusing assorted books but unable to settle down to read one.

I should be writing books, not reading right now, I thought.

My jaw tightened as my brain began to catalog all I had not done. English was my best subject and more than one teacher told me my writing showed promise. Still, I'd failed myself in that regard.

A niggling thought, maybe a mean mind gremlin, whispered, *You've failed in every regard.*

My stress headache drove me out of the library and outside. I found Rose weeding the garden by the pool. She looked up and waved. "I should have planted more sunflowers. It's late in the season to be doing it now. Next year I'm going to create a wall of sunflowers."

"*Mm-hm.*"

"Savvy? You okay?"

"Never better."

"Really?"

"A little headache. It's nothing. In some ways, I feel like I'm fully in my body, if that makes sense." I tipped my head back, inviting the falling sun's warmth. "We are all solar panels. I should have gotten out here to tan earlier. Where has this day gone?"

"They put on a great show, don't they?"

"Huh?"

"Sheila is a lovely person and Ryan's such a nice guy. When they get together, it's electric."

"I saw them. It was hot," I admitted.

"They'll be pleased you thought so."

"They...they knew I was watching?"

"Ryan rigged a little sensor on the gate from the main house. They put on their sex show for almost all the new guests."

I covered my face with my hands. "Dammit! They're freaks!" What I really meant was, I was a voyeuristic freak.

"They're living their truth. Sheila can't get off unless she has an audience. They'll do it again for you if you like. They love to oblige."

If they knew I was watching, did they know what I did while I was watching? I was too embarrassed to ask. Rose's laughter was not unkind but she did laugh a lot.

My aching head in my hands, I muttered, "No, no, no." Much to my disappointment, I discovered I could not turn back time and erase the afternoon by wishing hard.

"I decided something," I said. "I want to write. I penned a lot of short stories in school and won a couple of contests. I want, no, I *need* to write."

"Nice! What are you going to write about?"

"For starters, my time here. You're going to be in it, for sure. Is that okay?"

"That would be great. Make me taller."

"You're already tall."

"Yeah, but wouldn't it be great if you could write about having sex with a giant woman?"

I laughed. "We haven't had sex yet but...yeah. Giant woman. Like Lilliput. I could tie you down."

Rose's eyes sparkled with interest. "I'm in!"

I slipped my sandals off and stepped into the pool. The air was cooling so the water felt very warm. I lay back with my hands over my head so I could cling to the side of the pool. I let my body float. I spread my legs wide. "Wet," I said. "So...wet. Look! I'm making a single entendre!"

"Savvy, I do believe you're flirting with me."

"I realized I was being an idiot before, turning you down. Can't deny biology. Wanna come in? The water's warm. We could heat it up some more. Wanna come?"

Rose waded in with her clothes on. She placed one hand on the small of my back and the other behind my head. She massaged my neck and shoulders gently.

"I don't feel sore in the shoulders, anymore," I said. "Rick worked wonders. You know what I'd like now? My head hurts a little, but this isn't a physical thing. It's a mental thing. I was in the library thinking about all I haven't done yet and...enough." I reached behind Rose's head and pulled her mouth to mine. I kissed her deeply and slowly. Her lips were so soft.

I remembered Sheila's tongue flicking over the tip of Ryan's hard cock. Floating and kissing and getting more turned on by the minute, dizziness hit me. I had to stop to catch my breath.

"I think I should write erotica, but I haven't had enough sex to write it authentically."

"A travesty," Rose replied.

I caressed her left breast. Her nipples were hard under my palm. I thought of puppy noses, probing my hand, asking to be petted, begging for attention. "Can you help me, Rose?"

Rose kissed me again and again. "I'll fuck you with my tongue and suck your clit until you scream," she said. "I can hardly wait to open your box of heavenly delights."

"Box of heavenly delights,? Really?"

"I can't wait to shut you up with my twat," she said. "I'm going to muzzle you with my muff."

"Your muffle!"

"Yes. I'll ride your tongue." Her expression was wistful.

"My heart chakra is opening," I said. "It kind of hurts. Like somebody's got a crowbar trying to open me up so I'm not such a bitch. I've been such a tight-ass. Am I? Damn. I am, aren't I? My heart's telling me I'm right. My heart chakra does not lie. My heart chakra's a bitch, too."

"I like a girl in a wet t-shirt," Rose said. "There's something about fabric clinging to a heavy rack that's better than starting out naked. It's like Christmas. Undressing the object of my affection is like unwrapping a present with a great big red bow on it."

"Rick said something like that. He loves Christmas for the anticipation. If he likes the holidays so much, he should remember it's better to give than receive. He should have at least given me head. Speaking of which, I've got a splitting headache."

"Water and dizzy do not mix. Are you dehydrated?"

"Hypoglycemic, maybe. I don't know."

"Time a snack and some sleep, then?"

"Already?"

"I think so."

"Aw!"

"C'mon. Tomorrow morning, we'll go someplace special."

"And then?"

"Want to come upstairs and unwrap my present? I got a box of delights — "

"You're very tempting, but not tonight, you've got a headache. We've got pain relievers if you want."

"Okay," I said. "But I better get laid soon or I'm giving you guys one very tough Yelp review."

"We might make you wait a little. We deliver in the end."

"In the end. Ooh, anal! I haven't really tried much ass play. I haven't even tried pussy yet."

Rose pulled me close and whispered in my ear, "You're going to love mine. I can't wait for Rick to pound you from behind while you've got your beautiful face between my legs. I love having my pussy licked while the girl on my clit moans and screams. Are you a moaner or a screamer, Savvy?"

"You're a tease, too. Gawd, you angelic people are evil to us poor sinners."

"Let's get you off to bed, lust bunny."

"Get me off. Ha!"

"Don't masturbate tonight. Just go to sleep and watch what dreams may come."

"Don't diddle myself? Why not? Does evil come out if I do?"

"No, but I want you to ache for it when satiation finally arrives."

"When?" I demanded.

"If you're feeling up to it, how about tomorrow?"

"Don't clown me."

We made the long journey up to my room and I pulled off my wet clothes. Much to my delight, my day wasn't done. I stood naked before her. Rose handed me a towel but I refused to take it. I held both hands above my head, spread my legs, closed my eyes, and tilted my head back. "No. You do it. I'm a virgin. Sacrifice me."

Rose held the bath sheet at each end dried me off tenderly I kept my eyes closed hoping that she'd kneel between my legs and tongue me.

"I should go," she said.

"You should stay. And do me."

"But — "

"I, Savvy Needs, being of sound mind and aching clit, hereby demand that you satisfy my raging sexual desires, so help me God."

"Um — "

"What? You want me to sign something? Do me!"

"I do love you telling me what to do."

"Especially since I'm what to do!"

"You're sure."

"I've never been more sure. I've been thinking about you since the moment I stepped on the dock. I was shy. Boldness is better."

I shut up when Rose looped the towel behind me and pulled the towel back and forth. Her clothes were wet and clung to her small breasts and taut torso. She pressed against me as she dried my back.

I smiled. "Your clothes are wet and you made me wet again."

Without a word, she proceeded to dry my boobs, less gently this time. I was so turned on, I trembled.

"Better?" she asked.

"Nope! Still wet. Go lower."

I felt one of her hands slide down my belly. My legs were already spread. I gasped as she brushed against my bush. My eyes popped open and I went up on my toes as Rose caressed my vulva and slipped her thumb over the hard marble of my clit.

"Oh, yes!"

"How's that?"

"Delores says hello and she's pleased to meet you! Very pleased!"

Rose stared into my eyes as she teased me, swirling a finger around my clit before dipping into the mouth of my vagina, tentative and gentle.

I clenched my jaw. Through gritted teeth, I pleaded, "Keep going."

"Sorry. You made me break my policy."

"Keep going. Don't be cruel."

She bent her head to my breast and sucked my left nipple into her mouth. Rose slid a finger up and down my wet slit, up and down, around the clit and back down to the entrance to my pussy. She kept playing with me as she lifted her head to kiss me.

I moaned into her kisses.

"You are so beautiful," she told me.

"Please, make me come."

"I can't stop now, can I? Or can I?" She stopped and grinned. I wrapped my arms around her, trapping her to me. I took her right earlobe in my mouth and bit down. She moaned and returned to stroking my wet slit.

I lifted my left leg to wrap it around her waist. She held me, solid as a tree as she stroked me harder. "Yes! Yes!"

"Bite my ear again. Encourage me."

I did as I was told. I had one foot on the floor and I was up on my toes again. I moaned louder and moved my hips back and forth, faster, urging her to make me come. "Faster. Please. Harder! Faster! Please!"

Waves of pleasure washed over me. The sudden heat and force of the spasms of my climax took me by surprise. I was still coming as I toppled backward to the bed. Rose ended up on top of me, still stroking. The spasms of joy kept going. "Oh, fuck! Fuck, yeah!"

After a moment, I stopped shuddering. "Oh, Rose."

"Oh, Savvy."

"Did I hurt you?" Her earlobe was red, but I hadn't broken the skin.

"I'm fine."

"You really are," I said.

"Want to muzzle me? Muffle me?"

"What about your headache?"

"Did I have a headache?"

"Climb under the covers, lust bunny."

I did as I was told. However, instead of peeling off her wet clothes and joining me, Rose pulled the covers over my naked body and up to my chin.

"To be continued," she said. "See you in the morning, but shit, you should know, I am damn hella turned on."

"So stay."

She winked as she turned off the light.

I began to get up but my knees had turned to jelly and the bed was spinning slowly in midair. From the door, Rose called, "See you in the morning."

Mercifully, I didn't mull and worry and think. I closed my eyes and cherished the memory of her touch.

Later I awoke in the dark. I'd collapsed into bed so early I was, once again, up in the wee hours. It wasn't quite 4:30. Feeling refreshed, I got up and lingered under a shower of hot water. The house was quiet so I got dressed and went downstairs to make coffee with a French press.

Dawn found me out by the pool in a blanket with a pen in my

hand and a notebook in my lap. I tried to recapture every moment and nuance of my encounter with Rose in words. I remembered her touch, her tongue on mine, her taste. Then I wrote of my voyeuristic encounter with Sheila and Ryan.

I smiled as I wrote at the bottom of the page: *And Rick Barrister, you're next!*

32

R ose appeared by my side around 8:30. I stood, took her in my arms, and gave her a hard squeeze.

"I like the way your breasts squish against me," she said. "It's a great way to start the day."

"Getting a late start?" I asked. "You're usually up early."

"I was up very late. Rick gave me a long, delicious massage. You were supposed to get one last night but since you were unavailable —
"

"You could say I got a massage."

"Twat massage."

"Is that okay?"

"Better than okay. Loved it."

"Not as much as I did. Makes me wriggle just thinking about it. I want more."

"You'll get more. Feeling better, though?"

"All I needed was a little sleep and...well." I nodded to my notebook. "You know how I got stressed about not doing some things? Writing helped. I think getting the words down got the guilt about not writing out of my system."

"Sounds therapeutic."

"It was, though I wish I didn't miss out on my massage."

"I was glad to take your place. Thanks!" Rose turned and lifted her skirt. She wore no panties so I could see her left ass cheek was still red. "Got spanked!"

"Did that hurt?"

"I wouldn't have come so hard if it didn't sting a little. I'm much better now, so thank you again!"

I reached out, hoping to take up where we left off. Rose dropped her skirt, turned around, and kissed me hard on the lips. We paused in the moment, our arms wrapped around each other. I was thinking about how she wore no panties and how I'd like to return her favors. Instead, she slowly pulled back and held a black credit card out to me. I didn't take it. "What's this?"

"Shopping spree. Let's go into Victoria. I'll drive."

"I can't take more charity, Rose."

"Sure you can. We want you to have the full experience like any guest."

"Nice, but — "

"Savvy, when somebody wants to do something nice for you, let them. Accept tips. Relax and enjoy. People who aren't assholes enjoy doing nice things for others. Letting us do something nice for you makes us feel good. Win-win."

My pride got in the way. I shook my head.

"This is the dance people do around money," Rose said. "They're scared of it, embarrassed by how much they have — "

"Or how little."

"Okay, here's what's going to happen. You'll say no a few more times and then I'll insist. You'll pretend to feel better about it because I'll be insulted if you don't accept. Then we can go and have fun."

"Would you be insulted?"

"Nah. I'd think you were being silly and buy you a bunch of stuff you don't need on my card instead. If you take it now, we'll save a lot of time and you won't have to return something that doesn't fit or doesn't suit you."

"You do make a compelling case." I took the card. "Thank you."

After I took my notebook and pen up to my room, I raced back downstairs, eager to see the city with Rose. I realized that, for a change, I ran with enthusiasm. At home I jogged a few nights a week, plodding along with dull doggedness. Usually I, like most on the dirty side of thirty, ran with the desperate air of people trying to push back Death, too aware of aches, pains, and mortality. Moving with joy, I felt fresh and young.

I kept running until I met Rose out front beside a low, wide building. I found a trailer that carried several canoes and one Tesla. A long silver bus was parked beyond the garage. Rose popped the locks on the electric car and we climbed in.

"Sorry, I have to ask. What's the limit on the credit card?"

Rose laughed and nodded toward the back seat. "How about you don't buy more than we can take home in one trip?" She pressed the accelerator and we raced up the long driveway.

"Whoa, horsie!"

"You're fine, sweetie. Try not to claw at the upholstery." At the gate, Rose pushed a button on the visor and the iron wall slid open to the road.

"Hanging with you guys is fun, but I also feel like I haven't done much with my life."

"Nobody has it all figured out but, hey, never too late to do something big. Not until you're underground and they put a stone over your head. We're all in a race with the Reaper."

"I wish you wouldn't put it that way."

"I like to think I'm in tune with Nature. Untimely deaths are Nature being a bitch. I try to think of timely deaths as mulching and recycling, making room and giving some other flower a turn at blossoming."

"I try not to think about my mortality at all...though it occurs to me I was just thinking about it! Being happy reminds me I'll soon be sad. Twisted, right?"

"If you see the world as it is, ignoring death is difficult. Nobody has all the answers. We just try to use the time we've got. More pleasure, less pain. I don't overthink it. If I did, I'd never do anything."

"Besides the intricacies of bodywork, what's Rick's favorite subject?"

"Pick a topic, he'll listen. He seems to know something about everything."

"What's it like, living with him?"

"We're both so busy, we don't spend that much time together."

"But you live in the same house."

"I have gardens to care for. We come together over guest visits. Heh. Get it? We come together over guests?"

"I know you're not into labels, but you're into men, too, right?"

"Best of both worlds, baby!"

"You ever think maybe you and Rick should be together, like a couple?"

"We're friends"

"Fuck friends?"

"What we have covers all the bases. I had the flu last winter followed by bronchitis. He took care of me as well as any husband would. Friends are good to each other. Friends are the family you choose once you move away from home."

"What's the endgame, though?"

"I'm not sure what you mean."

"You were talking about death. It doesn't usually come all at once. I mean...when you get older, what will you do?"

"Dunno. When we're old, maybe more of my clients will be elderly. The same questions apply to anybody with a job. Could I be a plumber forever? Could I still be a nurse until my last breath? Most people won't manage to fire on all cylinders deep into old age, but sex and caring can be for nearly everybody for a long time."

"But when you're older and need a hip replacement or something?"

"I s'pose we'll hire younger people to keep up the high sexual pace."

"If Rick keeps working here, won't he eventually become a dirty old man?'

"We're sex-positive people, Savvy. That label is ageist. It disenfranchises our elders from their sexual birthright. Kind of sad, don't you think? I look forward to the privilege of becoming a GILF."

"GILF?"

"Where have you been? You've really never run across GILF porn? Grandmas I'd Like to Fuck?"

"Ha! Sorry, I'm still way out of my element here."

"You were nervous about taking the next step past bi-curious. What changed?"

"I finally let the burning lust take over without my pesky negative thoughts getting in the way. You, Rick, Sheila, and Ryan really fired me up. I decided my body is for more than carrying my brain around. The whole package needs attention."

Rose turned onto a larger highway to take us into Victoria. "I guess you can only hear shit or get off the pot so many times. At some point, you gotta take that dump."

"Where's Rick today?"

"There's a problem in the supply chain. He had to fly to Seattle for a meeting. You'll see him tonight. He'll apologize in person when he sees you. One of his companies is expanding operations so he got called away. He was disappointed you weren't able to make your massage appointment last night."

"I'm sure he didn't mind making do with you."

Rose shrugged, seemingly unconcerned one way or the other. "Plenty of time for all of us."

"It's hard to imagine you being anywhere else but here."

She glanced away from the road just long enough to bless me with a smile. "Thank you. And yes, I probably wouldn't have a lot of patience for the sexual conduct rules handed down from HR in some accounting firm. I'm very lucky to be where I am. If I had a regular job, I wouldn't be tearing off to Victoria to shop and show you around." She waggled her eyebrows. "I can't wait to introduce you to lots of things."

"Oh? Like what?"

"Well, if you're ever worried about the whole lesbian label, you can always do what Sheila and I did."

"Which was?"

"French kiss me around a cock. If there's a cock between us, we're straight as arrows, right?"

I laughed so hard I farted. Then I started singing "A Whole New World" from *Aladdin* as she drove into Victoria. I sang at the top of my lungs. I am not a particularly good singer and I said so. Rose told me my enthusiasm made up for my lack of talent.

For the rest of the ride into Victoria, I giggled so much I thought I might pee my shorts.

"Are you high?" Rose asked.

"High on you," I said. "High on being here. High on life. Fucking finally!"

33

Victoria is lovely, a city built for tourists to enjoy. It's small enough to walk to the most interesting attractions. Water taxis shuttled back and forth in a marina packed with boats. Tour buses maneuvered smoothly along the road edging the harbor. Tourists and locals alike strolled along the shore and no one hurried. We stared at the snow-capped Rockies and people-watched.

"What do you want to do first?" Rose asked.

"You mentioned a bookstore?"

"My shrine! This way to Old Town! My fave bookstore throws shade on all others." After a short walk, we came upon a building that looked like it had once been a bank: Munro's Books.

"Alice Munro was one of the original owners," Rose explained.

"Who?"

"Famous Canadian short story writer."

"Famous Canadian? Famous short story writer? Those are things?"

"Smart-ass."

"Sorry. We don't study such things in Alabama"

"She won a Nobel Prize so — "

"I know Hemingway, Mailer, Shakespeare and...Jesus, I just realized that we only ever studied old books and dead authors. I guess nobody has written a book worthy of note besides J.K. Rowling and George R.R. Martin. We didn't study that stuff in school either, though."

"Since moving into the spa, I find a lot of time to read," Rose said.

"You're making me glad I bit you last night. We Hill People don't have time to read. We're too busy trying to make fire by banging rocks together."

"I'll show you a better way to bang, baby," she replied.

We walked into Munro's and my jaw went slack. Row upon row of tall dark bookcases stood beneath colorful tapestries. With its high ceilings and airy feel, the space was vast and filled with browsers exploring a forest of books.

"I used to read a lot in high school and university," I said. "I'm not sure how I fell out of the habit. How do you stop doing something you love?" I was about to say something maudlin about my dead marriage, too, but I quashed the urge. I immediately felt better for shutting up about Doug and hoped it was the beginning of a trend.

"I've got new ambitions to feed. Whatever reference material a writer needs to start, I'm sure I'll find it here," I said. I already owned a few books on writing. I had read and reread Stephen King's *On Writing* several times. If I was going to write about the retreat, however, I figured following in the footsteps of the king of horror wasn't precisely the way to go. "Do you think they'd have a book on writing erotica?"

"At least one, I imagine."

Rose pointed me toward the shelves. "Browse. No rush. Take your time. We're in heaven." She went off on her own to peruse books on garden design. Meanwhile, I savored the elusive pleasure of dallying. There was something special about this bookstore that made me want to camp out. Kids fantasize about getting locked in a toy store overnight. Munro's was my toy store. I read book descriptions. I looked through first chapters, and sampled first lines. I needed to know what bait successful authors used to hook readers. I wondered what my hook would be.

When I decided I had no clue what my first chapter could look like, I lapsed into fantasy. I pretended there were stacks of my first book beside a signing table. I pictured a line of readers, each waiting for me to sign the book I'd written. I'd smile and nod and write something unique, witty, and pithy for each fan. Then I remembered my stage fright and decided I'd just sell everything by mail or on the internet.

Wandering those aisles, I felt lighter. My shoulders didn't feel like concrete anymore. The muscles in my neck were no longer like taut piano wire. The magic of Rick's massage stayed with me and I finally began to appreciate the work he had done. I could even see a difference in my feet. My toes weren't pointed off at 45-degree angles as I walked. I felt taller.

I muttered to myself, not quietly enough, "Well, that makes sense. Lesbian sex makes one taller."

An old woman looked up from the book she was perusing and an old man gave me a sharp look.

"Sorry," I said. "I've just had my first lesbian experience. It was lovely and I didn't realize I was talking aloud."

The woman smiled. The man gave me a wink. I reddened, giggled, and flounced off. I realized then that my life featured insufficient flouncing.

Rose had a great impact on me, but my mind kept drifting back to Rick. Embarrassment about my tantrum had worn off quite a bit and I looked forward to seeing him. As an apology, I ended up buying a book on sea kayak design for Rick. For Rose, I found a pretty book about dried and pressed flowers. I used my own money to buy the gifts since it felt ridiculous to do otherwise.

For myself, I found a book on writing erotic romance. As I flipped through, the sex scenes were pretty coy. I wondered how explicit I should be. This couldn't be a romance, exactly. Could it be erotic literature? Or was I too hifalutin? I was a bitter divorcee trying to figure shit out and taking too long to do it.

Then, as I lingered over romantic travelogues, I found inspiration. Every rags-to-riches journey had to start with an inciting incident. I remembered that little from basic English composition classes. If writing erotica was to liberate me, I'd have to be as honest as possible. I'd already read many romances but I preferred erotica, much of which doled out hefty portions of slam, bam, who's next? The erotica I'd read was mostly short fiction. It was the travelogues that gave me the idea to marry my sexual liberation with travel stories. I had traveled for work, so why not write filthy romances set in exotic locations?

By the time Rose met up with me at the front of the store, I was dreaming of escaping the travel business and taking off on literary flights of fancy instead.

Rose asked me how I was doing. "Well, I'm making progress. I freaked out that old couple over there. I have some ideas about how to move forward if I can get past my biggest obstacle."

"Which is?"

"Me. What if all I've got is a shitty life and a shitty story? Nobody wants to read the path I'm on. I'm bitter. I was bitter, I mean. I'm working on it."

"So write about that. Write your way out of it. Everybody's life is a story. You're a work in progress. That's cool because it's relatable. Are there successful authors or books you remember that you could emulate? If others have done it, you can, too."

My parents kept *Reader's Digest*, the Bible, and *Ladies Home Journal* out in plain sight. Gay Talese's stories about swinging key parties were tucked away where they weren't supposed to corrupt me. Snooping through my father's nightstand, I'd found a few paperbacks beneath his handkerchief collection. I remember *The Happy Hooker*, *The Story of O* and a Jackie Collins book I was pretty sure was my first encounter with the word bitch in print. *The Bitch* was the title.

Mom kept Danielle Steel books on her nightstand. She caught me looking at those when I was little. She called those books "private reading material" and declared I wasn't old enough to read them. I obliged her wishes as long as I could. I was slightly more sneaky when I returned to them when I was thirteen, furtive, and horny.

In university, I'd read Anais Nin and Henry Miller. Her writing was frank and sexy. Miller's sexual adventures were definitely written from a male perspective. Was it from *Tropic of Cancer* or *Tropic of Capricorn* where a guy is in a tub with a couple of women? He pees in the bathwater and they freak out. That was weird, but the scene I remembered best was a young woman getting the opportunity to give ol' Henry a blowjob. He wrote, "She dove for it."

I didn't remember anything much from the erotica I'd read that was only about sex. Likewise, the Harlequins I'd read were pure romance with sprinklings of sex. I didn't dislike them. I'd read quite a few, in fact, but that was part of their problem. Those light romances tended to meld together in my mind. There is even a website dedicated to helping romance readers keep track of which books they've read. They are often so alike it's easy to confuse them. The men's names tended to make me giggle, too. I've never met a Dirk, Rollo, or Brock in real life. When I thought about what to write, my mind kept coming back to Anais Nin. Her adventures seemed dirtier and more daring, making love in back alleys in Paris. Her stories weren't just about sex. They were about how sex expressed her worldview.

Nin wrote about being an empowered woman who refused to be confined by what society expected of her. Her writing was a prism to a way of thinking that was lost for a long time. She showed another way for a woman to be empowered, unembarrassed by her sexuality. Nin wrote diaries that exposed her inner life in detail.

Simone de Beauvoir was another inspiration. A feminist who threw off all patriarchal expectations, her lovers included women and men. She hooked up her wall-eyed friend and colleague, the existentialist philosopher Jean-Paul Sartre, for the ménage à trois experience. She also wrote travel essays to pay the bills and that got me thinking of how I could keep writing, using every day in a new place as fodder for my work.

"I don't know anybody who writes about sex spas and turns themselves inside out about everything. I'm going to look like a nut. I didn't have sex for three years. Either people won't believe me or they'll think I'm a weak loser. I don't want to look like an idiot. I've got the weirdness, Rose. I've got it bad."

My breath was coming faster, and I wondered if I was about to hyperventilate, pass out and possibly die at the front door of the bookstore begun by Canada's most beloved short story writer.

Rose took my hands in hers. "Plenty of women share your experience. Maybe you can help them get past the bad part faster. If how you reacted to divorce is your weirdness, make your weirdness work for you."

"I don't know."

"Why all the sudden self-doubt?"

"It's not sudden. My crisis in confidence is why I'm here in the first place." Staring in her green eyes, my breathing began to slow and my heart stopped trying to escape my ribcage.

"You've identified something to work on. Write about it."

"I do admire your confidence, Rose," I confessed. "And by admiring, I mean resenting and envying."

"What set off this episode of mini-panic?"

"I don't know. Habit maybe. I was feeling ambitious and up to it a few minutes ago. Looking at all these books! I think the stuff I could write isn't what readers expect. A book of mine could never end up on a bookshelf in this store. Sorry, I'm waffling. I feel like a little kid at the end of a diving board debating about jumping into a pool."

Rose shrugged. "If you don't fit other people's expectations, either change their expectations or write what you love. You don't have to be careless. Just care less."

"Say that again."

"The retreat is largely about letting go of the non-aligned things other people expect of us."

"Non-aligned things?"

"We work outside the norm because the world's unreasonable expectations are meant to control us."

"I see." I must have looked like a beaten puppy.

"I hate to see you so intimidated so early on," Rose said. "I should have taken you to a dumber bookstore."

As we walked out into the sunshine, I thought about what books might be vaguely like what I could write. From what I gathered, the common advice for hardcore sex writers was to stick with short stories and novellas. People sold full-length novels in the romance genre, not erotica. But was that all I wanted to write. Sex scenes kept me reading. Maybe they would also keep me writing. Sweaty bouts of slamming ham without a story weren't my thing. I wanted to tell a story to unite the episodic pussy poundings.

Most heroines in mainstream romances were young, fairly innocent girl-next-door types. Most were at least ten years younger than me. That seemed pretty crappy, to be a write-off in my mid-thirties. I turned to Rose. "If I have my way with you as I plan, I could write about that."

"Something will come to you," Rose said. "You might find you get a confidence boost when you're wriggling like a fish on the end of my tongue."

"Like a fish on your tongue? Bad metaphor."

"You're the writer."

"I don't think I am. Not yet."

"Then write and you will be. I'll be your first reader."

"Really?"

"See? You've already got a fan."

Bizarrely, that silly declaration helped me. Then I remembered Rick's instructions from our bodywork session: *Calmer. Softer. Longer. Relaxed. Deeper. Heavier. Warmer. More relaxed. Calm. Repeat.*

And I wasn't whining anymore. I was breathing deeper and planning my new career.

34

As I sat with Rose at a restaurant in Victoria with the Seussian name of Red Fish, Blue Fish, I pondered what literary giants I'd fail to emulate. Watching the ocean roll gently in dappling sunlight, I didn't envy those women their Bohemian lifestyles in Paris. They had the Eiffel Tower, awards, acclaim, and a legacy. However, I was luckier because I was with Rose. I'd finally settled down — softer, longer, relaxed, deeper, heavier, warmer...more relaxed...calm — and given myself over to hope.

Rose stared at the boats going by and chewed her tacone (a fish taco served in a waffle cone). Her nipples stood out under her t-shirt. It was probably the cool breeze that got them perky, but I preferred to think it was me.

"Rose? Do you think it's too late for me to write about becoming an empowered woman? I'm too old for that shit, right? Isn't that kind of a given by now?"

"Never too old to find your voice," she said.

"But aren't we all beyond the worst stuff?"

"Savvy, in Texas they want women to pay for burying their miscarriages. It's like the lawmakers want to make sure would-be mothers are sad enough about their loss. They want women to buy rape insurance. Our struggle for personhood is real and it's everywhere. Empowerment is not complete. We thought we made gains but we're just getting started. I have friends in the States who feel they have to carry ID when they go to a public bathroom. They're worried they'll get assaulted by someone for going to the wrong toilet because they don't look female enough. I knew queer kids from my high school who were bullied. One who killed herself."

"I'm very sorry that happened."

"Me, too. They were nice people. We weren't beyond the worst harassment then. We still aren't. Things are getting better, but not for everybody. The sexual revolution isn't over. Sexual liberation is still an unrealized dream for many, many people. The oppression is global and systemic. I understand why you think it's safe here. But if you and I were to hold hands in a public place, even here, are you sure you'd feel totally safe?"

I reddened. "Well, generally yes...but not from everybody. There are assholes everywhere. That'll never stop."

"I'll settle for the assholes being quiet," Rose said. "We don't have to change everybody's mind. We have to change enough people's minds that the assholes are afraid to misbehave. If nobody thinks they're safe hurting me for being the way God made me, that'll do."

"I've felt afraid to be me," I said. "I'm bi-curious. I knew it but I didn't come out. I wasn't being real until last night. I've been hiding in my hetero-bubble."

"So what are you going to write?"

"I'm going to write that you're right."

She smiled. "Well, of course, I'll love being told I'm righteous. The definition of a genius is anybody who agrees with me!"

"I'm going to write smut with a message," I added.

"That's a thing?"

"It will be."

"What's the message?"

"I'll find out when I write it. Maybe it'll become a message with smut. I might not write what is expected of erotica. I might not even have a genre. I'll write the truth as I see it. Part of my truth is I like to read raunch and I want to write it. If I don't fit in a genre on a bookstore shelf, I'll have to create my own little niche for the like-minded like you and Rick are doing. It might not sell or it might turn into something big, but I've got to write it my way. I can see it turning into half a self-help book if you and Rick don't hurry up and fuck me senseless."

"We can do that," Rose said. "With pleasure."

"You know, it occurs to me that my only measure of success so far has been making the rent each month. God, I've been so limited, so boring. It had to be done, but at least people with hobbies, like going to concerts or something, have something tangible to show for their efforts. I don't even have a drawer full of ticket stubs! I'm starting late!"

Rose put down her tacone. "One way to tell if you're running your life right is your days consist of remarkable events. More remarkable events mean more marked time because you're excited to pay attention. Time can go fast or slow. If you pay attention to everything, you slow things down and you keep the details. When life is mundane, we aren't enthused about taking everything in. With sharp focus, time can slow or it can speed up, depending on how you process the experience."

"So I need more peak experiences."

"That'll give you more to write about. Remember, when you write it, make me taller. And smarter. Give me bigger tits while you're at it or I shall be very cross."

Her smile warmed me. "Help me with the research. Give me more orgasms."

"Where's the shy woman who almost fell off the dock and blushes easily?"

"She got teased. She doesn't want to be teased anymore."

"We've created a monster."

"Well, this is me now. Deal. I'm saying what I want out loud. I want you and I want Rick."

Rose reached out to squeeze my shoulder. "Rick will take care of your needs, Savvy. I can handle it if Rick won't. But he will. He wants you."

"He said so?"

"I saw how he looked at you at dinner on our first night together."

"What's better, do you think? To change your life for the better a little at a time or to make a radical change? I'm thinking of ditching my travel business. It's ditching me so why not rip off the bandaid? Kelly enjoys the work, but it's past time I got out."

"Depends on you. You're ripe for change. People can change quickly if they decide to," Rose said.

"I didn't used to think so, but you might be right. I'm thinking of forgiving Doug. I mean *really* forgiving him. I've been holding on to my anger and I didn't know how to get rid of it."

"What's changed?"

"When you made me come last night, I didn't think about how miserable I was. Orgasmic joy pushed the anger right out of my head. Give me more of that and I can erase him from my history, like clearing a computer disk of old junk."

"Sounds like fun," Rose said. "I'm in. Get the orgasms. Then you can write about it. Could pay dividends. And don't worry about the writing. Just do it."

"Thanks. I get really excited when I think about sex with you. I get wet thinking about sex with Rick, too. I'm up for the adventure of becoming a drooling, multi-orgasmic wench. I can't wait to see where this goes. I like the idea of being dominated sometimes, but making a man beg smacks me hard in the tingly bits, too. When it comes to writing, I'm going to be nobody's bitch."

"Cool. Sounds like you're ready to erase a lot of history, archive the pain, and replace bad files with sexy files. What are you thinking of calling your book?"

"Too early to say but, somehow, the title's got to allude to doing all that good stuff and still sound sexy."

"Good fucking luck," Rose said.

"Good Fucking Luck," I echoed. "I'll keep that title in mind as Plan B."

After lunch, we visited a high-end sex shop. Rose had surprised me with the gift of a butt plug. I laughed at first. It was the sort of gag gift I'd seen at bachelorette parties. I told her so and instantly regretted my admission. Butt plugs were no joke to Rose.

"Experiment with this toy first," she'd told me. "Then you can graduate to anal beads."

"Oh, sweet mother-of-pearl! Slow down, Caligula!"

Rose leaned close and whispered, "I'm excellent at tying knots. Got a merit badge in Girl Scouts. Maybe I should pick up some velvet rope. You'd look good tied up in red velvet."

"I'm trying to picture you in the Girl Scout uniform. I can't imagine you without the tattoos."

"Yeah, if only my guide leaders could see my rope work now! I'd give those suburban moms something to dream about. Sex and ropes plus is a heavenly art all its own. The aesthetic is very precise when done right. It's a shallow, vanilla take to focus on simple domination and submission. Getting tied up signifies trust and a whole new level of intimacy. It's giving up power to get what you really want. BDSM is a dance."

I gave Rose one of those laughs that is obviously fake and nervous. "*Heh, heh, heh, heh, heh.*" I was turned on, too.

35

When we returned from Victoria, I invited Rose up to my room. "I need some help forgetting my old life. Is it true there are inner lips and outer lips?" I teased. "I have to research that issue deeply."

"I look forward to helping you with that," Rose said, "but I have to run. Special plans tonight!"

She wrapped her arms around me and I dropped my bags to press her to me. She kissed my neck with long, slow kisses that lit me up. Then her lips traced their way up to my ear as her left hand dropped to my ass to give me a hard squeeze. Finally, she kissed me on the mouth.

I pressed into her as I circled the tip of my tongue on hers. The sensation was gentle and warm but soon became more urgent as lust surged through me. It came to me why kissing is so exciting. What we do to each other's lips and tongues is a prelude, an audition. It shows the delights we'll perform with our mouths when we sink to our knees.

Rose pulled back after a few minutes and gave me a wink and a smile. "So much to savor."

"So much to look forward to. Time slowed down for me there, in a really good way."

"I'm glad I have your attention," she said. "See you soon!"

I poked through the purchases I'd made in Victoria. As I looked up from the items spread out on the bed, Rick appeared in a doorway. He had a strange habit of doing that. His hair had been cut a little shorter on the sides and he was freshly shaved. He wore a powder blue linen dress shirt and black jeans. His sleeves were rolled up past his elbows, drawing my gaze to the muscles in his forearms. I wondered if doing massage alone could build that degree of definition. Did he pump a lot of iron, too, or was it all the kayaking?

He knocked on the doorframe. "May I come in?"

"Sure. Vampires can't cross the threshold without an invite."

"Are you still mad at me?"

"Embarrassed, not mad. Was that what the credit card was about? An apology? I'm the one who's sorry."

He shook his head. "No need, and if I were going to apologize, I'd apologize. I wanted you to have a good day, that's all. I didn't like how we ended your massage."

"So I will get more?"

"Of course, if you want. Did you have a good time in town?"

"Honestly? Fantastic! Thank you! Rose is helping me let go and that relaxation exercise you taught me helps, too. Misery doesn't just love company. Misery insists on it. Low self-esteem and frustrated life goals got me there. Past time I changed all that, huh? I'm doing better."

I glanced at the bed and regretted it was covered with the stuff I'd bought. Rose had promised me I'd get more orgasmic satisfaction. Had she sent Rick upstairs to do the deed?

"I've decided to revisit an old passion. I want to write books. But I don't want to mess it up and that makes me nervous but — "

"But your anxiety is smaller than your urge to write."

"Yes." I didn't sound convincing.

"Write what you want, your way."

"That's the only way I can do it so...cool."

He looked at the other bags on the bed. "What treasures did you find?"

"Some gifts for friends, mostly."

I'd bought lube, a vibrator, and three pieces of lingerie at the sex shop. Rose insisted I get rid of my granny panties so new, lacy underwear spilled out of one of my shopping bags onto the bedspread.

Rick nodded to one of the bags. "More sex toys are bought in Victoria than any other city in Canada. They say it's because of the elderly population. I like to think our clients contribute to that statistic."

"I love Victoria. We went to Munro's, too." A defensive tone entered my voice. I wanted Rick to know I wasn't just hanging out in a sex shop all day.

"I'm sorry I couldn't take you on a tour myself. We had an engineering problem with solar panel couplings that required my input. I have nothing else scheduled for the rest of the week. I was hoping we could spend time together if it still suits you?"

"Have you spoken to Rose yet?"

"She tells me you're ready for the boyfriend experience. She says it's urgent we get right to it."

"That's where you get me off, right?"

"Usually."

"Well?"

"I told you. I'm a romantic. We haven't had our first kiss yet."

I stood tall and went up on my tiptoes to bring my face close to his. "Ready!" I closed my eyes.

I felt his hands on my shoulders, pressing down gently. "Can't have a first kiss without a first date."

"Seriously?"

"The first kiss is important."

"You've already seen me naked."

"Not according to plan."

"I touched your dick."

"Over the pants. Doesn't count."

"I want to have sex."

"Me, too."

"Do you?" I could feel my irritation and impatience rising again. "You're a sadist. I feel like I'm at the dinner table watching everyone else eat. I watched Sheila and Ryan eat each other."

"Sheila and Ryan's show is usually a fourth-day treat, but Rose thought you needed to get on the fast track."

"They fucked like there's no tomorrow. And who knows? There might not be. I have to catch some dick while I can."

He took my hand. "Then come with me. No time like the present."

"To the basement? Are we going to the sex dungeon?"

"For a first date? Savvy! I'm amazed at you. So lusty!"

"It's not sudden! I've had a long dry spell. The drought is done and I'm wet!"

He chuckled as he pulled me after him. "C'mon."

"Where are we going?"

"How about a boat ride?"

"I'm listening."

"Champagne in the moonlight?"

"Eh. The bubbles tickle my nose."

"Cherry Kool-Aid under the stars?"

"Now you're talkin'!"

36

The moon was so bright our shadows followed us past the pool and through the gate to the right. Rick held my hand as we walked through the woods. Wooden lattice arches like I'd seen that morning punctuated the path. Skeins of tiny white lights, like stars, twisted through the ivy to show us the way. We passed darkened tennis courts. Further on, I saw a few low buildings.

"Is that where you keep the chickens?" I asked.

"Chickens and goats. I'll show you our little hobby farm in daylight. The goats are great at keeping the grass cut back," Rick said.

"Do you kill your own chickens?"

"Rose wouldn't let me," he said. "We only eat the eggs. When we have too many chickens, we send them to people who need chickens for eggs."

"Nice. But why goats?"

"Rose got me into them. We breed them to go to people in need. In many countries, goat's milk and cheese can instantly pull a poor family up into the middle class. Every country needs a middle class to keep things humming and the wheels turning."

"You send them across the world?"

"That would be inefficient. We buy goats abroad to help poor families abroad. The goats we breed here are for poor families in Western Canada and the Western United States. We took an idea that already worked in Africa and used it here. Unfortunately, they're still needed. A lot of municipalities won't allow goats within city limits so we get the goats to people in need in rural areas. For urban areas, we're working on rooftop and community garden initiatives. Rose is in on those projects. Urban agriculture is up her alley."

"You're building up good karma."

"I believe in instant karma. You do good, you feel good." Rick shot me a broad smile. "I do sell my body, but so does any coal miner."

We paused for a moment to listen to the ocean surf meet the shore. Otherwise, it was quiet. I breathed deeply, feeling my lungs fully expand.

"I have a sound machine at home," I said. "Bought it at the drugstore. It plays recordings of a jungle, a forest at night, and ocean waves. It was supposed to make me chill out. I wanted to relax and sleep better."

"Did it help?"

"It made me think how I wasn't actually experiencing those things, so it didn't help much. The real thing is better, much better. Thank you for bringing me here, Rick."

"My pleasure." He put an arm around my shoulder and gave me a squeeze. "Your pleasure is my pleasure."

We came to a high spot on the path and paused again to look out over the Pacific. The bright moon showed a calm sea.

"Every day presents lots of choices," he told me. "I'm so happy you chose to come here, Savvy."

"I had a lot of doubts, but since I got my tantrum out of my system —"

"Don't worry about doubts. People who are sure of everything are certifiable idiots."

"You sound too sure about that," I said.

"I have doubts sometimes."

"What do you worry about?"

"Finding the right people to connect with. We're in dark times.

Darker times are coming if we don't turn the ship around. People are the engine. Love, passion, and compassion are the fuel."

"If you have to ask, I've screwed up," he said.

"If fulfilling your vision comes down to people," I swallowed hard. "I've been scared all the time, for a long time. Before my marriage broke up, I was scared. I blamed my ex for a lot. Not altogether fair. I knew we were in trouble. I should have left him before he found his mistress. I gave up on my first dream. I'm embarrassed it's taken me this long to even begin to turn things around."

"You got a bad bounce, Savvy. All that matters now is now."

Rick pulled me close, his hard body against mine. I could barely make out his face in the dim light. In his tight embrace, I gave myself over to his warmth. I rested my head on his shoulder.

"It's time we focused on your short-term goals with you."

"Such as?"

"Making love in the moonlight." He bent to kiss my neck. All my worries about admitting my failures fled. All I could think about was the sweetness of his kisses. I tilted my head back, hoping his lips would cover mine. Instead, he kept on kissing my neck and burying his face in my hair.

I pulled him as close as I could. I hadn't dry-humped since high school, but I started rocking my hips against his hard-on. It was as if my hips were obeying an ancient command ingrained in biology. I felt young, a little silly, and passionate. I was so passionate I was almost mad.

"My, God!" I pulled back to get a better look at his face. "You're a Svengali mind-control robo-vampire from the future! I love what you're doing to my neck! How about you rip my clothes off?"

"Soon."

"Monster."

Rick leaned closer and whispered. "I don't bite unless you want me to. Do you like your nipples nibbled gently? Or are you a nipple clamp kind of person?"

My throat went dry. "Um...."

"I thought you'd laugh — "

"I'm still wondering if I'm a nipple clamp gal. I don't think I'm into that...however..."

"Yes?"

"When Rose showed me the sex shop, she took me on a tour of the displays as if she worked there. She treated it like we were at an all-you-can-eat buffet. She suggested I try a little bit of everything to see what I liked."

"Rose has an open mind. It might be contagious."

"*Mm.*" With Rick so close, holding me tight, I was open to trying anything. I hugged him tighter, squashing my boobs into his chest, hoping for more kisses.

He pulled back slightly to hold my face in his hands. "You're so lovely in the moonlight."

"Yeah, yeah, do me."

"With sex, I drag out the anticipation as long I can before you start stabbing me in the spleen with a cheese knife and a rusty spoon."

"Got a rusty spoon on you? For a moment there, I thought we were having a moment."

"We were. We are. But I don't want to rush."

"This isn't rushing."

"When a violin's bow draws out a long sweet note, the tension and vibrations build."

"What?"

"I want to play you like a violin."

"I want to blow your whistle."

"Ooh, Savvy. That's not first date talk."

"Looks like Rose is going to get a lot of sex from me tonight. *All* the sex!"

He smiled and took my hand again. "If you're trying to make me jealous, that won't work. You've got a good shot of making me feel envy, though. C'mon."

We arrived at a long pier. A lighthouse on a high hill pulsed its beam over a boathouse. A cabin cruiser rocked gently in its dock, running lights lit.

Rose leaned out and waved from the stern. "Boat's ready!"

"Boat? Looks like a ship to me. Are you coming, Rose?" I asked.

"I've had you to myself all day. Tonight, Rick gets to wine and dine you. Or, Kool-Aid and dine you. Or something."

"Something?"

"It's date night!"

"You don't need a crew for this thing?" I asked Rick.

"Nah, we aren't going far out. Calm sea, you and me."

He climbed aboard. Rose gave me a hug and told me to have a good time.

"I am going to get laid tonight, right? I'm feeling the need, guts-deep!"

"Hey, if you don't get laid, or even if you do, you know where my room is. When you come back, you're welcome to come to me. We can all enjoy each other without it becoming a competition."

I was stunned at what a dim asshole I could be. "No possessiveness? Nobody feels threatened? At all? You people are from Mars."

"Don't pout," she said. "It's sexy on you, but don't. Remember, if you come to see me and I'm asleep, wake me with your tongue. I love to wake up that way, don't you?"

"I've never woken up that way."

Rose kissed me on the cheek and gently groped my left breast. "Poor baby. You've been deprived too long! I can't wait to help you catch up! The sex-starved are the best fucks. Them and the chicks with all the roses for tattoos!"

She giggled as Rick started the yacht's engine. At her touch, my nipples were erect. My engine was already running.

"Toodles!" Rose called before loping away along the pier and into the dark. She ran like a gazelle.

"Ready?" Rick called.

I should have brought the butt plug and the lingerie, I thought.

"Ready for anything," I told him. "If the so-called boyfriend experience takes much longer, I might get cranky."

"We can't have that," he said. "And I'm more than ready, too."

37

W e anchored at the edge of a small bay and Rick joined me in the bow. Few pleasure craft sailed in the Haro Strait at that late hour. To the east, San Juan Island seemed close.

"The sky is clear and the stars are close," I said.

"Poetic."

"Not very. It's the sky that's the poem."

"A lot more poetic than saying 'Gee, not a whole lot of light pollution out here, huh?'"

"You're quoting a client you liked a little less, aren't you?"

"You caught me."

"You sure do have a strange way to make a living, Rick."

"When you think about how people live, a lot of it is pretty strange. Give me money and I'll give it back when you die. That's insurance. Stay in this room and count things when it's sunny outside. That's accounting."

"Sell your precious time to fulfill other people's dreams," I said. "Most jobs...my job. Sex with strangers doesn't get old, though?"

"I only have sex with friends," he said. "And don't you find there is a special energy at the beginning of any relationship, no matter how short it might be?"

"Been a long time since I dated."

"Changing a stranger into a friend is a great feeling. First dates are so powerful: the attraction, the dance between being too close and too far apart. How soon before you can hold them and feel their body against yours? Will they return your kiss? What will they be like? Will they moan? Will it be fun, funny, or serious? There's so much going on in the first flight of getting to know someone — "

I looked up into his dark eyes and shivered a little. The ocean air had turned cool, but my trembling was not all about the dropping temperature.

"It gets cold on the water at night no matter what time of year it is," Rick said. "Rose left you something to wear." He reached into a basket and handed me a sweatshirt and sweatpants that bore the emblem of the University of British Columbia.

I didn't think they were especially sexy but I pulled them on, anyway.

"You look great," Rick said. "Very collegiate."

"UBC, huh?"

"Rose's alma mater."

"Wearing this, I feel like a college girl again."

"Did you enjoy that time?"

"I don't think I used the time well. All I really wanted to do was read and stay out of the workforce for four years."

"You don't strike me as a lazy person."

"I can't afford lazy."

Rick sat on the deck and opened the picnic basket. "We have a galley below, but I'd rather stay out here if you aren't too cold."

I gazed up at the blanket of stars. I couldn't remember a time when I saw the Milky Way so vividly. "Out here is fine. What's in the basket?"

He pulled out a wine bottle and handed it to me. "One for you and one for me."

"Cherry Kool-Aid?"

"Of course."

He pulled out a bowl and set it between us. "Strawberries dipped in chocolate fudge. Rose said they're orgasmic, or almost that good."

I tasted a strawberry. "Oh, my god. Maybe I don't need you!"

He laughed and I relaxed. The water lapped at the boat. We watched the distant lights of a large ship in the strait.

"I didn't mean to be a travel agent. Nothing wrong with it, but I planned to be a journalist. Didn't work out, though. The whole profession kind of went under. The job used to have respect. Now a lot of them don't even have self-respect."

"Did you consider blogging or setting up a YouTube channel? Maybe a podcast? Seems a lot of journalists ended up doing that sort of thing."

"Didn't think of that. I needed to pay bills. I can't imagine how I would have monetized that stuff fast enough."

"It can be hard to see a way out when the bills are coming in."

A twinge of annoyance hit me. Unfortunately, I acted on it. "You're young and rich, but you've heard word of the little people's struggle from across the sea, huh?"

"You sound angry."

"I want you to understand where I'm coming from. I'm thirty-four, divorced and...isn't there some stat about how I'm more likely to be killed in a terrorist attack than find a good man or something?"

"I don't think that statistic could ever be true of you, Savvy. I don't think it was ever true for anyone. If it was, it must have been before the internet streamlined dating."

"*Hmph.*"

"I've had rough times. There were a few close calls when my dad and I were trying to get the solar panel business off the ground. I thought we'd lose everything."

"You're saying you know my struggle?"

"All start-ups have precarious times where you're trying to build fast from small to big. People fall off that financial bridge for plenty of reasons all the time. Me, my mum, dad, and my wife almost lost everything before we got to this point."

"Your w-w-what now? You have a wife?"

"Rose didn't tell you?"

"Nope."

"I guess you didn't see the name of my boat, either. You're on the *Lucia*."

"Where is she? You divorced, too?"

"Widower."

"I'm sorry. How does a guy your age become a widower? I'm sorry! My mouth flaps faster than my brain thinks sometimes. I shouldn't have...."

"Lucia died in a helicopter crash," Rick said. "We were in Blue River. We went down hard. It was bad. Lucia and the pilot died. I'm glad the pilot died or I would have had to kill him. It was his fault. He was showing off, trying to impress us. His recklessness flew us smack into a glacier."

"Awful. When was this?"

"Three years ago."

About the time I found Doug with Patsy, Rick was going through his own slice of hell. "I'm sorry. When you meet somebody who seems to have it all, it's easy to think it came easy and they don't know pain."

"I understand," he said. "Have another strawberry fudge orgasm. I love to watch your eyes roll back when you feel pleasure."

"You move on quickly after dropping a bomb. 'Oh, by the way, my wife died in a helicopter crash. Have a strawberry!'"

"I'm changing the subject."

"I thought you wanted me to have the boyfriend experience. Shouldn't I get to know you, too?"

He shrugged. "I don't want to be a downer. Talking about a dead wife could kill the mood."

"So you never talk about her?"

"Not much."

"Then let me give you the girlfriend experience. What was she like?"

"She was a tiny blonde with the ambitions of eight people."

"Of course she was. And gorgeous, too, I suppose."

"Lucia wanted to accomplish a lot, to see the world. She had a funny little nose. Turned up a little. I thought it was cute."

"Your nose is a little funny, too. I bet you were the perfect couple. What did Lucia do?"

"She was my first lawyer. My dad and I were putting together the company and we needed contracts looked over. She was fresh out of law school, a little older than me. She was learning the ropes, but she was sharp."

"A whirlwind romance?"

"I knew her for less than a month before I proposed. Foolish, really, but I love to fall in love."

"Not foolish. You're a romantic."

"We didn't spend enough time together and then she was gone. She died in my arms. The first year was all depression. That was one of the times we almost lost the company. Dad's the solar panel engineer. I'm the dealmaker."

"And then?"

"Then I realized life is short and I should use my time better."

"And so you became a Bohemian. Where's your dad now?"

"South America. He was supposed to come back, but he met someone down there and decided to stay. He sent Sheila back in his place."

"Sheila? As in Sheila and Ryan?"

"The same."

"He sent her back?"

"He wasn't going to use the ticket. Mom and Dad's marriage was open long before he went on his extended business trip. I talk to him once a week or so. He's sourcing rare earth minerals for us down there with his new wife."

"Can I ask you an extremely personal question?"

"This feels like we're going backward, doesn't it?" He smiled, not unkindly.

I pictured myself back on the massage table, legs spread and begging for a fuck and a fresh wave of embarrassment washed over me. I'd only thought of Rick as a big cock attached to a handsome man before. Learning more of his history, I saw him as a human being with a real life. "We're having the get-to-know-you better picnic," I said. "What would Lucia think of the spa?"

"She would have hated it if she were alive. I was totally committed to her. Sadly, she's not around anymore so...there you go."

"Is the retreat your attempt to find someone like Lucia again?"

Rick shook his head. "People are unique. Even twins are different. You can't replace one person with another. I've always found the story of Job offensive. God takes away Job's wife, kids, and everything else. In the end, all Job's suffering is supposed to be okay because God gives him a hotter wife, more land, and more children. That deal doesn't work for me. Everyone is precious."

"Is the spa about your escape from mortality, like a life-affirming thing to deny your pain?"

"That's what it would be if this were a romance novel."

"Not a lot of man-whores in the romance novels I've read," I said lightly.

"What got me out of depression was time, exercise, and ambition. I woke up one day and realized if I didn't get out of bed and make some deals happen, my company would fall apart. Then I'd never get out of bed again."

"So you got out of bed, saved your company, and...?"

"And decided to do something to get myself out of my head. Something life-affirming."

38

W e ate and drank and took our time. I told him about growing up in Alabama. He told me about traveling in Brazil. After a while, we even fell into silences and I sensed neither of us felt the need to rush to fill those empty moments. Comfortable silences are a good sign.

"Pretty nice out here," I said finally. "Got a blanket?"

He got to his feet and disappeared below for a moment. Rick returned with two thick blankets. He draped one over my shoulders. "Better?"

"No. I want to show you something. I remember this from growing up in Alabama." I spread both blankets on the deck, grabbed his hand, and pulled him down beside me. We lay side by side looking up at the stars.

"When the night sky is cloudless like this, ignore your peripheral vision. Look straight up at the stars with nothing else in the way. See? You can pretend you're in space."

We lay there for a while, holding hands and staring up. My senses felt especially sharp. The small space between Rick's body and mine felt electrified. I was enjoying one of those peak experiences Rose had recommended. "Are you going to kiss me soon?" I asked.

"Between the boat and the stars, this is damn romantic, in case you were wondering."

Before he could answer, a falling star shot across the sky. We turned to each other, nose to nose. Our lips touched. Warmth flowed into me. It was a soft kiss, gentle and unhurried. The next kiss was longer and slower. He tasted of strawberries and chocolate fudge. I suppose I did, too.

With our third kiss, I realized Rick was letting me set the pace. I slipped the tip of my tongue across his lips, then our tongues met. I melted into him and stopped counting kisses.

I squeezed his broad shoulders, running my hands over his muscled torso. Rick ran his fingers through my hair. I kissed him deeper as I pushed my hand under his shirt. His abs were like a topographical map.

"Wait." I pulled back and sat up. "I saw this in a movie once." I stared into his eyes as I unhooked my bra and pulled it out through the sleeve of the shirt. At least I tried to. It occurred to me, halfway through, the actress in the movie had no sleeves and plenty of room to maneuver to yank the bra out. She didn't have to fight with a big underwire bra, either.

Rick chuckled and helped me when I got stuck.

"Shit," I said. "Not quite as smooth as I pictured in my head."

He let out his deep rumbly laugh. "Tonight, we're a couple of teenagers making out under the stars."

"One of us feels like an awkward teenager."

"Then don't put the bra trick in your book. Imagine it went as you hoped. Either way, you got the effect you wanted."

I looked down at his crotch. "Yes, indeed," I said, appreciatively.

"No one's around. It's you and me and the ocean. You and me and an ocean of kisses, as many as you want, Savvy."

"Only kisses?"

He pulled me to him, his hand beneath my sweatshirt caressing my skin, lighting up my nerves. Rick returned to kissing my mouth, but he caressed my breasts, too, kneading them, feeling their weight in his hot palms. He moved on to my nipples, massaging me gently.

"Oh, god!" I gasped. "You've found my buttons."

"Tell me what you like."

"What you're doing with my nipples is awesome. Do it harder."

He did as I asked.

"*Ooh*...harder!"

He pinched my left nipple and I plunged my tongue into his mouth as I ground against him.

He did the same trick with my right nipple and I moaned.

"I love to make you moan."

Despite the cool air, I was sweating. "You asked me a question earlier. I didn't know the answer but I do now."

"Which question?"

"I might be a nipple clamp kind of gal. I want to experiment."

"Then we won't waste more time, will we?"

I didn't answer him with words. Instead, I reached down and rubbed the bulge in his jeans up and down.

"*Mm*. Yes." He ran the tip of his tongue across my upper lip slowly.

"You aren't going to run away again this time, are you?" Desperation had crept into my voice.

"The boat's not that big." He reached down and cupped my pussy through my pants. My heat radiated into his palm. "And I'm not going anywhere."

I thrust my hips forward, urging him to stroke me as I groped his thick cock through the fabric of his pants.

"Tell me, Savvy, you're the writer. What do you feel?"

"Your thick cock through the fabric of your jeans."

"I mean, what do you feel?"

"Electricity. Like what you're doing to my tits lights up circuits and makes my clit buzz."

"Go on."

"Like my hips are rocking into your hand on automatic. My pussy lips open. My twat is soaked. I want you to fuck me, Rick. Rail me. Don't hold back. If you hold back, I'll scream. Make me scream for the right reasons."

I pulled up my sweatshirt. His hot mouth found my left nipple, sucking hard. I moaned my approval as his hand slipped under the waist of my pants.

My hands were busy, too, struggling with his belt and unbuttoning his jeans. "Buttons instead of a fly? Really?" I asked. "A zipper would be faster."

"Let's make this moment last."

"No! Suck my nipples harder!" I demanded.

Rick didn't stop, but he didn't do as he was told, either. Instead, he flicked the tip of his tongue over my right nipple. He moved back and forth between my tits as I gripped his cock.

"Rick?"

"*Mm-hm?*"

"Your cock still isn't out of your pants and I'm getting hungry."

His left hand found my clit as he raised his head to suck my upper lip.

"Oh, *Geeth-thuth!*" I called out.

He slowed, circling my clit slowly, almost touching it but not quite.

Frantically, I abandoned his straining rod to reach down and pull off my pants and underwear, desperate to give him easy access. I managed to get one leg free before I fell back. I got up on my elbows to try to get the sweatpants and underwear off completely.

Rick eased one finger into me.

I pushed down on his hand. "More!"

He thrust two fingers into me. I cried out as I fell back again, muscles tight and toes curling at the strain.

"Your eyes really do roll back when you're having a good time." He stopped moving his hand and when I bucked my hips, he moved with me, denying me the stimulation I needed to come.

"I'm having a great time," I panted and pleaded. "Now get your cock out and give me what I need."

I'd fantasized about my ideal man for three years. In my reveries, the perfect man's face was always in shadow, his body hard and ready. Now I had the real thing. I needed Rick inside me. I wanted him in my mouth and pussy.

I wanted to be fucked so hard the world would go away: no future, no past, just this moment. I wanted to come so hard I'd forget every petty worry, every debt, and all my fears. I needed a good Now.

"Don't hold back, Rick."

He didn't.

I panted as Rick played with my clit. "Let me come! Make me come!" I bucked my hips against his hand, trying to get more pressure.. Then I had a brainstorm. He'd teased me. Maybe I could tease him. "Can I tell you something?"

"Of course."

"Let me tell you about the first blowjob I ever gave." I didn't wait for him to reply. My words came out in a rush between short, shallow breaths. "I didn't know what I was doing, but I got the job done."

I reached for his delicious-looking bulge again. He rewarded me by sliding his fingers over my clitoris. I shuddered and grabbed his head with both hands. I sucked his earlobe between my teeth. "Do that again," I begged. "Harder!"

He did as I asked and I talked faster, in a race with my own orgasm. "He was my high school boyfriend. I was babysitting a couple of little kids who had gone to bed and the parents weren't supposed to come back until late. He came over after I put them to bed. All we'd done was some necking and heavy petting until then. He was too shy to ask but I knew what he wanted."

Rick circled my clit again and I shuddered.

"Who wouldn't want that from you?" Rick said.

"Damn right. Anyway, we were on the floor in front of the TV under a blanket, rubbing each other up and down. I'd taken off my bra before he came over. All my buttons were undone. I remember thinking if the parents came home early I could button up quickly. I was scared because I knew they'd know what was going on anyway."

Rick flicked my clit again before teasing the opening to my vagina. My legs trembled. "Ooh, you're a bad man!"

"I wanted to do this the second I saw you." Rick lowered his head and sucked my nipples. My words came faster, desperate that he not stop what he was doing to my tits with his lips and tongue.

"The boyfriend complained he was sore. I asked where and he kind of pointed at his crotch. I'd heard of blue balls. I felt sorry for him. I said, 'Poor, baby! Your pants are too tight!' He was kissing my neck. I reached down to open his fly. He unbuckled his belt for me and I squeezed him gently, not sure what to do next."

Rick moved up to kiss my neck. I reached out to cup his balls and managed to get another button of his fly undone. Rick abandoned my clit and I gasped as he eased two fingers into me again. I cried out and began to shake. I thought I'd come then but he didn't move. "Then what happened?"

"I-I asked him, 'Do you want me to kiss it better?' He nodded and I pulled his cock out from his underwear like I'm trying to do with yours!"

Rick returned to circle my clit with his thumb. He shifted down again to hover above my nipples. His hot breath caressed them, but he didn't take me into his mouth.

"I gave my boyfriend's cock a lick up the shaft. I didn't know what to do. Girls talked about treating it like an ice cream cone so I did. I licked it and then I moved up the shaft. The head of his cock was pink. Slowly, I covered the tip with my mouth and sucked on it."

Rick rewarded me by sucking my right nipple hard. The electricity burned into my belly, starting a fire there.

Abandoning the struggle with his button-fly jeans, I got a hand under the waist of his underwear. I grabbed his cock. It was thick and warm, smooth and silky skin over a steel core. "Oh, fuck!" I said. "It's bigger than I thought."

"You turn me on, Savvy. You really do."

"Prove it!"

"What happened with the boyfriend?"

"He didn't come the first time I sucked him but he liked the sensation so much, we figured it out soon enough."

Rick fell into a rhythm, plunging his fingers into me.

"Do that thing with my clit again!" I begged.

"Not quite yet," he said.

"W-what? You — "

"Why are you telling me about your first blowjob?" Rick asked.

"Because I thought you'd be interested in me telling you about the blowjob I'm going to give next." I didn't think I was into dirty talk. Turns out, my pump was primed.

I struggled to catch my breath as I spoke. "I'll suck your cock! Just let me come! Please!"

Instead of giving me the friction I needed, Rick slipped down between my legs to lick me. I spread my legs wide.

"Slower," he commanded.

"Alright. I'll...I'll pull out your penis and — "

He raised his head, adding to my frustration. "Say, 'cock.' It's better. The words penis and vagina sound so clinical."

"Fine!" I grabbed his hair and pulled his mouth to my clit. "I'll pull out your cock and run my tongue all over it. I'll lap at your balls. I'll flick my tongue around the head."

At this, Rick flicked the tip of his tongue fast on my clit. My eyes rolled up, his hair in my tight fists. I mashed him into me. "Yes! Yes! There! Right there! Oh, fuck! Fuck, yeah!"

I almost came but Rick pulled away.

"What the hell are you doing?" I demanded.

He moved up to kneel by my head. I pulled his pants and underwear down savagely and grabbed his cock with both hands, sucking him to my mouth. As soon as my tongue began to slather the shaft, he reached down and found my aching clit again.

I licked his balls, sucking each one into my hot mouth gently before returning to the head of his cock. I did exactly what I told him I'd do, afraid he'd stop again.

Rick moaned his appreciation. He moved to one side to use both hands on me. Side by side, we were 69ing each other. I took that as my cue to really go to work on him. I pressed down, getting as much as his sweet monster into my mouth as I could.

His hands and mouth were busy, too. One hand had found my asshole and, though he didn't press in, he was doing something ingenious with his fingers, flicking back and forth and round and round.

My slit was open and wet, welcoming his probing fingers, first one, then two.

I moaned and grabbed his taut ass, urging him back and forth, making him fuck my mouth as I struggled to accommodate his long, thick cock as best as I could. He was careful not to gag me, keeping his thrusts slow and not too deep. I wanted all of him in my mouth. I wanted him in me.

Rick flicked the tip of his tongue across my clit again. I moaned with pleasure and pulled back a moment to encourage him. "If you stop now, I can't be held responsible for what I do."

His deep chuckle vibrated into my twat, setting off even more intense sensations. He'd already brought me to the precipice a couple of times. It would take little more to put me over the top.

I pulled back for a moment to beg, "Come! Come in my mouth and make me come!"

To my surprise, he pulled away.

"No! You goddamn tease!" I held on to his dick, gripping him hard, reaching with my mouth. He pulled away farther. I let go. I didn't look him in the eyes. I was transfixed by his cock. "C'mon, man! That's just wrong!"

But Rick wasn't done with me. He pulled me to him and kissed me sweetly. "I want to see your face when you come." He squeezed me tight before tipping me over backward onto the blankets. The moon bathed us in ghostly light.

He held me tight again, kissing my neck, my lips, my breasts. Then Rick surprised me by rolling to his back, pulling me atop him. "Guide me into you."

Still trying to catch my breath, I obeyed and rose to kneel over him. I grabbed his dick and slowly sank. I'd been so well prepared by his foreplay that, when I impaled myself, I could accommodate his girth and length without discomfort.

My sweatshirt was half off. I pulled it off the rest of the way. The contrast between the cold breeze and our slick, hot sex drove me to fuck him harder to stave off the slap of the sea air. He held my breasts, kneading them.

"Pinch my nipples again," I said. "Like before."

He complied and I rode him harder. The boat rocked gently beneath us. I threw my head back. Bathed in pale moonlight, Rick looked like a moving statue. I felt every inch of him. I rose up, squeezed him, and thrust back down hard. I'd almost come so much that now, contrary to my expectations, I was finding it harder to achieve orgasm. That was okay, at least for a while. Warmth spread deep in my belly. I took up a relentless rhythm. It wasn't about coming anymore. It was about enjoying the ride longer.

I gazed down at Rick's handsome face. "I've never had sex on a boat before."

"I thought I had, but the way you go at it — "

"Bullshit artist." I smiled and redoubled my efforts, speeding up the pace, driving my hips into his. I was rewarded with his appreciative moan.

"Are you ready to pop?" I asked.

"Are you?" He ran his hands over my nipples before grabbing my hips, urging me to ride him even harder. The electric circuits in my pussy sent a renewed buzz.

Rick pulled me down to him, wrapping me tight, pressing me to his chest. I arched my back, and he took over all the work.

"I love what you're doing to me," he said.

"I love it, too. Shut up and fuck me like you mean it. Make me come hard."

I put my hands on his shoulders and lifted up into a squat as Rick bent his legs to meet each of my thrusts.

"Oh, yes," I said. "It's finally going to happen."

He kept one strong hand on my hip, urging me on. With his other hand, he reached down between us. I knew what he was about to do and I gasped in anticipation. His hand lingered around my clit, not quite touching it.

"Please, Rick. Please. I can't take anymore. I can't!" To my surprise and to his, I shouted a command, "Play with my clit!"

He did. I moaned louder. We fucked harder. We were doing it together, building to the release. The warmth in my tits and belly turned to electric fire as the first wave hit me. It had been so long. Rick had made me wait so long! I'd forgotten what an orgasm could be. No vibrator could compare to this intensity. I squeezed my eyes shut and held my breath, stifling a screaming orgasm.

Then the second wave hit and my shout echoed across the water.

I kept riding through it. Rick kept thrusting. His hand was still on my clit. He kept up the stimulation as the walls of my pussy clenched. My delicious spasms did not stop. I froze and bent, my hair hanging in his face. My mouth dropped open, and he rose to take my lower lip between his perfect teeth. The deep spasms continued as I plastered myself to him, wriggling to pull his arm out from between us. My clit couldn't take any more stimulation. I was on my knees again, crushing my breasts into his chest. "Oh, fuck!"

Rick slowed his pace as he grabbed my hips with both hands and thrust deeper into me. That did the trick.

The third wave hit as he rolled me to my side and I wrapped my arms around his head. Panting, I tried to catch my breath as the shudders slowly ebbed. He was hard as a rock and still in me, not slipping out.

Rick reached up to pull my hair to the side, out of my eyes. He smiled. I smiled back.

"Holy shit," I said.

"Holy shit," he said.

I looked down. We were still joined, one frantic beast at rest, but ready for more. Frankly, I was confused. "Um, this is maybe a stupid question I'm not supposed to ask but...um...did you, uh — "

"I didn't come," he said. "You almost made me come, but I managed to hold back."

"Bullshit."

"Nope. Didn't come."

"How? I mean...you — "

"Tantra, Savvy. Tantra."

"Wow. That's what Sabine meant by a magic cock. Okay, you've got skills I didn't really believe existed."

"Tantra is real. Google it if you want. But let me hang here with you a little longer, at least until the cold drives us to get our clothes back on."

"Er, so, I'm trying to decide whether to be insulted. In case you wondered, I came like a tidal wave."

He laughed and shook his head. "If I came every time I had sex, I wouldn't be ready when you're ready for more." He kissed me sweetly.

"And you want to have more sex with me, right?"

"Oh, yes," he said. "Very much more. You are so beautiful."

"Is that the next stage in your plan?"

"Forget the stages. This week it's you and me."

"And Rose, too?"

"And Rose."

Rick rolled me onto my stomach. I thought I was going to get another massage. Instead, he pulled me up to my hands and knees. I gasped as, with one hard thrust, he entered my pussy from behind.

I kept saying, "Holy shit," as he fucked me again.

It took me longer to climax this time. Soon, my breasts swung in a faster rhythm as I pushed back on his big cock. I felt every inch of him as he stretched me, filling every inch. I cried out and bit my lower lip. I arched my back to meet each thrust as Rick reached around with one hand. His fingers found my clit as he pounded me from behind.

I should lie and write something profound or at least funny. "Holy shit" was all I could say as my eyes rolled up and I came and came and came.

And came.

I'd been made to wait a long time. Rick proved he was worth that wait.

39

The next morning, Rose knocked on my door. She found me cross-legged on the floor at the foot of my bed. I held my new journal in my lap. My pen, filled with peacock blue ink, was poised over a blank page. I didn't even give her a chance to say good morning. "I'm still debating about the beginning. I'm stuck."

Rose smiled as she passed me to pull back the curtains. "Let's get some light on the subject. What's the problem?"

I squinted as sunlight flooded the room. "Ugh. Can I start my book with my husband fucking his girlfriend's tits? That'll turn people off, right? There's too much to tell and I don't know how to do it."

"What have you got so far?"

I flipped back a few pages and showed her what I'd written about the boyfriend experience.

Her eyes widened as she scanned my tight scrawl. "This all happened on the boat last night?"

"It was epic. I've got the big sex scene and I've made a lot of notes. I don't know if I'll tell the whole thing."

"So the beginning is the real snag?"

"And the ending. But what is the beginning? Almost falling off the dock when I got off the seaplane? Makes me sound goofy. Meeting Sabine at a party? Sounds weird. Should it start with meeting you and Rick?"

"What would you say is the inciting incident?"

"Shitballs. I was afraid of that. I wouldn't be here if I hadn't come home early and found Doug and Patsy going at it in my bed. I can't start the book with disgust and humiliation...can I?"

"You have to trust readers are going to understand what you're doing, Savvy."

"A bunch won't."*

"Of course, a bunch won't. There are drunk drivers on the highway, too. Still, we dare to drive. Label it erotica. Label it a new kind of erotica. It doesn't matter, just tell your story. Who's your audience?"

"I dunno. Bitter divorced women who don't want to be bitter? Horny geo-engineers who can stop climate change by putting mirror satellites in space? Horny biologists who know how to immunize honeybees against pesticides? Or women who don't want to care anymore because they're free to have the lives they want? I've got the same problem you guys have with the spa."

"How's that?"

"I've got a marketing problem."

"May I suggest something?" she asked.

"Please."

"I choose to live true to my nature. Instead of falling into the deep groove of what's gone before, how about you do that? Just tell your truth. People who resonate with your pain and envy your pleasure will get on board. The rest won't read it, anyway. Haters aren't anybody's audience. I don't know shit about marketing, but the truth of what you feel is attractive. Rick would tell you to choose to become the person you really are, living consciously."

"How?"

"By deciding to change. Peak experiences break old patterns. Challenge the assumptions people make about how the world is supposed to work. Change is what many are looking for, no matter what age it is or what age they are. You've already changed, haven't you?"

I shrugged off the question. I'd had a hard time falling asleep the night before. I wanted Rick beside me. Instead of joining me in bed, he'd kissed me sweetly and left me at my bedroom door. I wanted to keep him in a cage...or be in his cage. I guess I had not yet progressed beyond hand-me-down ideas of possession and ownership. Now all I could think about was Rick and the book. I hadn't raised my consciousness enough to let go of selfishness.

"I'm glad it went well last night," Rose said. "You guys got off to a rocky start."

"Until we got off. I haven't been fucked like that since...since never."

Rose reached out and kissed my forehead. "I won't pretend I'm not disappointed you didn't wake me with your tongue last night. But we have more nights."

"Sorry," I said. "I was exhausted."

"Sex is a sport," Rose said. "We have to train, keep in shape, and practice, practice, practice!"

I debated whether I should ask my next question. Rose seemed so relaxed and open. I acted uptight and controlled compared to her easy, comfortable sexuality but I plunged in. "Rose? Have you ever seen the movie *Pretty Woman*?"

"Sure. Julia Roberts and Richard Gere. Hooker meets billionaire and she becomes Cinder-fuckin'-ella. It's been years, but I remember the broad strokes. Why?"

"He takes her to the opera and she finds out she loves it. It wasn't part of her world and then it was and she can't go back to the streets. I'm worried I can't go back. Do you ever have people who come here and refuse to leave?"

"It would help more if you went back out in the world to spread the word."

"You haven't seen how dark and dingy my apartment is. The shower has two knobs, but both give me cold water half the time."

"How do you want to change your life, Savvy?"

"I want to change everything. Now that I've got the cobwebs out of my cooch, I feel like I should declutter my apartment. I've been holding on to things. I told myself I kept knickknacks for sentimental value. Now I'm thinking it was a way to hold on to the past. I don't even like the past. I've got photographs of my trip to San Francisco. I don't need to keep the bib from lobster night at Fisherman's Wharf."

Rose laughed cheerily. "There's a lot of power in a reboot. You sound motivated."

"The kung fu power in Rick's magic dick is strong."

"This is the pattern break you needed. Everybody needs to step back once in a while, forests and trees, trees or forests."

"Yeah, yeah. Stepping back. I've heard it before."

"But now you feel it in your bones. It's important to reassess. Reboots happen less and less now. The speed of life makes us rush into the future too much. When it comes, the shake-up has to be a big event to get us to recalibrate."

"What do you mean by the speed of life?"

"We operate on a different clock here. Back home at your job, I bet there's no separation between on-hours and off-hours. People are always working and they either don't — or can't — take time off. Even if they're going to their kid's play they're distracted by their phones."

"I definitely read less than I used to. There are too many distractions."

"You can fix it. You're a writer. It's like editing your life."

"Editing usually means deletion."

"So? What's in your life you can do without?"

"I've got a junk drawer full of old batteries. Those must be dead by now. I've got old keys. I don't even know what locks they're for. Then there are my bookshelves. I've got books I'll never read again. Why keep them? And old clothes...god, I'm a hoarder!"

"I doubt you're more of a hoarder than most people. Pack it all up. Sell it or give it away. Get it out of the house. Edit."

"Makes me nervous," I admitted. "On the other hand, I remember moving into my first apartment. I didn't have any furniture so, even though it was a tiny place, it seemed huge. I had my whole future ahead of me then and — "

"You still have a future ahead of you."

"I'm older now."

"If you think you're too old to change, you must be dead. I don't think that's true, is it? Shall I check for a pulse?"

Thinking of the fucking I'd just had, I grinned. "No, I'm definitely not dead."

"Then you can still grow and change."

"Okay, Princess Moonbeam. Everything's hearts and flowers. Happy? What's next?"

"Yoga?"

"I'm not that flexible."

"Then we really need to open your hips. There are few things more attractive than a woman who can spread her legs wide."

I thought it was another of Rose's come-ons. It was. She was also serious about yoga.

40

D ressed in shorts and white t-shirts, Rose and I faced each other. The big living room's cork floor was warm under my bare feet. I'd assumed we'd use an instructional video on the big plasma screen TV. Instead, Rose served as my yoga teacher.

"When you write your book, I'm totally gonna come off as the crunchy granola, Birkenstocks, free love, kale, and chickpeas hippie chick, aren't I?" she asked.

"I'll try not to fall into using too many clichés...but yeah, kinda probably...yes, definitely actually."

Rose's stretchy shorts were very short. Her shirt was plain white and she wore no bra. As the session progressed, she led me through a progression of yoga poses. We began to sweat and the exercise soon turned into a wet t-shirt contest. She stared at my tits openly. Her hard nipples pulled my gaze as she led me through the asanas.

She encouraged me to slow my breathing and to breathe deeper. I'd dabbled in yoga years before and I was pleased to find I could still do a lot of the poses. It took more effort than I recalled, but I kept up. My balance sucked so my Tree Pose looked like a twig pose, wobbly in a breath of wind. Rose told me to visualize strong roots reaching through my feet. I was skeptical, but as I stood on one leg I became more stable and held the pose longer.

Downward Dog was harder than I remembered. It took a few minutes for my legs to relax. My arms began to shake.

Rose gave me a break by giving me an easier pose before returning to Downward Dog again. "Your Achilles tendons are a little tight. Relax into the stretch and allow your heels sink to the floor."

It took a while, but my legs eventually loosened and I got my breathing under control.

"Let's try a sexy one," she said. "This is one of my favorites."

"A sexy one? *Heh*. Of course it's your fave." I wiped the sweat from my eyes with my forearm. "What do I do?"

Rose drew her yoga mat close to mine and sat facing me. She spread her legs and motioned for me to do the same. She put her feet on the inside of my ankles and reached out so we clasped hands. "Nice spread, Savvy."

"Thanks."

"Don't be nervous."

"People telling me not to be nervous makes me nervous."

"Press your ankles together."

"Hashtag: Something I thought I'd never hear Rose Sinclair say!"

I did as I was told. She resisted the movement so my feet didn't come any closer together. When she nodded for me to stop, she gently pressed outward. Magically, my legs stretched farther apart.

"How'd you do that?" I didn't know my legs could spread so wide.

"Something Rick taught me. It's a kind of assisted stretching technique. Press in again, a little harder this time."

My legs trembled, but I kept up the pressure.

"Not so much," Rose warned. "Just enough to get the muscles on the inside of your thighs to contract."

When I stopped, my legs slid apart even wider. I concentrated on relaxing into the stretch.

"It's called Proprioceptive Neuromuscular Facilitation," she said.

"Oh. That."

"Fastest way to the best stretch there is."

"I used to be pretty flexible. I didn't think I could get this degree of flexibility back!"

Rose placed her feet farther up my legs so the soles of her feet were below my knees. We repeated the exercise, slow and gentle. My gains in flexibility were tiny but measurable.

I felt like I was doing porn star yoga.

"You okay?"

"Y-yes. I'm okay. It feels good."

"Every stretch should feel good. If you feel any pain or you're reaching your limit, you've gone too far. The muscle will contract if you try too hard. Breathe slower and relax into each stretch, letting it happen. Take your time. It's like Tai Chi or doing anal: the slower, the better! Cool, huh?"

It took some time, but Rose was patient. The session was part yoga, part physiotherapy. She reminded me to relax into each stretch. "Always a pull, never a pain. Don't hold your breath. Let it come easy."

We took frequent water breaks. As I moved around the room, I became looser. I wasn't sore or stiff and I even felt more graceful.

When we got back on the mats, Rose had something new for me to try. "If you liked that, you'll love this." We sat facing each other again, our legs spread so they formed a diamond, Rose ran her hands up my arms until we clasped elbows. Gently, she pulled me toward her so, with both of us still spreadeagled, I bent forward from the waist. "Now, pull back."

As I breathed in and tried to straighten. Rose gently resisted. I felt the muscles on either side of my spine contract.

"Breathe out and relax."

I was surprised to find how far I could bend forward after one stretch. We repeated the exercise and, each time, my head came closer to Rose. "This feels great!" I said. "I've never been so loose."

"I love a loose woman," she said, "but I suspect you can go farther."

We did another stretch but, this time, my low back didn't stop me from bending farther forward. The muscles in the back of my thighs were too tight.

"We don't want you to tear a hamstring. I'll make it easier for you."
Rose gently removed her feet from the inside of my calves. She
scooted forward so we were closer together and my feet were at her
knees. "Spread me, Savvy."

As I pressed with my feet, her legs came farther apart, seemingly
effortlessly. "Wow. You are bendy!"

"Enjoy the view."

My gaze had slipped down to her breasts again. "Um...yes. That
feels better for me," I said. "My thighs aren't burning at all."

"Try this," she said. Clasping my elbows again, she pulled me
forward until my face hovered above her lap. "Feel the stretch? Not
too much?"

My mouth was an inch from the mound of her mons pubis. I felt a
familiar warm tingle through my groin. "Can you stretch me a little
more?" I asked.

"Okay. Pull back again," she said.

I tried to straighten and she resisted my pressure. This time, as
the muscles in my lower back relaxed and I bent forward, the movement was easier. My mouth came to rest on the thin fabric of her
shorts.

"Take a long breath in," she commanded.

Again, I did as I was told. Her scent was light. I wondered how she
would taste. I'd tasted my own vaginal juices. Would hers be the
same?

Rose pushed her pelvis forward. "Now breathe out through your
mouth."

I exhaled and she welcomed the heat of my breath. She let out a
long sigh and a shiver shot through her pelvis.

"Tell me what to do and I'll do it," I said.

Rose let go of one of my arms and pulled the fabric aside. The
pale flesh was hairless except for a neat strip of red pubic hair,
trimmed and narrow. "You know what to do," she said.

"Tell me."

"Start with a long, slow lick up...and *slowly* down."*

I didn't want to look like an amateur. Appearing tentative might seem like an insult. I did as I was told without hesitation. As Henry Miller would say, I dove for it. Rose tilted her hips forward as she yanked her shorts farther aside. A sweet offering!

I explored her with my tongue, pausing to kiss her clitoris before moving back to slow, torturous licking. She was wet and her slight tang made me crave more. I loved the animalistic need we shared. I wanted to reach between my legs and play with my clit. I wanted to sit on her face and let her tongue me. Instead, Rose held me fast as she rocked her pelvis up and down against my tongue.

"More!" she pleaded.

The tip of my tongue found her clit again and I circled it as Rick had done to me the night before.

"Oh...yes...."

I flicked the tip of my tongue over her clit as fast as I could. She trembled and gritted her teeth.

She sucked in air as I pulled away from her clit to explore her deeper. I happen to have a long tongue. I pictured it as a stir stick making tight circles as I strained to reach into her as deeply as I could. Then I switched it up with something I'd read somewhere about drawing the alphabet with the tip of my tongue. I got the feeling Rose preferred the I and the O most so I stuck with those letters for a while.

Rose moaned, "Almost...almost...."

Sensing her orgasm was on its way, I clamped my mouth on her clit and sucked hard. I moaned and let the sonic vibrations run through her. "*Uuuuuuuummmmmmmm.*"

Rose cried out and let go of my arm to slip her hand behind my head. "Do that again!"

"*Uuuuummmmm?*"

"Yes, that!"

"*Uuuuuummmmmm!*"

Rose came in long spasms, freezing her in ecstasy before the shakes hit her again. The taut muscles of her inner thighs contracted. She couldn't take more. She pulled away and fell back and pulled her thighs tight together as she continued to shake.

Tingling, I sat back slowly. Watching the aftermath of my work, I couldn't help but grin. I'd always wondered what it would be like to give a woman head. I told Rose so.

"And?"

I grinned. "It tastes like 'more, please!'"

Rose rolled to her side and reached up to wipe my face with a soft, warm palm. "Your chin is shiny, Savvy."

"I wonder why."

"Naughty girl."

"So this is yoga," I said.

"You're bendy, too," she said. "A natural."

"I've never got into such a deep stretch until now," I said. "On the other hand, nobody offered a reward at the end of the stretch."

"You like my reward?"

"It was kind of awkward," I admitted. "Not exactly how I pictured it."

"I hope you're about to say, 'but.'"

"If I could skip all the yoga and get straight to dessert, I could go deeper with my tongue."

"Sounds delightful."

"I do owe you a wake-up licking."

"I owe you now," she said. "I'll let it be a surprise." Rose rolled up on one elbow and put her hand behind my head. She pulled me closer until my lips were an inch from hers. "You're lovely, Savvy."

"You are, too."

"Kiss me."

I was not merely bi-curious, anymore. I was bi-enthused. I'd been timid too long but I was relieved to discover it wasn't too late for me to be me.

41

L unch, served on the balcony beside the library, came in the form of tall glasses of mixed berry smoothies, veggie egg white omelets, and sweet coffee.

Afterward, we climbed into a big Brazilian hammock together to watch the boats go by. I felt younger. Climbing into a hammock with another adult seemed a little silly, but that was a remnant of what people might think "back in the real world," where silly was a bad thing. I've since learned to appreciate the word more. Silly is fucking glorious.

With our arms wrapped around each other, we swayed in that hammock, enjoying the view and togetherness. Rose told me about living in Philadelphia. "I've moved around a bunch and done some travel for the spa, but I'm done with that now. I don't want to live anywhere else but Vancouver Island. I'll die here."

"Morbid much? Don't talk about dying. I want you to live forever."

"Nobody manages that, so we gotta use the time well."

"What kind of work did you do, traveling for the spa?"

"Research, mostly, scouting for the best ideas from other spas and figuring a way to improve ourselves. There's new technology to explore. Rick wants to do more with hydrotherapy, cryotherapy, saunas, and flotation tanks. His next plan is to start opening gyms that focus on longevity and aging, physiotherapy, and functional strength. He's even talking obstacle courses for circuit training, gami-fying fitness. The idea is to improve the body by aping hunter-gath-erer societies. He figures we'll age better and get more blood flow to the brain and genitals."

"He's sure got a lot of enthusiasms."

Rose rolled her eyes in faux misery. "I had to tell him I need to focus on our work here or he'd pull me into a dozen projects."

"Still, doing research at spas sounds like a great job. I'd love that!"

"It was fine. I did enjoy it. I missed my work here too much, though."

"You love plants that much? I'd rather be exploring exotic desti-nations."

Rose looked surprised, as if I'd missed the point entirely. Turns out, I had.

"This retreat is where I found my purpose," she said, "but I don't live for plants and sex. My purpose is to bring joy to my friends. Bringing joy gives me joy. Something wrong, Savvy?"

"Me. I was wrong. I've gotten this all wrong. I came here because it was a sex spa."

"Sex got you here, yes. So what?"

"I missed what Rick was trying to tell me when I got here. You've both been showing me by example, but I was too caught up in my bullshit to see it. I ended up here because I needed answers and a way out. I've been too distracted by my neuroses and history. Rick looks great in a skintight wetsuit. That was distracting, but I've really fucked this up in my head."

Rose gave my arm a squeeze. "When people arrive at our door, there's always a reason. Rick would say we all focus on the problem so hard, we lose sight of the solution. You aren't alone."

"Everybody's looking for answers and a way out, right? When you told me Sheila used to be a successful lawyer, I honestly couldn't imagine why she would need this place. I was only thinking about money and status, not happiness. I didn't have my head on straight."

"I've found our guests almost always know their answer already. They just need to step back and commit to doing something with that knowledge. You came here because your friend suspected the potential for sex would get you on the plane, right?"

"Kelly was right. I got on the plane but...my head is clearer now."

"Sex was your fantasy because you weren't getting any. You've had some. Got anything else going on when you look deeper? Is that your purpose? It's okay if that's the answer."

"Oh, I know now there's more to do. I thought the best I could do was fuck away bad memories, as if coming here was some kind of defiant act. Instead, I'm making new memories, good memories. That's what's helped me clear my head. I have a lot of shit I need to forget. It's been hard to let go of the divorce trauma and all. I was so scared all the time...."

"And?" she prodded. "Go on."

I did have my answer the whole time. I'd known my purpose before I got on the plane. I'd known the truth since I was a little kid.

Rose read my face and broke into a broad grin. "You've got it now, don't you?"

"I've finally got it again, yeah. Writing is my purpose."

"Didn't you decide that already?"

"I did. What I'm saying is I have to get out of the travel agency altogether. Not next year or the year after. Right away! The business has been circling the drain and sucking away my soul, my energy, and my time. I have to get back into writing, make it my primary thing. Between my marriage and divorce, working and hating everything, I wandered away from what I was supposed to do. The answer was staring me in the face the whole time, but I was too embarrassed to look it in the eye. There's enough money in it for one person, not two. Kelly can have it. She's always enjoyed the work more."

"So you'll get out of your travel agency. What's next for you?"

"I'm not sure of the details yet, but the divorce gave me plenty to write about. I started writing again soon after I got here. I hardly thought about it. I just did it and started to feel better, you know? More engaged. I have been such an idiot! I don't care if I have to declare bankruptcy or if I pay my bills temping. I won't starve. It'll be hard, but I'll get by. Maybe it won't be great, but at least I'll be doing what I should. I've spent too long trying to make the agency work. Even if I could make it succeed, I'd still hate my desk at the mall."

"How will you do it?"

"I'll have to abandon Vancouver. Too expensive to live there. I'll find someplace, maybe do shifts selling coffee or something. No more spreadsheets and worrying about the payroll. I'll get a paycheck and stop worrying about the back end of the business. I'll do anything as long as I can grab some time to write every day. I'll work on books and stories instead of just thinking about it."

"You're sure?"

"Changing my life is going to take more than making notes in a notebook and pecking away at it. I thought I hated my life because Doug and I broke apart the way we did. It's much more. I hate the business I've tied myself to. I'm drowning. I been acting like failing at my business is the worst thing I could do and holding on for dumb reasons. I didn't want to admit this to myself. I'm still afraid of telling my parents. Isn't that crazy? I'm a grown woman. It's time I acted like it and told them the agency won't work out."

Finally, I'd found myself. "Finding myself" suddenly had a meaning that didn't sound crunchy-granola-hippie-poser stupid. With each of life's detours and disappointments, my answer was in me the whole time: Pick up a pen, vomit my pain, organize my thoughts, and do what I was meant to do.

I sniffled a little. "You know, I think I just got something written on my heart. That's what Mom would say when something hit her deep."

Rose stroked my hair gently. "What's written on your heart?"

"Even if I'm good at something, that doesn't mean I should do it. Even if I'm not great at something, that doesn't mean I shouldn't try. I tried to do everything right and I still fucked it up. I'm starting fresh. It's not too late."

"People lose themselves sometimes," Rose said. "All you have to do is what you know you're supposed to do. I'm sure you'll be okay."

My tears began to flow. I put my head on Rose's shoulder and she hugged me tightly.

"You want to talk about it?"

I shook my head. "I don't need to talk anymore. I'm not crying because I'm sad. I'm crying because...it's not happiness, exactly. Relief. These are tears of relief."

Rose held me tighter in a sisterly embrace. She didn't say anything and neither did I and that was perfect. I just let the tears come. I let it out and let it go. I don't know how long we lay there swaying in that big hammock, our legs intertwined and me blatting like a little kid.

When I finally pulled back, Rose kissed my wet cheeks. "Better?"

"Much," I said. "Thank you. I just realized, my best times aren't all behind me. I've got stuff to look forward to. Even if I don't, I can change that. I'm ready to move forward, for real this time. I can feel it."

"Exciting, isn't it?"

"I don't think I've felt this way since I moved out of my parents' house to go to university."

"That mood you got right now? Smells like potential."

"I just have to write and write and get laid more. I was so afraid I'd had all my good times already. I'm not afraid now. I can handle being poor. I'm already poor. May as well be a writer with no money instead of a travel agent with no money."

Rose kissed me on the cheek hard. Her kiss wasn't sisterly, but it wasn't sexual, either. It was a sweet congratulatory gesture. I loved her for it. I liked myself much more, too.

Don't doubt it: A conversation at the right time can make a huge difference in a life. If you're having conversations with people who aren't helping you toward your purpose, it could be you're talking to the wrong people. Maybe the good information isn't hitting you at the right time or you aren't really listening.

One of my therapists might say I'd opened my heart chakra by recharging my root chakra. My daddy would say, "Sometimes you gotta clean the bird shit outta your ears." Staying at the retreat with

Rose and Rick flushed out my fears so I could listen to myself again. Giving and receiving head cleared my mind. Sex was my process to getting unfucked.

When I left Vancouver Island, I would not return to my sad little corner of the mall. I didn't know all the good things that were ahead of me then. If I'd known the future, I would have given up sooner. Every success guru talks about determination, hard work, long hours and never taking no for an answer. Very few mention that failing at a career you hate and getting the hell out is a twisty success.

42

R ose lay beside me in the big hammock sucking on ice cubes. We'd got up to pee and pulled two new books from the library. Rose was dozing off and on with a copy of *The Subtle Art of Not Giving a F*ck* open in her lap. The fact that she wasn't really reading it seemed kind of perfect.

I read a few chapters, but the ocean pulled my gaze. The water was a moving painting. Boats under full sail sliced the whitecaps of the Haro Strait. I imagined they had no destination. The crews of those sailboats were exactly where they were meant to be, doing what they loved to do. The means was the end: Nowhere to be and few imperatives beyond the moment. What a wonderful way to live.

Planes flew overhead from time to time. For a change, I felt no pang of yearning, wishing I was aboard one. I wasn't far from Vancouver, but I was worlds away from my old life. My Vancouver life almost seemed like it had happened to another person. I tried to remember the last time I'd lingered over a meal or a book there. I couldn't think of a time when I didn't have to get up and rush to get a bunch of things done. Even when I was on vacation, it seemed I'd had to hurry to catch a charter bus. All my trips had been hurried tours, trying to take everything in so I could sell travel packages to people without sounding like an idiot.

"Good morning, ladies. A dollar for your thoughts?"

I looked up to find Rick slipping into the lounge chair beside us. He stepped softly for such a big guy. I never seemed to know he was coming until he appeared.

"You know what?" I said. "I know your secret identity! You're Sex Batman!"

I thought Rose was asleep under her sunglasses, but she giggled, "Sex Batman!"

Rick looked mystified. "Come again?"

"Thanks, I'd love to come again. But really, here you are, a rich, young guy with scads of money hiding out in a secret fortress planning to save the world. You're Sex Batman!"

"Does that make me Alfred?" Rose asked. "I don't know about being the butler. I picture myself as the ginger with the tits in *The Rocky Horror Picture Show*."

"Ooh, I love *Rocky Horror*," I said. "When I was a teenager, we lived in Galveston for a summer. I dressed up and snuck out to go to a midnight show at an art theater. I threw toast at the screen. That might be the craziest thing I've done...until lately."

I wondered what happened to the girl who threw toast. I suspected that I wasn't becoming someone new. I was returning to the person I was meant to be. "Maybe I should title my first book *The Girl Who Threw Toast*."

Rick gave me the side-eye. "Write it before you decide on a title. *The Girl Who Threw Toast* sounds like an Oliver Sacks book about an obscure psychopathology."

We all burst out laughing. I had to concede the point.

"I danced onstage at the Met," Rose said.

"The Met? Really?"

"Not really the Met. It was *a* Met. It was an after-hours club in New York. Three in the morning, I danced on stage in a cage. Drunk out of my mind, I had new tattoos I wanted to show off. A bouncer from the club tried to stop me until I took off my shirt and skirt. I danced in my thong and bra until dawn."

"Wish I'd seen that," I said.

"The cage bars were thick enough I could hang off them. I don't remember much of the details except for a trio of good-looking Hispanic girls stared at me all night. Two had an acute case of Resting Bitch Face, but the cutest one was into what I was doing. I undulated for her."

I quirked an eyebrow. "Undulated?"

"Three years of belly dancing lessons, baby!" Rose handed me her book, got up, and lifted her shirt. Her tight abdomen rippled as she waggled her butt. Then she lifted her hands above her head, closed her eyes, and gave us a short demonstration. Rose shook her ass with skill and finished with a maneuver that made me think she had an invisible hula hoop around her hips. When she was done, Rose gave a coy curtsy.

"Nice!" Rick and I chorused and clapped.

"I love a hot dance club," Rose said. "It's the second-best workout there is."

"What's the best workout?" I asked.

"What happens after the dance club," Rose replied. "I've got to get out dancing again. When's the last time you went out, Savvy?"

I shrugged. "University...maybe a little after graduation?"

Rose pursed her lips in a way that let me know she didn't want to judge but she was judging. "If you don't dance, you get stagnant. Standing water gets sour or dries up. Same with people. Unless somebody really doesn't like dancing or fucking, we gotta dance and we gotta fuck. Most people do like dancing and fucking, but their brains get in the way of their bodies."

"I was just rereading *The Dharma Bums* — " Rick said.

"Oh, here we go," Rose said.

"No, this is cool, I promise," Rick said.

"Hunky guy says something nerd-tacular in 3, 2, 1 — go!"

"I was reading the introduction by Ann Douglas," Rick began.

Rose rolled her eyes. "Who the living hell reads Kerouac for the introduction?"

Rick raised a hand. "Human potential movement nerds."

"Nerd!"

"Feel better?"

"Much, thanks," Rose said. "Please, do go on, boss."

I giggled.

"There's a quote in there from Langston Hughes about Harlem's jazz joints," he said.

Rose gave him an imperious look. "Who?"

"Doesn't matter. He said the music was so powerful that bebop was 'letting midnight out on bail.' Isn't that a great turn of phrase? There's a new study out that suggests some people have more sensitive auditory nerve centers. They feel the effects of music so much, it literally gives them goosebumps. There's preliminary talk that the right music could help people with depression, get them to access positive emotions they can't reach otherwise."

Rose considered this. "That is interesting. I have to admit, there are some pretty stirring songs in *Les Misérables*. The big anthems, especially. Some of those songs make me want to overthrow the government of France."

"Watching *Rocky* and listening to Michael Buble songs makes me work out harder," Rick said.

I was still stuck on that turn of phrase about music. "'Letting midnight out on bail,'" I echoed. "Damn. I could write a long time and not come up with that. Hemingway said he was trying to write one honest sentence. I only wish I'd written 'letting midnight out on bail.'"

"Savvy and I were just talking about her writing. She's decided to commit to it exclusively."

"I'm feeling very optimistic all of a sudden," I explained. "I just need to write something that resonates with readers, a book that might last a little and reminds people I was here. A book that squeezes a little sense out of the everyday stuff that doesn't make sense."

Rick nodded. "That is a need."

Suddenly self-conscious at being so goddamn earnest, I turned to Rick, eager to deflect and move on. "What about you, Sex Batman?" I asked. "What's the craziest non-sexual thing you've done?"

"You mean besides falling in love?"

Rose pulled an ice cube from between her lips, tossed it at Rick's chest, and missed. "Nothing sappy! She said crazy!"

"You mean like running with the bulls in Pamplona?"

My eyes widened. "You've done that?"

"Hell, no. Whenever I see that video, I'm rooting for the bulls a little."

We laughed.

"Okay, so? Give," I demanded. "Craziest thing?"

"Peyote ceremony."

"Peyote?"

"I was a huge fan of Hunter S. Thompson's writing. He was crazy but always in an interesting way. I've read *Fear and Loathing in Las Vegas* several times."

"Have you even read a book from this century?" Rose asked.

Rick ignored her. "In high school, I wanted to try to duplicate Thompson's experience. After the helicopter crash and losing Lucia, I remembered that. I went to Vegas but I couldn't find anyone who would sell me mescaline. I almost ended up in jail when I asked the wrong person."

Rose perked up. "You never told me that part."

"About almost being arrested? Not much to tell. I ran really fast. Then a friend hooked me up and took me into the desert. I did peyote under the stars."

"Did you have a vision quest?" I asked.

"I did."

"And what was the revelation?"

"It didn't come to me in words," he admitted. "However, I woke up in a motel room in Reno the next day with no clear memory of how I got there. I sketched plans for the spa on motel stationery that morning."

Rick had the look of a man who was still in that hotel room, stuck by profound inspiration. "What's tough is not knowing someone who shares your worldview. Being alone is tough. Our culture idolizes the rugged individualist, but that's a myth. We are emotional, cooperative animals and we need each other to survive and thrive. The components to manufacture something as simple as a pencil have to come from all over the world. We need each other to get anything positive done."

"Hallelujah and yeah, yeah, yeah! Spread the word and don't skimp on the compassion." Rose said. "Now, who's up for some sport sex?"

43

R ick took my hand. I looked back at Rose, expecting her to follow. Instead, she gave me a happy wave. "Lick ya later, Savvy. I'm still in afterglow mode." She lay back in the hammock and settled in for a nap.

He led me to the elevator. As soon as the doors closed, he picked me off the ground and kissed me. I liked that feeling of literally being swept off my feet. We descended to the basement.

"Good yoga session this morning?"

"Yes. Very stimulating. I didn't know I could stretch that far."

"Rose told me she was going to give you some training."

"She did."

"Sore at all?"

Anxious and eager, I admitted that my neck was a little tense. "Is massage on the menu?"

Rick reached up with big, warm hands to cup the nape of my neck. I smiled and closed my eyes, leaning into him as he kneaded my neck and shoulders. He frowned and pressed the side of my neck, somehow finding a tender spot instantly. "Ooh!"

"It feels like I'm pressing hard, but I'm not, I promise."

The pain ebbed. I slowly tilted my head away from where he was pressing. My right ear came closer to my shoulder as the stretch took effect.

"The body will change if we persuade it rather than coerce it," he said. "Like with people, push too hard and you get resistance. Invite people to change and they are drawn to explore what they could become."

"That the secret of persuasion?"

"One secret, maybe. Nothing works on everyone. There are people who are allergic to water. Can't help everyone."

I thought of how hard I worked to get my mouth down to kiss Rose's snatch. I had the motivation to change because I wanted to please her. "I loved Rose's brand of yoga."

"There are many kinds of yoga. Ashtanga can really raise your heart rate. Did she show you that or — "

"Rose got my heart racing."

He looked at me sideways and smiled. "Oh. I see. Rose Yoga. Nice. Are you sure you're up for a post-workout massage?"

"Up for anything. How about you?" I brushed the tips of my fingers over the front of his pants gently before applying more pressure to the length of his cock with my palm. "Are you up for anything, Rick?"

He answered me with another long, deep kiss.

We didn't go to the massage room where he had treated me before. Instead, he pulled a different shoji screen aside and we entered a room with a huge jacuzzi. The lighting, cast by pot lights, was subdued. A barefoot woman sat on the edge of the tub with her back to us. She wore a sarong around her waist but that was all.

She rose and turned to step into the light. Sheila had given me a private sex show with Ryan and now we were face to face. She smiled as she wiped her hands on a towel. "Just checking the temperature. All is prepared for you, Savannah."

"Thank you. Please, call me Savvy."

She reached out to shake my hand while giving me a little bow. I thought she would be formal, but then she stepped close to embrace me. Her bare breasts pressed into me as she gave me a long, warm hug. "You've seen me around, yes?"

I blushed. How could I forget? I'd never heard any woman refer to her vagina as a hot pocket.

"Can I get you anything before I go, Savvy? Tea?"

"No, thank you. I'm fine. We had lunch."

"Excellent!" She turned to Rick. "I'm going to take care of those contracts."

"Find me later when you need signatures."

"All set." Sheila went up on tiptoes and kissed Rick on both cheeks and did the same to me.

Before she left, Sheila took both my hands in hers and gave a toothy grin. "To get the full effect, have an edible before you get into the jacuzzi. So glad you came, Savvy. So glad!" She closed the shoji screen behind her and I was alone with Rick again.

I hadn't noticed the plate on a nearby tray. Rick picked it up and offered me first choice. There were two chocolate brownies, two slabs of banana bread, and an assortment of lollipops.

"I recommend you only take one," Rick said.

I thought of Rose getting out of her mind drunk. I imagined Rick naked under the stars in the desert. I thought of the girl I'd once been, the teenager who dared to sneak out to go to a movie forbidden by her mother. I wanted to be the girl who threw toast at the screen at *The Rocky Horror Picture Show* again. I smiled as I picked up the banana bread.

"It's potent. Better have half of that."

Defiant, I ate it all in a few hurried bites. Then I picked up the cherry lollipop and sucked it between my lips.

"Ooh, you're bad."

"Nobody ever died of a cannabis overdose."

Rick chuckled. "True. You're safe."

"But are you?" I swirled my tongue around the lollipop suggestively. "With this tantra thing, you don't come, hm?"

"Not until it's time."

I reached for his crotch and rubbed up and down slowly. "How do you not get blue balls?"

"The trick is not minding. And lifting heavy things eases the pressure."

"So you won't mind if I try to make you come? I made Rose come. I've never made two people come in one day. Looks like a fun challenge."

Rick pulled me close. I could feel his hard-on through his jeans.

I took the lollipop from my mouth and we kissed passionately for a few minutes, taking our time.

I pulled back to ask, "Do you like the taste of my cherry?"

"I like the taste of your lollipop."

"I wasn't talking about the lollipop."

"I love the taste of your cherry."

Rick didn't leave me alone to undress this time. He helped me out of my clothes and I helped him out of his. As soon as he was naked, I grabbed his cock.

"Take it slow," he suggested. "You still have to finish your lollipop before you start on mine."

"Okay," I said, staring at his erection. "But there's this thing between us."

He laughed and pulled me toward the jacuzzi. "We have all day," he said. "And it's not all about sex."

"Oh, please! You aren't going to tease me anymore, are you?"

"Sure, I am. But not forever."

The water was warm without being too hot. The tub looked like it could fit ten people but I wrapped myself around Rick. "I'm willing to share my pot lollipop." I kissed him again.

The combination of the warm water and Rick's hard body against me excited me to no end. I raised one knee to feel the soft skin of my thighs slowly rub up and down his rigid cock. "Poor baby, always putting off coming all over me."

"Ooh. Savvy! You're making it hard for me."

"I know! Have you lost your train of thought yet? Maybe you'd like to do something else? Like me?"

He laughed and splashed me in the face. I splashed him back. Before it escalated to a water war, he held up his hands. "Wait! Wait! I have something you'll enjoy!"

I grabbed his cock and pumped it up and down slowly in my fist. "Uh-huh. Tell me." I loved the feel of it in my hand.

Rick reached out to click a button on the side of the tub. The water erupted in bubbles. Then he turned on his side to hold me tight. I felt his hands reach around me. Under the roiling water, he began to caress me.

"I like that," I said.

"You might love this."

"Huh?"

He slipped behind me and, with both hands, maneuvered me toward him. "Ready?" Rick positioned me over two jets of warm water. It was as if a pianist with warm hands was playing with my vulva, fast and firm.

I gasped and shuddered. "Oooh!"

Rick slipped around me again to kiss my lips.

I put both hands on his shoulders to steady myself as I arched my back. I pushed closer to feel the pressure hit me just so. "That's a sensation."

"Pleasant?"

"Oh, yeah," I panted. My eyes glazed over. "Uh-huh...I've never done something like this.

"Good?"

"Uh...huh." My mind was mostly on the pulsing jet of water. I reached between us to grip Rick's cock again. I held tight, but I didn't move. I wanted to tease him, too. He stared into my eyes. I felt absorbed by his gaze. Or maybe that was the marijuana in the banana bread kicking in.

Finally relenting, I stroked his dick up and down. I couldn't help myself. I became more aware of the hard topography of his penis: the shaft, the veins, the pink head rising above the jacuzzi's waves. I sucked harder on my lollipop, imagining it was Rick between my lips. I closed my eyes. His cock tasted like cherries.

"Savvy?"

"Mm? I imagined myself on my knees as jets of water pounded my pussy and ass and clit and breasts. I could see his huge cock sway into view as I opened my mouth to suck him deep.

"Savvy?"

I opened my eyes. Rick held a full bottle of bubble bath above the agitated water. He dumped the whole thing in. The water thrashed and foamed as bubbles grew around us.

I broke into a belly laugh. I couldn't stop laughing. The water was soon so soapy, we slid up and down each other's bodies. We giggled, as unselfconscious as children.

As the mounds of bubbles grew, rose, and burst around us, each one felt like a soft kiss on my skin. That was as new a sensation as the pulsing jets of water pushing and pleasing me.

"Are the edibles starting to work on you, Savvy?" Rick asked.

"You're a unicorn and I want to ride your horn."

He laughed. "It's weed, Savvy, not acid."

"I know. It was a joke, dumbass. No offense. Now, would you mind terribly fucking me hard? Fuck me terribly hard, mind you. Hard fucking terrible me, mind. Fuck my mind, hard terrible. Fucking hard mind me terrible. Ooh. Wordplay!"

"You are so crazy. Love it."

"Crazy chicks are the best fucks. Try me, you'll find out."

44

My lollipop had melted away in my mouth. We stood to wash off the bubbles. I couldn't stop giggling as Rick dried me off with a fluffy bath sheet. He kissed my lips and I held him tight.

"I really like you." As soon as I said it, I knew it sounded as if we were in junior high and I had passed him a note in the library.

I could have fallen back into self-loathing and embarrassment, but Rick's gaze didn't waver. "I really like you back."

"What's next?"

I gasped as his right hand slid from my left breast to between my legs. He stirred me gently and slowly. "How about a massage?"

I moaned. "To work out the knots?"

He was doing fine with the knot of my clit, but he stopped to pick me up and carry me.

"Well, don't I feel like a little princess!" I said. "You are strong!"

"Were you expecting me to throw you over my shoulder in a fireman's carry?"

"Or a caveman's carry. Whatever gets us to horizontal quickest."

I'd thought the shoji screen at the end of the room was a real wall. It slid aside with a whisper and we were in a massage room I hadn't seen before. This massage table was bigger. Its legs looked thicker and more solid than the first. I caught sight of two dangling restraints at the corners of the table. They were thick cuffs of leather lined with fur. Tingles and warmth rose from my clit to my belly as I pondered the possibilities.

Rick lay me on the massage table and told me to flip on my stomach. I lay on a soft sheet. This time there was no top sheet or blanket to cover me.

For this massage, he'd be naked, too, and that was a glorious sight. I'd made fun of romance novels and erotica with hot guys on their covers. The cover models' abs always made me think of cheese graters. However, those guys do exist in real life. Some of them, like Rick, even have big dicks that touch their tight bellies when erect.

"Do whatever you want," I said.

"I love your invitation. Let's start with you in the massage position. Lift up a little." He slipped pillows beneath my hips and feet as I placed my face on the face pad. Both his hands settled on my low back and I spread my legs wider instinctively, shivering at his touch.

"Cold?"

"I'm good." The room was warm. It wasn't the temperature that made me tremble.

"You had quite a workout this morning, didn't you? We'll start with some sports massage to loosen you up."

I was about to protest but, as he moved around the table, the stiff girth of his erect cock brushed my arm. I gulped. "Do me!"

"Do you want a safe word?"

"Do I need one?"

"Everybody needs a safe word sometimes," he said.

"How about 'Dougie?'" I suggested.

"Your ex-husband's name?"

"He'd hate that."

"Makes sense. The last thing I want to hear is anything about your ex." Rick chuckled as he pulled my hair forward so he wouldn't get massage gel in it. He leaned down and I felt his hot breath on the nape of my neck. He ran one finger down my spine slowly, light as a feather.

Tingles radiated out from my backbone and I gasped in surprise. "You've got the magic touch."

With that, Rick surprised me again. I thought he was kidding about the sports massage. He began to work up and down the sides of my spine. Gentle but firm, he pulled and pushed at my flesh. As the muscles began to relax, he was less gentle. Then he went deeper.

"I thought I was already fairly limber after yoga but, wow. After this, I should be ready for the circus!" *Or the orgy,* my horny brain added silently. "Massage me, please, but don't stop there."

"Relax and do nothing," Rick said. "I'll drive."

The next part of my massage proceeded much like my first. Rick moved from trigger point to trigger point, alternating between long strokes and pressure on specific spots. He was the baker. I was the bread. As he continued, his kneading turned my body to putty.

As I surrendered to his work, he increased the pressure. Rick seemed to enjoy making me moan. Occasionally, his erect cock brushed up against my bare skin: my arm, my hand, my hip, my ankle. As he moved around me, I concentrated on when and where his hard cock might brush up against me next.

"If your erection lasts more than four hours," I said, "aren't you supposed to consult a doctor? Or do something about it with me? Ooh!" I gasped as his hand slipped between my legs and spanked my taint lightly.

"It's time we moved on to the heated oil, isn't it?"

I had lots of lubricant between my legs already. I lay still, but my brain was busy.

Music came up slowly. I'd been so focused on Rick's work I hadn't been aware the room had been quiet before. It was slow jazz, something I recognized but couldn't quite place at first. Then I remembered: "What You Won't Do for Love" by Bobby Caldwell.

I heard his palms rub together briskly before they settled on my low back again. I was pleasantly surprised at the heat of the massage oil. It was almost hot.

"Nice," I said. "You worked on me a long time without the oil."

"Once the oil comes into play, it's for glide. It's more for relaxation. No more trigger points, I promise."

"My nervous system isn't so nervous, anymore."

He worked the same areas as he had before, but in a different way. It was as if the massage had started again and what I really wanted was for him to flip me over and fuck me like he was mad at me. Rather than acting like a petulant child and throwing a tantrum as I had before, I decided to let Rick do his thing.

When I concentrated, I could feel what he was doing, how my muscles were reacting. The strokes had become longer and connected. The warm oil left my skin tingly. Some strokes started at my toes and went up my body to end at my shoulder and neck.

Soon, he slipped a hand between my thighs, less than an inch from my vagina. I gasped and squirmed.

"Do you want me to stop? Feels like you strained your adductors," he mused.

I thought of how wide my legs had spread during my sex yoga session. I'd probably pushed myself too fast so I could snack on Rose. "I can't imagine how that happened."

"I bet I can guess."

"No secrets from you. I can't figure out how I went without sex for so long. Now sex is all I want. The weird thing is, I keep getting a sexy massage from this hot naked guy, but he won't fuck me!"

We laughed until he cut my laughter short by circling the opening of my vagina and sliding two fingers up and down my vulva. When I gasped and wriggled, he held his fingers still. I rocked my hips against his hand. The sensation was pure pleasure.

After a moment, I got up on my elbows to look back at him. "I'm naked and at your not-so-tender mercy. See the look in my eyes? That's my naked lust look." I turned on my back and spread my legs wide, an offering. "I don't want you to stop, Rick. I want you to go deeper. When you're done with your hands," — I stared at his hard dick — "I want you inside me and I want you to come. How about it?"

"I'll finish work on your neck first."

"Rick!"

"Then I'll blindfold you and tie you down."

"You enjoy teasing me too much. You, sir, are a sadist!"

"If so, I'm the sweetest kind of sadist."

"Good thing I'm a masochist." I stared at his hard dick again, mesmerized. He'd been erect a long time. Holding back must have made him ache for release, too. "As long as you do me, all will be forgiven."

"Hey!" Rick chuckled. "My eyes are up here!"

I glanced up at his eyes long enough to say, "I wasn't talking to you."

Then I went back to staring at his meaty cock hungrily.

45

Only human, Rick must have been eager, too. He asked if I was ready for the blindfold.

"Oh, yes."

He lifted my head gently as he pulled the blindfold over my eyes. "And the restraints?"

"I guess so, if you don't want me to grab your cock and start jerking it. Can you honestly say you don't want that, Rick?"

He leaned close, pulled my hair back, and kissed my ear. "I want it all."

Rick moved around the table, from wrist to wrist and ankle to ankle. My legs were spread. My hands were pinned to the sides of the table beside my hips. He'd buckled me in well, but not too tight.

"I'm helpless," I said. "What are you going to do to me now?"

"You know."

I wriggled and smiled.

I sensed that Rick left my side for a moment. When he returned, he dripped three drops of warm oil on each of my nipples. It was hotter than before and, as it slowly cooled, the tingling became more intense. "Oh, gawd!"

"You can call me Rick," he said.

"Should I call you 'Master?'"

"That's some next-level stuff," he said. "Right now, I want to enjoy your body without having to make you think."

"I'm not thinking. I'm feeling."

"That's the great thing about blindfolds." He closed his hands on my breasts. My nipples poked up between his fingers as he kneaded me.

I gasped with pleasure as he cupped my breasts, massaging them lovingly. His slow strokes moved down my torso before returning to my breasts.

As intense as the sensations were, there was still something meditative about what he was doing. As Rick caressed me, the world went away. I might as well have been in space, light-years away. This feeling was singular, unlike anything I'd experienced. Rick had mentioned being worshipful as he worked. I melded with his hands as if the hot oil bound us together in an experience beyond massage and past sex. This was sacred and profound.

Every stroke up and down my body was like whipped cream on hot chocolate on a fall day, like wrapping myself in a hot blanket fresh from the dryer on a Sunday morning, like chocolate mousse on a hard dick.

Rick's every move contained such depth and richness of care. He knew my nerves. I thought of a classical musician playing an intricate instrument. I became that instrument and he played me. A warm ache spread down from my breasts and into my belly. I moaned not from orgasm, merely from anticipation.

Rick's mouth closed on my left nipple. He sucked hard.

My clit buzzed from need. My brain wasn't working anymore, but my body was talking. My nipples stung from want of sucking.

My clitoris ached for his touch. *I am Need,* I thought.

My box yearned for his cock. *Fill me!*

With another long stroke, his palm brushed my vulva. I shuddered. Before returning to my tits, his fingers sunk into the top of my thighs to pull my legs a little wider apart.

I gritted my teeth. "Rick! Please!"

"You have the most lovely full lips." The tip of his tongue traced mine. His mouth closed on my upper lip and he gently sucked as his hand found my clit.

Though my legs were bound, there was enough slack to allow me to spread my legs wider as I arched my back. He continued tonguing my upper lip, matching the rhythm of his finger.

I cried out and shuddered as the first orgasm hit. "Ah! Yes! Yes!" My legs went straight as pleasure shot through me.

"You are especially lovely when you come," Rick said.

"Make me especially lovely whenever you want," I panted. My cheeks were hot and, as he moved to my side, my fingers did not merely brush his hard cock this time. He allowed me to take it in my fist. I gripped him hard, afraid he'd take it away if I gave him the chance. "Got you now, Sex Batman."

He ran his palms up and down my body. Everything tingled.

"Ready for another orgasm?" he asked.

"Mine or yours?" I asked.

"You are so very lovely." I was still blindfolded, so I shuddered with surprise when his lips found my left hip. Rick kissed me gently, almost a tickle.

"I'm pretty sensitive now," I said. "I came so hard, I don't know if I can do that aga — "

His hot mouth found my pussy. My heart pounded as I wriggled against my restraints. He was clever with his tongue. My clit was too sensitive so he focused his efforts on exploring my pussy.

"*Ooooh. That...is perfect.*"

He pulled the blindfold off. I raised my head to look down my body. It wasn't Rick licking me. Rose stared at me as she parted my labia with the tip of her tongue, licking, pressing, loving, slathering me slick.

"Order her to fuck you with her tongue," Rick whispered in my ear. "She loves that."

"Rose?"

"*Mm-hmmmm?*" She hummed her reply and my eyes rolled up in my head.

"Oh, fuck! Fuck me with your tongue, Rose!"

Then she really went to work. I was in bliss, galaxies away from my bills, any petty concerns...even my past. Only the Eternal Now existed and Now wasn't merely pleasant. Now was labia-licking, pussy-eating, clitoris-loving, say-it-with-me, all-caps, in italics and bold: *FUCKING GREAT!*

46

R ick gave my neck rich, lingering, searching kisses.

I gripped his cock hard and wouldn't let go.

Rose alternated between tonguing my twat and teasing my clit.

Rick covered my lips with his. I moaned into his mouth as our tongues played over each other.

I stiffened and my legs went straight as my toes curled. Rose, sensing my building climax, stopped short of making me come.

"Bitch!" I cried.

Rose ignored my pleas for mercy and climbed on top of me. She kissed my neck as Rick had. I felt her hard nipples graze my own. Then she bent to allow me to suck one of her pink nipples into my mouth. Rick took Rose's other tit in his mouth. I watched her smile widen as her green eyes grew heavy-lidded. We pulled at her nipples with our lips and teeth.

I stopped to whine, "Rose, you didn't let me come! My vengeance upon you will be a terrible wrath."

She grinned even wider. "Remember what I wanted to do to you?"

"Which time?" I asked.

She climbed higher, straddling my head. Her pussy settled on my mouth.

"*Mmmmmm*," I hummed into her clit.

Rose groaned. "Told you I'd shut you up with my muff."

I pumped Rick's cock in short, urgent strokes, matching the speed of my hand with that of my tongue on Rose's clit. Soon, I felt her stiffen.

Her will was stronger than mine. Rose was willing to put off orgasm to prolong her pleasure. She positioned herself so I couldn't reach her clit. I could still reach her vagina. "Your turn to fuck me with your tongue, Savvy."

I didn't hold back. I pressed into her as hard and as far as my tongue would allow. Soon, I didn't have to raise my head at all. She plunged her fingers into my hair, holding me fast as she ground against my busy mouth.

"Rick?" Rose said. "I love her. Make Savvy moan, please! Make her moan into me!"

Without a word, Rick pulled away from my hand. I grasped for him, but I'd reached the limit of my restraints. He loosened the bonds at my ankles. At first, I thought he was freeing me. Instead, he gave my ropes more slack to spread my legs.

I felt his thumb on my clit and I squealed at the sensation. He wasn't too gentle now. I didn't want him to be gentle. I thrust my pelvis up, eager to accept him inside me. He obliged, taking me in one deep, savage thrust. I moaned with pleasure into Rose's twat and tongued her ever harder.

Rose stiffened above me again as she rubbed her clit furiously, chasing her orgasm, determined to catch it. When Rose came, she bucked her hips and howled a long note of approval.

I was lost in sensations. My face was wet. Rick began to thrust into me as Rose, her breasts heaving with exertion, rose off me. We all shone with sweat and the massage oil from my body.

Rick grabbed my hips and lifted me into each thrust, filling my depth.

I became nothing but lust and need.

Rose came to the side of the table, one hand on my left breast, the other on my clit, making sure I got maximum stimulation. Pleasure, I discovered, is a song. I moaned incoherent lyrics. I babbled my delight, totally given over to my body's signals. I wasn't just receiving Rick's cock. I was receiving every sensation from every nerve.

Sensing I was building to my climax, Rose deserted my clit abruptly. I didn't get what she was doing at first. Then I felt her release the bonds on my ankles as Rick lowered himself on top of me. He increased his pace and began pounding my pussy in earnest, his thick shaft stimulating my clit with every fast, deep thrust.

With my legs free, I wrapped them around Rick's back, urging him on, locking him to me. Rose pressed on my hips, angling my pelvis up. Not knowing what she was up to, I cooperated. I felt her separate my ass cheeks. I looked up into Rick's face, he gazed back, intense and focused.

Rose slipped down to tongue my anus and I squealed again. She slathered us with her tongue, first my asshole and then Rick's balls. With her free hand, she pressed on Rick's buttocks, encouraging him to fuck me harder. As each thrust grew more urgent, Rose pulled back for a moment.

Undeterred and undistracted, Rick fucked me hard and well. I met each thrust, fucking him right back.

Rose stepped back to watch us, both hands between her legs, stroking softly, slowly, luxuriously. She was so beautiful. Rick was so handsome. I felt lovely, too. If gravity suddenly went away, I'd still have kept my legs locked around Rick as we floated toward the ceiling.

Rose stepped forward and freed my arms. "Take him, Savvy. Take him all the way. He will come with you."

Rick moaned and nodded his agreement.

I wrapped my arms around him and buried my face in his neck. We fucked and fucked our way toward orgasm. It was fierce and animalistic, as if I was riding a horse bareback and holding on for dear life.

My eyes rolled up in my head. "I'm going to come!"

"Me, too," Rick moaned.

Just as we were about to reach the end of the sweet, hard ride, Rose poured the rest of the warm oil over us.

Rick and I came together in wave after wave of pleasure.

47

The next morning I awoke in my bed with someone under the covers lapping at my vulva gently.

I muttered sleepily, "Five more minutes, Mom! I don't want to go to school!"

The person between my legs chuckled. It was Rose, of course. Rick laughed beside me.

My eyes flew open. "Oh! Good morning. I didn't think you stayed with the guests overnight."

"You're an extra special guest."

I smiled, but my cheek was wet with a single tear. "I never want to leave here."

"But you have to go," Rick said.

Rose lifted her head to speak. "It's the heroine's journey — "

I reached down and guided her back to business. "*Sh*. Tend to your knittin'. The adults are talking."

Rose chuckled again and went back to licking me, harder this time. I noticed her hand slide up to fondle Rick's cock, too. I wasn't jealous. I wanted to help.

Rick put an arm beneath my head and pulled me to him. Rose moved with me and Rick reached down to cup my upper thigh. He lifted my leg so I remained vulnerable to Rose's talented tongue. I felt his hard chest against my soft breasts. He kissed me tenderly. Sleep was forgotten.

"Sweet dreams?" he asked.

"Yes, but I didn't know reality could be better than dreams. I really don't want to leave."

Gently, Rose pushed a finger into my pussy. I gasped and shuddered a little as I stared into Rick's dark eyes.

"I have something serious to discuss," Rick said. "Are you sure you can concentrate on a happy alternative?"

"Uh-huh."

Rose might have taken that as an insult to her skills. She immediately began flicking the tip of her tongue across my clit.

"*Mmph*," I said.

"Write about the retreat. Spread the word. We'll help you set up so you can concentrate on your new mission."

Rose began pumping Rick's erect cock beneath the duvet, apparently eager for him to hurry up and get to the point. He reached down to caress my breasts before leaning forward to kiss me softly.

Rose stopped what she was doing to both of us, "Make her the offer, boss."

"We think you should visit more of our spas."

"More? There are others?"

Rose slipped down to tickle my anus with her hot wet tongue.

"We've got big plans for world domination. We need to build more."

"Where would I go?"

"Every location is next to the ocean. I have several ideas where we might expand. A couple are complete. Others are under construction. If you could start immediately, that would be great."

"I don't know," I said. "Kelly ill have to run the business alone and I didn't bring my passport and — "

Rose eased a finger into my ass. The tremor she sent through my core startled me with its insistence.

"Okay! Okay! I can stop by my apartment on the way to the airport! I can pick up my passport but..."

Rose stopped what she was doing. "But?"

I tightened around her finger. "That's my butt."

A woman's voice, soft and friendly and familiar, came from the doorway. "I brought your passport."

Startled, I turned to find Kelly staring at me and smiling. "We can go as soon as you're dressed. Well...as soon as you guys are done and dressed."

I stared at my friend, speechless. Between the bedsheets and my embrace with Rick, I was covered. Still, I felt naked. Rose laughed between my legs as she increased her lingual efforts, working toward my clit again.

"Remember when Paul and I went through that rough patch?" Kelly asked. "I went away for a few days to sort things out. I worked it out here."

"I told you we get our clients by word of mouth," Rick said. "I hope your book will help us find more converts. Our expansion efforts won't succeed if we have to convince everybody one at a time."

"What do you want me to tell them?"

"Tell them everything," Rick said. "Compassion, passion, pleasure. Care for yourself and others more. Tell them they can free themselves of other people's expectations and enjoy their lives more."

"And urge them to stop doing all the stupid shit people do," Rose added. "Let's avoid all that."

"Rose, darling?" I cooed.

"Yeah?"

"Eat me."

Rose left my pussy to pull back the sheets and come up for air. "I have something more to say. Forget all Rick's philosophical complexity and bullshit. Tell 'em to fuck their way to happiness. If they love themselves and others, Nature will do the rest."

Naked and eager, Rose moved up and moaned as she lowered her mouth over the head of Rick's rigid cock. Kelly smiled as she dropped my passport to the floor. She undressed on her way to the bed. Her eyes did not leave mine.

I smiled, looked to Rick, and kissed him. "Before I forget, something about the book. How do you feel about being compared to a galloping beast as you fuck me?"

"Weird."

Rose lifted her mouth from Rick's cock long enough to say, "Purple prose."

I ran my fingers through her short hair and pushed her down again. Her eyes watered as she deepthroated him.

Kelly pulled off her bra and slipped her panties down her long brown legs. I waved for her to come to me.

"Looks like you aren't such a tight ass anymore, Savvy."

"I haven't really gone full anal yet," I said.

"Still so much to learn," Kelly replied.

"Who's minding the store?"

"We got a new corporate client who handles high-end spa packages."

"Oh?"

"Sheila drew up the contracts," Kelly said. "I'll be handling the travel arrangements for all of Rick's clients. You write books."

Kelly crawled into the bed beside me. She cupped my breasts and massaged my nipples gently for a moment before reaching between my legs. She ran her fingers up and down my vulva slowly, teasing me, making me moan.

I leaned back into Kelly, my lips an inch from her mouth. "We should celebrate our good fortune. If only there was a way to celebrate. I can't think...*um...ooh*...what should we do?"

"Savvy," Kelly said. "Shut up and kiss me."

I kissed my best friend for the first time as I reached for Rick's cock.

48

Three months later, after trying out a few assignments abroad for Rick's corporation, I was about to officially become a citizen of the world. I'd scouted a new spa location in Thailand, researched buying a gym in Austin, and looked into recruiting a chef from a whole food restaurant in Munich. Instead of going back and forth from Vancouver, my next step was to travel from country to country. I sublet my apartment in West Van so there was no home to return to. My job was to find the best people to join our network of employees, suppliers, contacts, and clients.

On my last trip home, Kelly drove me to Vancouver International. I was so nervous I needed to pee even though I didn't really need to pee. I'd purged my old life thoroughly. My office at the mall was a memory and would soon become a frozen yogurt store. My partnership with Kelly had graduated to an online business. I'd sold or given away everything — books, clothes, all those knickknacks I used to have to dust, even my photo frames. Any photo I wanted to keep was digitally recorded. When it was all gone, I was left with one small suitcase and my laptop.

As thunder rolled overhead, traffic around the airport was slow. Kelly glanced over and caught me fidgeting. "You okay, Savvy?"

"Oh, don't mind me. Just sweating audibly. Do you realize I've got one bag and a one-way ticket out of here? I used to have more makeup than could fit in one bag!"

"Where you're going, you won't need much clothing. Just buy more sunblock when you get there."

"Yeah. You're right. I think that's on my list."

"You've got your passport and a ticket to ride. That's all you really need."

"That and my laptop, my notebook, a pocket full of hubris, and a head full of wishes."

"What are you feeling, buddy?"

That sounded like a Rick question. Ask anyone how they are and they are programmed to answer, "Fine, thank you." Ask them what emotion they are experiencing and you get a real answer. Kelly had learned her sex spa lessons well.

"I feel like I've cut all ties to Earth and I'm floating away. I'm homeless!"

"You'll always have a couch in my basement if it all falls apart, Savvy."

"I'd be too embarrassed to take you up on that. I'll become a troll. I'll live under a bridge in Phuket."

"You know this is okay and you'll be okay, right?"

"My mom's betting on the troll thing."

"What did your dad say?"

"He wouldn't come to the phone. Mom wanted to talk."

"At least your mother is keeping the lines of communication open."

"When I said she wanted to talk I meant she wasn't done berating me when I hung up on her."

"Sounds like you only have one alternative."

"Murder-suicide and the sweet release of death?"

"You're going to have to succeed. Your parents will come around to your way of thinking when you're putting them up in the guest cabin out back of your mansion."

I blurt laughed. "As if I'd let them stay in the guest quarters."

Rain began to beat at the windshield, another beautiful day in Vancouver. We turned off Grant McConachie Way and drove into the airport. "You don't have to park or anything, Kelly. Just drop me off before I lose my nerve."

"After all this, still nervous? Want me to turn around and see if we can get you a shift at McDonald's or something? Set up a Match.com account and meet some guys that way?"

"I'm committed...or should be."

"I know. Just testing."

"I have to move forward. No lateral moves and certainly not backward."

"Good."

"Sorry, I was really talking to myself. This is a big step. I've always had a return ticket. Even when Doug and I moved to Canada, I had an open-ended return ticket to Alabama."

"It's a big step, but you're up to it."

"I know. It's more excitement than fear now." Kelly reached over and gave my hand a squeeze as we slipped behind a taxi dropping off passengers at the Departures door. "I'm so proud of you, Savvy."

I could feel my eyes getting misty. "I figured out why I was an awful waffler. I hated what I was doing. I'm a writer who wasn't writing. I'm a traveler who wasn't traveling. No wonder I could never be satisfied. I was going to the drugstore for coconuts."

"Huh?"

"No matter how many drugstores you go to, you're in the wrong spot for coconuts."

"Ah. Don't put that analogy in the book," Kelly advised me.

I assured her I would not.

As we inched forward, Kelly added, "You know you aren't alone, right? That's what all those self-help books you read get wrong."

I perked up and asked her what she meant.

"Self-help is full of tactics and strategies and a whole lot of do this, do that. It's why I read Jodi Picoult instead."

I could feel my eyebrows do that thing where they get stuck

together in the middle. "What I've written so far is a new genre: Self-help Smut. So tell me, what do the self-help books get wrong?"

"They give the impression that life hacking is easy. It's simple, of course. Just about everybody already knows, deep down, what they need to do to help themselves. Those books don't seem to allow for failure and waffling, though. People go back and forth because they're human. They fall off the bandwagon. Dieters stop dieting and get scolded instead of encouraged. In the real world, we understand there will be dips and detours. You didn't write for years. Doesn't mean you can't now."

"So find a good dick and hop on and hold on?"

"Don't use that analogy, either," she said. "New habits and lifestyles aren't all or nothing is all I'm saying."

"I hear you, but I realized something since leaving the spa. I don't know how I'll get it in the book yet, but essentially, I know I'll never be satisfied."

"Sexually? Damn."

"No, no. I mean, with life. To feel good, I have to write every day. But happiness? I don't think it's a steady state. It's not a cruising altitude you stay at. It's a moment. It's an orgasm. It's a good book in a hammock on a lazy afternoon. Happiness is morning coffee and a kiss. It's that feeling you get after a good workout or when the power goes out and you light candles to play Boggle with friends. It comes and goes."

"You're going to have a lot more happy moments now," Kelly said.

"I'll try to string them as close together as I can, but I know I'll never be satisfied. Is that sad? Oh, my God, I'm my mother."

"No, Savvy. Your mother is everybody. Everybody is you. Everybody has doubts. We all go back and forth. People who don't doubt have gotta be idiots, right?"

I chewed my lip.

"Feel better?"

I leaned over and kissed her hard on the lips. "I don't know when I'll be back."

She gave me an awkward hug from her seat. "I'll see you when I see you."

A car horn honked behind us, startling us both.

"Don't get out," I told her. "Just pop the trunk. I'm ready."

The rain poured harder as I stepped out of the car and slipped the strap to my precious laptop bag over my shoulder. That's when I realized I'd forgotten to bring an umbrella. By the time I pulled my suitcase out of the trunk my hair hung wet in my eyes. I would have been annoyed, but I was leaving on a jet to the tropics in a couple of hours. What did I really have to complain about? I splashed up to the curb and waved to Kelly as she pulled away.

When her car receded from sight I tilted my head back and tasted the rain. I love the smell of a cleansing rain. The world feels fresh and new. "Goodbye, Vancouver."

I didn't think about my ex at all. This was not a tearful farewell. This was a new beginning. I turned to go and didn't spare another backward glance.

At the WestJet counter, a pretty young brunette flight attendant gave me a bright smile that warmed me. "Bonjour! How are you today?"

"Free," I said.

"Pardon?"

"Headed to Bermuda."

She tapped at her keyboard to enter the details of my flight. As I thanked her she began to point me toward the airport security checkpoint.

"No worries," I said. "I'm certain of the way."

Soon I'd be in the air jetting toward a new life, achieving escape velocity for good.

And for Good.

DEDICATION

The author would like to thank Sabine, Kelly, Paul, RB, and RS, always in my heart and in my pants.
To Gari and Rob, my long-suffering editors. You warned me my first draft was too much, but I got the length and girth I needed in the end!
Thanks also to KF, JK, and MY.
Finally, three cheers for Mojo. Your encouragement made me make so much happen. Knowing who I am (and who I might become) was one of the secrets to strength I didn't possess before I met you. And thanks for the laptop!

ABOUT THE AUTHOR

Savannah M. Needs is a former travel agent turned writer of erotica and self-help smut. This is Savvy's first book. An anthology of her sexy travelogue adventures is in the works now.

Find out more about upcoming book releases at her website, SavvyMNeeds.com.

www.ingramcontent.com/pod-product-compliance
Lightning Source LLC
Chambersburg PA
CBHW050339030726
47503CB00008B/2518